Concealed

The Taellaneth - Book 1

Vanessa Nelson

CONCEALED

The Taellaneth - Book 1

Vanessa Nelson

Copyright © 2018 Vanessa Nelson

All rights reserved. This is a work of fiction.

All characters and events in this publication are fictitious and any resemblance to any real person, living or dead, is purely coincidental.

Reproduction in whole or in part of this publication without express written consent is strictly prohibited.

Find out more information about Vanessa Nelson and her books at: www.taellaneth.com

For Mum and Dad.

For many things, but in particular for encouraging me to read, opening up whole new worlds.

Contents

1. CHAPTER ONE — 1
2. CHAPTER TWO — 9
3. CHAPTER THREE — 17
4. CHAPTER FOUR — 27
5. CHAPTER FIVE — 40
6. CHAPTER SIX — 53
7. CHAPTER SEVEN — 58
8. CHAPTER EIGHT — 67
9. CHAPTER NINE — 75
10. CHAPTER TEN — 86
11. CHAPTER ELEVEN — 93
12. CHAPTER TWELVE — 101
13. CHAPTER THIRTEEN — 105
14. CHAPTER FOURTEEN — 113
15. CHAPTER FIFTEEN — 121
16. CHAPTER SIXTEEN — 132
17. CHAPTER SEVENTEEN — 138
18. CHAPTER EIGHTEEN — 150
19. CHAPTER NINETEEN — 157

20.	CHAPTER TWENTY	170
21.	CHAPTER TWENTY-ONE	179
22.	CHAPTER TWENTY-TWO	189
23.	CHAPTER TWENTY-THREE	201
24.	CHAPTER TWENTY-FOUR	210
25.	CHAPTER TWENTY-FIVE	219
THANK YOU		229
CHARACTER LIST		230
GLOSSARY		232
ALSO BY THE AUTHOR		234
ABOUT THE AUTHOR		236

Chapter One

A STRANGLED CRY OF warning. She ducked. Too slow. The heavy tail slapped her face, spun her, and sent her sideways into bookshelves and a lungful of dust and ink. Coughing, she turned, the silver sheen of her defensive wards visible in the gloom, voice rasping as she spoke the words for a hold spell, power gathered in one palm before she flung the spell across the too-short distance. The drain of energy sent her a step back against the shelves, wood pressing across her back. She did not relax, heart racing, grabbing on to the shelves with her free hand, using that for an anchor as she began another hold spell.

The snake, several times longer than she was tall, fat with the scribes' precious archives, writhed under the hold spell, green and gold scales speckled with silver from her magic and green sparks that were the creature's own power. All Erith creatures possessed some magic, and this one was big enough to resist the hasty hold she had thrown. A full-grown adult, with fangs as long as her fingers. Shoving worry aside, she released her next spell, further loss of energy draining her defence, shimmer of silver dying, leaving her alone in the shadowed archive with the giant creature.

A sibilant hiss and turn of its head, flat gold eyes showing nothing, was all the warning she had. Just time enough to fling a hand up, protecting her face. Venom sprayed, coating her arm and hand, face only partly protected, sticky stuff burrowing into her skin. Cloth along her arm smouldered, acid working through to skin, burning.

Biting her lip against the pain, she gathered the last of her power for a final spell. There were untouched shelves of records behind her that the Erith would want protected at all costs. The Erith loved their records.

"Hold!"

There was no power behind the word, but Arrow froze anyway. The White Guard had arrived. A sheet of amber power, the White Guard's own wards, flooded the space, along with five tall Erith, the dark grey of their uniforms blending into the shadows.

A coil of something dark and thin flew across the space, settling on the snake. Some kind of netting. It tightened around the wriggling coils with a flare of amber, Erith magic holding the creature. The snake writhed across the floor, trying to bite its way free of the net, hissing as the amber sparked. The net bit into the snake's side as it fought its captivity, stripes of blood welling up then trailing onto the floor.

The snake's struggles scattered half-eaten fragments of parchment, and it twisted, a spew of venom aimed at the warriors. It missed. The warriors, far nimbler than Arrow, stepped aside, each moving with smooth grace despite the close confines between the head-high bookshelves. Satisfied the net was secure, a pair of White Guard, hands gloved against the venom, simply picked up the bound creature and shoved it into a large sack made of rough cloth held by the other three.

Forgotten for the moment, Arrow drew a much-needed breath. Five warriors had accomplished the capture in mere seconds without drawing a weapon, putting her own efforts to shame.

"No!" The wail of despair announced the arrival of Chief Scribe and his first sight of the devastation in the archives, sharp features tightening and fair skin paling still further as he took in the full extent of the damage. Even in his distress, he gathered his brocade robes close to avoid the damage, ornate clothing a stark contrast to the pared-down efficiency of the warriors' uniforms.

Glancing around as the scribe continued to lament, she felt a twinge of sympathy. The room which had until that morning been a large, ordered, collection of the Taellaneth scribes' records and correspondence, was devastated. The snake had eaten through most of the parchments, and a few of the bookcases, the air now thick with the sharp scent of ink, broken bookcases housing only ragged fragments of parchment, floor haphazardly covered with more fragments, sticky with blood and venom.

Arrow straightened before the Chief Scribe could notice that she had slumped, grimacing as the blisters on her hand burst, clear liquid dripping onto the floor to mix with the venom, parchment, and thin trails of snake blood. The skin along her arm was still burning. It had been a long day before the scribes' summoning and she wanted nothing more than salve for her burns and a long stretch of unbroken sleep. Neither was possible.

"That thing should be killed." The scribe spat his words, and for a moment, Arrow thought he was talking about her. He had expressed that view before, several times.

"It needs to be taken to a place it can do no more harm," the senior warrior answered, voice calm. Ruthless when they had to be, the Erith's elite warriors did not kill without reason.

She bit her lip to hold in a whimper, acid eating into her face, very close to her eyes. Ducking behind the bookshelf, out of the scribe's line of sight, she gave a nod of acknowledgement to the junior scribe who had cried the warning. The juniors were huddled in the internal doorway, blocking the light, their plain, dark robes blending together. They were all wearing similar wide-eyed expressions, amber sparks in their eyes further betraying their unease. Setting their worries aside, she made her way outside to the garden in the middle of the scribes' quadrangle, looking for the medicinal border.

Even though it was the heart of winter, there was no snow or frost in the Taellaneth's prized gardens and it did not take her long to find the necessary section of the scriptorium garden.

Sighing in relief, she dropped to her knees on the carefully raked gravel, and awkwardly plucked a handful of thick leaves, the fingers of one hand too swollen to use. Breaking the leaves open to release the sap, she coated her hand, then her face, in the greenish liquid, sighing again as the sting eased, faint, buttery scent coating her lungs, working some sap under her sleeve. Salve might have been an impossible dream. This was real.

"You stupid creature." The scribe's voice was close behind her.

She wobbled to her feet to face him and made the necessary bow.

"The archives are ruined. Ruined."

There was no point in telling Eshan nuin Regersfel that she had only arrived a handful of moments before he did, when the damage had mostly been done. It did not matter that the only way a full-grown creature like the snake could have got into the archives was because someone had failed to inspect and renew the scriptorium's defensive wards, protective spells that were woven over all Erith buildings. It did not matter that maintenance of the wards was the duty of the scribes, including the Chief Scribe. It did not matter that the scribes on duty had failed to notice the enormous snake eating through their records for most of the day, reacting with outright panic when the discovery was made, trying to deal with it themselves. Far from resolving the problem, they had sent the snake into a frenzy, and only then instructed the youngest of their number, by that time wide-eyed and incoherent, to find her and, apparently, also the White Guard.

Eshan nuin Regersfel saw no reason where she was concerned. And little restraint. He could not permanently damage her, because his master found her useful. Over the years, he had found many ways of inflicting punishment without damage, finding her defective no matter what she did. And if he was angry enough, there would be more direct punishment involved. He was angrier than she had ever seen him. She shivered.

Glancing past Eshan's shoulder, she saw the scribes had now gathered at the archive's doors, still huddled together for support, frozen expressions melted into worry, whispering furiously amongst themselves and doubtless wondering which of them would be sent away in disgrace. A position as scribe in the Taellaneth was the highest honour many of their families had achieved.

In front of the near-frantic scribes, the senior warrior approached Eshan, face grim as the Chief Scribe's fury continued. The four other warriors, the remainder of the senior warrior's third, gathered behind him, a pair of them carrying the wriggling sack between them, ignoring the snake's fury.

"The problem is resolved," the warrior told Eshan's back, voice cool. "The rooms are clear of any other snakes or eggs."

"Not before time."

Arrow's brow lifted a fraction before she controlled it. Eshan enjoyed a very favoured position in the Taellaneth, courtesy of the House he had been adopted into, and the lord he owed allegiance to, but there were limits. Although Arrow did not recognise the warrior, from the braids on his sleeves he was too senior for Eshan to use that tone.

"You need to renew the wards," the warrior continued in that cool voice. The Erith rarely made an obvious statement without purpose.

Apparently, Eshan did not realise he had been criticised, his pinched expression remaining.

"Go." The scribe waved a hand at the warriors. The warriors did not react, and simply left in stony silence, a calculated insult.

Hand and arm prickling as the sap worked its way through the wounds, eyes watering from the sting, Arrow waited for the inevitable round of questioning and blame, wondering what else Eshan would hold her responsible for. He had reason to be furious at the devastation of the archive, but a thank you to the warriors taking the problem away would be the least they were due, not his rudeness. Something else was bothering him.

Despite the whispering from the other scribes, he paid them no attention, apparently deep in thought for long moments before casting a narrow-eyed glance in her direction, tight smile crossing his face. He looked as though he had found a solution to a difficult issue. Arrow's stomach twisted. Whatever it was, she was quite certain she was not going to like it.

"We will discuss this later," he snapped to his scribes, prompting another round of dismayed whispers.

"Come," he ordered and stalked away, back towards the main building.

Careful to keep out of reach of his robes, Arrow followed the scribe along the immaculately maintained pathway that led to the main building of the Taellaneth, the specially constructed heart of Erith government. The building was vast, a one-storey single block crafted of stone the colour of pale sand, with a giant dome of brilliant blue stone rising in its centre, the cover for the Receiving Hall. The remainder of the building was devoted to less formal gathering rooms, meeting rooms and offices for the Taellan, the governing council for the Erith, an array of servants' quarters concealed below ground.

The scribe strode past the monumental sculpture that had pride of place on the close-cropped grass in front of the main building, and continued through the main entrance, the carved double doors standing open in Erith tradition to signal welcome. Arrow was rarely permitted through the main entrance, closely following Eshan as he continued along several corridors wide enough for five warriors to walk shoulder to shoulder, the scribe ignoring the handmade runners he stalked over and the exquisite carvings or paintings that lined the walls, and not pausing until he reached a set of closed double doors that led to one of the main meeting chambers.

"Wait."

Eshan spoke the necessary password for the door and slipped inside, a roar of noise spilling out along with the scent of Erith tea, curling into Arrow's stomach, a reminder that she had not eaten since early morning. Through the slit of the open door, Arrow could see what appeared to be the entire Taellan, all ten of them. No one was sitting around the oval meeting table; instead, they were clustered together, talking over each other, a few gesturing wildly, light catching their rings and sparking off the mirrorglass panels on the walls. Several pairs of eyes reflected amber, betraying how unsettled they were, an extraordinary display of agitation from a race that took pride in their civilised manners.

Before she had time to work out what they were discussing, the door closed behind Eshan and she was left facing her own reflection in one of the mirrored panels in the door. A cruel contrast. The Erith were a beautiful people to look at, being tall, slow to age, with precisely cut features and flawless skin which shaded from alabaster to midnight dark. The Taellan, among the most influential Erith alive, were dressed according to their station in silks and brocades, gleaming with health, individually stunning and collectively breathtaking, no matter how long she had had to get used to them.

The mirrored panel showed her a very ordinary face with pale, freckled skin tinted green from the sap and unevenly scorched from venom, unruly dirty blond hair in its usual tangled mess, escaping the pins she had shoved in that morning, grey eyes dull with pain, the silver sparks that denoted her power invisible. Apart from the silver in her eyes and the curve of her ears hidden under hair, she looked human. Definitely not Erith. And exhausted. It had been a long, hard day before she had been summoned to the archives and she had almost no power left and no immediate means to renew her energy. Her personal wards were slowly rebuilding, the use of magic pulling energy from her body that she could ill afford.

It was a trade-off. She could be defenceless and heal more quickly or gather some defence. She would always choose defence. The Taellaneth was no place to be vulnerable.

Blinking, lashes catching on sap, she looked away, familiar with her plainness, eyes skipping over the wall panels, each carved individually by master craftsmen. This was the Taellaneth, unsubtle symbol of Erith power and artistry. Every piece of it was beautifully designed and finely made.

In this building, the Taellan conducted much of their business at their Queen's insistence. And none of the Taellan had been in residence this morning. Arrow frowned. It was costly, both in money and magic, to travel so fast and so far, to bring all the Taellan together. There had been no disturbance in the grounds, and none of the chattering scribes had mentioned anything worthy of the entire Taellan's attention.

Mind turning on possible reasons for the gathering, Arrow straightened in automatic reflex when the door opened again, wider this time, and Eshan stepped out, a taller, older Erith with him, the other Erith's midnight blue robes plain by contrast to Eshan. The older, burnished-bronze skin finely lined with his years, small hints of white in his black hair, had no need of adornment. Seggerat vo Regersfel, head of House Regersfel, Eshan's master and leader of the Taellan. She bowed.

"Not a bad notion," Seggerat was saying to Eshan.

The scribe preened under the praise, cheeks flushed.

The elder turned his attention to Arrow. "There has been a disturbance among the shifkin. You will go and aid their investigation."

"My lord?" She blinked, wondering if she had heard correctly.

"A disturbance," the elder repeated slowly, irritated.

Arrow simply stared, wide-eyed, trying to absorb the startling command.

"My lord ..." Eshan leant closer to his master and murmured something, too quietly for Arrow to hear.

"Very well," the elder snapped, eyes flaring amber, a sure sign he was deeply disturbed. He glared at Arrow as if she were personally responsible. "The Prime's mate is dead. You will aid the shifkin in finding the truth of the woman's death."

"My lord." Arrow's bow was pure reflex, heart skipping, brain turning in circles. The Prime's mate. The shifkin equivalent of the Erith Queen's Consort. Dead. Unexpectedly, otherwise, the Taellan would not be meeting. And not by natural causes, or there would be no need for investigation or the uproar she had heard.

Another heartbeat and unexpected sorrow hurt her chest. The shifkin woman had been a stranger, but too young to die. Shifkin and Erith shared a common trait of long lives, with the oldest spanning centuries.

"Eshan, make arrangements." The elder's eyes, amber fading, flicked over Arrow. His face tightened with a familiar expression of distaste. "Yes, not a bad notion at all." He nodded to Eshan and returned to the room, noticeably quieter on his return, door closing firmly behind him.

"Get what you need. Transport will be at the gates shortly."

"Sir." Arrow's polite response was made to the scribe's back as he stalked away, slippers silent on the handmade runners.

She stayed still for several heartbeats, a dozen questions rising, none of them uttered. There would be no answers from the Erith. The oath-spells bound into her blood and skin, the price of her continued existence, stirred, reminding her that she had orders to obey and promising pain if she did not comply. Her pulse quickened, excitement and apprehension mixed. A venture out of the Taellaneth was welcome. And yet. The Erith and the 'kin had a long, bloody history of conflict, peace held just now by the thin width of the parchment on which their treaties were written. The conflict still burned under the surface and she had just been shoved into the middle.

Chapter Two

Night was gathering as Arrow made her way out of the main building, risking a reprimand by taking the main entrance. The twin moons overhead were as frosty as the air, the slivers narrow, the moons themselves—according to Erith tradition—locked in an eternal struggle for power.

She paused at the foot of the shallow steps, the sculpture catching her attention as it was designed to. Translucent stone that shimmered in daylight, now glowing a ghostly white, lit by small sparks of magic placed here and there on the grass around it. Six figures. Five that made up one third of a White Guard cadre. Some kneeling, others standing, weapons ready, in a loose circle around a war mage at their centre, his hands raised in spellwork. Each face determined, staring resolute at an unseen enemy. The master craftsmen who had made the sculpture had ensured that there was at least one face in full view, whichever angle the sculpture was viewed from. Arrow's view showed her a kneeling archer, bow drawn, arrow ready to let fly, protecting the war mage's back, the mage's stone cloak seeming to ripple in an unseen breeze. Erith runes, carved from the same stone, circled the sculpture in the grass, the title of the piece repeated over and over. Fallen not Forgotten.

A reminder, if one was needed, that the freedom and prosperity of the Erith came at a high price. Commissioned by the Queen, she had, according to rumour, stared down the entire Taellan when they had objected to having such a sacred memory on display for any casual visitor to see. It was a cornerstone of the Taellaneth, she had told them, that they should not forget.

And a reminder for Arrow too, that she should not forget the wonder in the world. Every time she stood before the statue, she was reminded of the first time she had seen it, her much smaller hand folded in the warm, calloused hand of

Nassaran, the elderly Erith who had cared for her until she had been old enough to begin studying at the Academy.

Her first memory of this statue was of being warm and safe, staring slack-jawed at the huge stone men above her, while Nassaran's soft voice told her the tale of the incursion and its end. His words had been low and full of emotion she had had no name for then, too young to understand. She just knew she was protected and cared for, and that the man who held her hand would defend her, as the stone men would defend all the other Erith who could not look after themselves.

Checking she was unobserved, Arrow made a brief half-bow to the long-dead third and mage. The last six, she now knew, who had sealed the last incursion. They had faced the Erith's greatest fears knowing they were the last line of defence, giving their lives in that defence. They were deserving of respect.

The stone eyes of the archer did not blink, still focused on a long-dead, unseen enemy, and she continued on her way, careful to skirt around the scribe's quadrangle. Eshan had taken a quicker route out of the main building to get back to his domain, the sound of his wrath a harsh counterpoint to an otherwise serene evening. More than one scribe would be leaving his service, she guessed.

The scribe's anger made little difference to the Taellaneth, the grounds a giant garden, meticulously planned. The Erith had moved fully mature trees and giant rocks from the heartland to form the garden with curving pathways, springing grass lawns, and an array of Erith plants that scented the air year-round.

As daylight faded, glimmerlights, tiny sparks of Erith magic, appeared here and there among the plants. Just enough light to allow the Erith to see clear as day, barely enough for Arrow to navigate by when it was fully dark.

By the time she reached her residence, a converted storeroom tucked out of sight behind a high hedge with sweet-scented climbing plants tangled through, her fingers had reduced in size to be usable again, sting dulled to faint irritation.

Her walk had given her time to plan what she needed and, much as she wanted to lie down on her mattress and sleep until morning, she could not. The 'kin lived closer to the human world than the Erith, so she changed her dark Erith clothing for dark, human-made clothing, the effort telling her how much she needed to rest. She could not remember the last full night's sleep she had been permitted. And there was no rest in sight. Get what you need, Eshan had said. She really needed sleep, knew that was not available, so would have to eat instead. Dressed in human clothing, she would not be permitted into the Taellaneth kitchens, but she was going out into the human world where there were fast-food venues that would not care what she wore. And which sold coffee.

She froze a moment, dull sparks of silver in her eyes flaring. Coffee. Hamburgers. Chocolate. Delicious, and forbidden among the Erith. A shiver ran through her. It had been many months since the Erith had sent her out of the Taellaneth. So long that she had wondered if they had forgotten her or, worse, had decided to keep her confined until her oaths expired. The hated magic that had bound her to the Taellan's will for over half her life. Oaths bound with an expiration date that was almost here.

Another shiver. Perhaps her last task for the Erith, and they were sending her to their old enemies. Maybe they thought that the 'kin would ensure Arrow did not reach the end of her oaths. It would be a tidy end, for the Erith, to her troublesome existence.

Arwmverishan.

The whispered word was so real that she turned and looked for the speaker, before realising that the voice was just a memory she was too tired to suppress. Another memory rose, a cacophony of young Erith voices shrieking the word over and over. That was from earlier that day, the new intake of students at the Academy horrified and fascinated by the half-breed assigned to show them how to draw basic runes. They had not learned much.

Arwmverishan.

Abomination.

The first word she had learned. Trying to repeat it, shape the unfamiliar letters, and managing only a sound that was like Arrow. A human word, meaningless to the Erith, but they had to call her something.

Muscles locked against another tremor, her jaw clenched, Arrow came out of memory to realise she had been standing still for several moments, and the oath spells in her blood were restless. She had been given orders.

Taking her knee-length, human-made, leather coat from its hook, she quickly checked its wards were intact, the faint sheen of silver at the very edges of her sight reassuring her. Then she pulled her battered messenger bag, also of human make, over her shoulder, settling it against her hip and glancing around in a final cursory check. She had restocked her bag after her last journey from the Taellaneth into human lands. As ready as she could be, she left, renewing the wards, using most of the tiny spark of power she had remaining.

Stepping out of her residence into the night, another presence brushed against her wards. The wards pulled more power, recognising a possible threat. This one had hurt her before.

"You really are an abomination." The cultured voice emerged from nearby shadow. A tall, slender Erith lord stepped onto the bare ground before her front door.

"Lord vo Regresan." Years of practice kept her voice even and calm, face expressionless, her apprehension and distaste hidden. The young lord, from any other background, would be recognised for the petty bully he was. Youngest offspring of one of the Taellan, and presumed heir to his House, he was fond of using that position to get his own way. Beautiful even by Erith standards, the lord seemed to gather the available light to him, golden skin glowing, impact of his presence distilled by the sneer across his sculpted face.

"You cannot wear that ... outfit."

"It is to fulfil a task for the Taellan." The Taellan did not like human-made items within the Taellaneth grounds. They were, though, highly pragmatic when it came to getting their will carried out. Something the young lord had yet to learn.

"It is an outrage. My father shall hear of your conduct."

Arrow thought that Gesser's father, Gret vo Regresan, likely had far bigger concerns. The older lord was also normally highly adept at picking his fights.

"Did you want something?"

"The tenth cycle has demonstration classes over the next few days. I require you to attend." Arrow could not recall the last time that Gesser had actually conducted the class himself. He was proud of his title as Assistant Teaching

Master at the Academy and wore his Academy robes with flair. The pride and flair had yet to extend to him actually carrying out his duties. Every teacher required Arrow's assistance from time to time, knowing she could not refuse. Gesser managed to require her assistance more than all the others together.

The tenth cycle was a new class for him. A moment's thought, and she realised that they would have reached the point of learning to keep their focus through distraction, including pain. Demonstration was required by a senior mage, or senior student, to prove that it was possible to hold focus. It was the least welcome demonstration duty across all Academy classes. Arrow had been the demonstrator for every class since she had passed her own tenth cycle, standing firm under hails of sticks, stones, magic, and in one case, knives, being thrown at her. The student throwing knives had received a raised eyebrow from the Teaching Master supervising the class, nothing more.

"I am unable to assist."

"You must. There is no one else." There was a hint of something in his voice.

Arrow lifted a brow. "My lord, the Taellan's command takes priority over classes. The Preceptor himself has decreed it."

"But..." His jaw snapped shut, eyes glinting with amber power. He was furious enough, and frightened enough, to try something remarkably stupid, she realised. He had struggled with that class when they had taken it together and had retaken it more than once. She did not need to look at his hands to know that he was drawing runes in the air. Not as powerful as those set with chalk, but still potent enough to harm. She took a step forward, calling up the tiny amount of power she had left, the pull inside telling her she was at the end of her reserves. The trickle of power brightened her eyes, sparks of silver growing.

"I have my commands, my lord."

Exhausted or not, abomination or not, she was more powerful than he was. He had damaged her extensively when she had been a student, her power constrained. Now there was nothing he could do.

The sense of power faded as he met her eyes, his face a mask, shoulders set, and fists clenched, faint amber points in his eyes flickering. Arrow held her ground.

Without another word, he spun on his heel and left. Watching his back, she allowed herself one sigh. The fingers on her right hand clenched, phantom ache from a previous occasion when the young lord had also not got his way. The bones had set well enough that she had use of her fingers, though they did not lie straight.

Forced with adulthood into more mature ways of seeking revenge, she would not receive more broken bones. Rather, she would find herself assigned every one of his demonstrations on her return. More than likely, her residence wards would be ripped open, the few possessions she had scattered to the elements. He, along with a few others, would not forgive her for succeeding where they had failed. She, with her impure Erith heritage, had graduated from the Academy, something fewer than one in a hundred students achieved.

Beginning the walk towards the Taellaneth gates, she shrugged aside the possibility of future punishment for another day. She had had to learn to pick her battles, much like Gret vo Regresan. Worrying about Gesser's likely reaction was pointless, as there was nothing she could do to stop him. Besides, he had a limited imagination, usually content to sit gleefully in the corner while she took his classes.

Her mood lifted with the realisation that, in her absence, and being the most junior member of the teaching staff, he would be forced to be his own demonstrator. The students were unlikely to use knives. Still, the class was uncomfortable for the demonstrator and Gesser would be required, for once, to earn his robes.

Steps a little lighter, she continued on her way.

The Taellaneth wall loomed out of the night. A vast structure constructed of wood and magic, the wall ran around the entire complex, standing higher than the top of the dome of the Receiving Hall, broken only by two sets of gates. One set led to the Erith heartland and was forever barred to Arrow. The other gates led to the closest border with the human lands, and these she was permitted to use from time to time.

The gates she approached were bracketed with a pair of watchtowers that rose even higher than the walls, apparently dark and deserted. In truth, they were staffed by White Guard, day and night, warriors stationed in the towers and on the ground. Between the watchtowers, one of the massive wooden gates was slightly ajar, the sound of raised voices greeting her.

"... cannot bring that thing in here," the sentry just outside the gate was saying to someone unseen, a mid-ranked White Guard from the braids on his sleeves, just visible in the light available. The sentry's companion on watch was standing a little distance away, taking no part in whatever argument was going on.

"I have orders." The voice, rough from past injury or disease, was faintly familiar. Arrow stepped through the gate.

"Good evening to you, *svegraen*," she addressed the warrior.

"There you are." The sentry barely looked at her, voice clipped. She could not make out his expression in the dark, but he would have seen her human clothing. "You are late."

"I am sorry," she said reflexively.

"Come on, then." The rough voice was impatient.

Arrow stepped around the sentry, nose wrinkling as she caught the very human smell of exhaust fumes. Coming out of the Taellaneth, the scent as always reminded her of her first exit. She had been exiled after she had accidentally started a fire that consumed most of one of the Academy's classrooms, shoved outside the gates and onto the first of a series of vehicles that would take her to Hallveran.

Today, there were no hands grabbing her. The roughened voice belonged to the Erith's chief mechanic, whose charges were housed in a warehouse-sized building a few miles from the Taellaneth gates, a warehouse that the mechanic regarded as his own personal kingdom and the vehicles under his care more precious than any offspring. Behind him, picked out in the limited star- and moonlight, was a vehicle of some description. Arrow's brows rose. The Erith did not normally permit any technology this close to the Taellaneth.

"Here." The sentry handed her a large leather pouch. "The Chief Scribe left this. Said directions are inside."

"My thanks." She took the pouch and turned to the mechanic, who was shifting from foot to foot, scowling. "Good evening."

"Well," he grunted, and turned to the vehicle, rattling off a description of the vehicle's make, model and mileage that Arrow did not understand. She could drive thanks to the mechanic's impatient tuition but had no comprehension of how the thing worked. Following him around the vehicle, she tried to memorise his words in case she would need them later as he pointed out various features that seemed important to him, nodding as he glared back at her from time to time.

"Fuel tank is full. Wards renewed last week." The mechanic held out the keys to her, knuckles gleaming white in the gloom. "Return her in one piece."

Interesting. He had decided the vehicle was female. She was tempted to ask him if the vehicle had a name, but simply took the keys, making a mental note to stop as soon as she could and renew the vehicle's wards herself. The mechanics were as weak in magic as they were strong in their love for human technology.

She gave the mechanic appropriate thanks and was about to offer to take him back to the warehouse when she saw that there was another vehicle, farther away from the gates, waiting to do just that.

Under the watchful eye of the White Guard sentries and the disapproving glare of the mechanic, she managed to get into the driver's seat, start the vehicle and pull away from the Taellaneth without embarrassing herself. It was only while she was driving along the one available road, heading towards the faint lights of the nearest human city, Lix, that she realised she had forgotten to turn on the headlights.

She muttered a curse in the private space of the car's interior, found the appropriate switch, lighting the road in front and her fingers tightening on the wheel for a moment. Such a basic thing to forget. Sent by the Taellan to the shifkin, the weight of the elder's command pressing her into the seat, there was no option to fail in her task or return without answers. The oaths would not let her. She could not afford mistakes.

Chapter Three

*G**O TO FARRAWAY TOWNSHIP and offer aid to the shifkin.*

The single line of directions, written in the Chief Scribe's hand with none of his usual precision, was all the visible authority she had. As well as the haste of the note, the packet from the Chief Scribe had been far less than the comprehensive information she normally received when sent outside the Taellaneth, containing little more than that one-line note and funds for her journey. The lack might be due to speed. Perhaps.

But she was often sent on tasks for the Taellan at short notice, sometimes returning from one errand to find another waiting for her, and Eshan had never provided anything less than three fingers' width of paper for her to review, and for much simpler tasks than she faced just now. On one memorable occasion, he had provided her with a hand's width of paper simply to purchase a new telephone for the Erith's administration complex, tucked in the shadows of the mechanic's warehouse.

This last year alone, she had been given a dozen tasks outside the Taellaneth grounds, each coming with a heavy packet of information and funds. Now she had been sent on perhaps the most important task and had nothing more than one sheet of paper. It was deeply worrying.

There were no map directions, but Arrow did not need them as, like the Taellaneth, there was only one road. Farraway Township was where the shifkin Prime, Zachary Farraway, made his home and the only settlement on Farraway Mountain. Ruler absolute of all shifkin, the Prime's own lands stretched beyond the actual mountain to the foothills and farmland beyond, the Prime as personally wealthy in land as only a few Erith Houses. And, like the Erith lands, it was somewhere she had never thought she would get to visit.

The 'kin were as intolerant of visitors to their lands as the Erith, and she could imagine that the recent death of so prominent a figure as the Prime's mate would not have improved matters. Apprehension coiled through her. She had met a few 'kin. The Erith traded with all races, even those they despised, and found her useful for business they disliked. She had dealt mostly with lower-ranked 'kin sent to transact and, rarely—where the occasion warranted it—more powerful 'kin who had an aura about them which made her want to keep her back to a solid object and some magic to hand.

She spent a good part of the journey frowning, turning possibilities over in her mind. There was nothing to indicate that the shifkin knew she was on her way, or why the Erith's assistance had been requested. The shape-shifters were more than competent with human technologies that might aid their investigation and disliked the Erith as much as the Erith disliked them. Their joint history was centuries of regarding each other as natural enemies and brutal conflict with high losses on both sides. The Erith Queen might have insisted that there would be peace. The peace was mere decades in place, set against hundreds of years of open hostility, and among the Erith that Arrow knew, many still openly sneered when the shifkin were mentioned, regarding them as little more than upright beasts. Arrow did not know enough shifkin to understand how they felt about the Erith, judging that they must find some benefit to the peace as it continued to hold.

A knot tightened in her stomach as she realised that the elder had not actually said that the shifkin had requested Erith assistance. It was entirely possible that the Erith were simply sending her to find out what she could, or for some other reason that she could not work out. She had lived among the Erith her entire life and they still surprised her in their actions and motives. She had long since learned that the only way to survive was to be as quiet and efficient as she could. Just not too efficient. She was already marked by the silver power she wielded and her seemingly human features. Standing out more would draw too much attention.

Having driven through the night, fuelled by human fast food and the oath spells that would not let her rest, Arrow thought she was refreshed and ready when she turned off the main, human-made highway, only to discover that the mountain road, the only access to Farraway Township, was not smooth or well-maintained. A mass of churned-up snow met her eyes in place of the clear, smooth road surface she had been travelling on. The vehicle slid sideways the moment its wheels touched the snow and it took all her limited driving skill to bring it to a halt, her palms sweating on the steering wheel, heart going too fast. Recalling some of the mechanic's more obscure words, she had eventually worked out how to fit snow chains to the vehicle's tyres and was glad she had done so as the vehicle crawled, slowly, up the mountain.

The leather of the steering wheel was indented with finger impressions by the time she completed the hazardous, narrow series of hairpin turns that wound up the mountainside and arrived at the township, set in a shallow, wide basin amid the Farraway Mountain range, higher hills and peaks rising all about.

Her first impression was wonder. The entire area she could see in the slightly pink early morning light was covered in snow. She had never seen so much of it. Would not have believed it possible. The snow lay as a great blanket across the entire township. Some paths had been cut through it, but most of it was untouched. This thick layer of white was a version of winter she had never encountered, with the Taellaneth gardeners managing the seasons with the same care they tended their plants, and the only other place she had seen in winter was Lix, where there was never this much snow, and what snow there was became churned to grubby slush on city streets.

Her next impressions of the shifkin heartland were conflicting. Chaos and silence. There was no ordered design. Buildings were set randomly across the basin, coated in snow, no harmony with their neighbours, different designs competing for attention, tall trees here and there adding to the disorder. Her eyes landed on a red house to one side of the basin. The end of it, which was all she could see, looked like a giant triangle poking up to the sky, the colour cheerful and vibrant under a snow-covered roof. A turquoise blue house nearby was a blocky construction, its peaked roof shallower, its colour clashing with the red. And next to the turquoise and the red houses was a yellow house whose shape made no sense to her eyes, a seemingly hexagonal construction with what looked like purple stripes. Mixed in with the bright colours were plain wooden houses, simple box shapes with pitched roofs and no decoration, easier on her eyes among their gaudy neighbours. A little over two dozen buildings, perhaps, though the snow was heavy enough in places to make it hard to count. Despite the evidence of life, the place appeared deserted. Even through the vehicle's protective wards, the township was still and too quiet.

Looking around and wondering where she should go, she spotted one building much larger than the others with a tall radio mast on its roof high above the trees and snow, and followed the road towards it, ending up at an open space in front of the building, snow cleared enough that the tarmac was visible.

The space was dominated by a wrecked vehicle tilted on its side, underside exposed, one wheel entirely missing, another twisted, the metal frame holding the tyre bent at an odd angle. Driving around the wreck, she could see that the front end had been mangled, the metal plates ripped and torn with deep, gouging marks that looked like they were made by claws along the shiny red surface, top ripped up exposing a cream interior that showed no sign of blood or battle. She swallowed. Left in the open, the space carefully cleared around it, the wreck was an obvious warning. One she had to ignore.

Stopping her own vehicle, she dragged her attention away from the wreck to the sign attached to the building, near the double doors: "Farraway Township Municipal Offices". In smaller writing underneath was a list of services the offices provided, including hunting permits. There were lights on in the building, and a shadow moved past one of the windows, the first sign of life she had seen.

Even prepared for winter, the biting cold shocked her when she got out of the car. The vehicle pinged as metal cooled in the frigid air, breath clouding in front of her as she hastily fastened her coat and put on her hat, gloves, and scarf. The Taellaneth was never this cold.

As ready as she would ever be, she gave the wreck, somehow much larger now that she was outside, another quick glance before moving away from the car. A bare few steps and she stopped. She was no longer alone. In between heartbeats, several shapes had gathered at the edges of her sight. Keeping otherwise still, she moved her head slightly, finding perhaps a half-dozen shifkin surrounding her.

Two were in animal forms, the wolf-like shape that all 'kin could adopt. The ones in human form were clearly not human. They were under-dressed for the weather in a variety of casual outfits, jeans, T-shirts, and sweatshirts, not affected by the cold, and moving with the smooth, casual grace of the master predators that they were.

"Come to play, little girl?" The voice, speaking the common tongue, was too close to her ear.

Arrow bit her lip against an undignified squeak. Her limited dealings with the 'kin before had been in neutral, human-managed territory, calm and controlled. Out here, deep within their borders, her senses were filled with shifkin. The hint of wild in the air, the trace of unfamiliar power against her skin and her personal wards, the bite of winter, savage and untamed.

"I am sent—" she began.

The 'kin just behind her made a low sound, a growl from a seemingly human throat.

"Not interested."

"I—"

"You stink," he told her.

She wondered if she really did smell bad after a night's journey and opened her mouth to try and speak again.

"Not interested. Not welcome. Get back in your little toy car and get off the mountain."

He tracked around to stand in front of her, lips slightly raised to show white teeth, eyes full of hate and anger as he stared directly at her. A challenge, among the 'kin. Often self-preservation, among the Erith. She held his eyes. A deep blue, a colour rarely found among the Erith, in a face that looked entirely human, tanned from outdoors. The oaths she carried, binding her to service to the Erith, would not allow her to leave with her task unfilled. She had tried to escape before. More than once. The oath spells would lock her body in place if she tried to run, bring her to her knees in pain if she disobeyed an order. So, despite her racing pulse and the flare of her wards, sensing danger, she held her ground.

"I am sent to lend aid." She managed a full sentence, the words of the common tongue strange to her mouth after so long within the Taellaneth.

"Aid?" He sneered, lifted a finger, and poked her on the arm. A casual gesture but it sent her stumbling back against the car. Shifkin were strong. Strong enough to tear her apart like the mangled wreck she could see past his shoulder.

"We're closed." Another 'kin was close by, the two of them crowding her against cooling metal and glass. "Go away."

"I cannot," she said, lips stiff with cold and fright.

"Go. Away." The second 'kin was more powerful than the first, the wash of his anger and power making her skin and feet twitch with the urge to move. But she could not. The oath spells stirred, sensing denial of her purpose and she suppressed a shudder at the loathed sensation of the spells' magic waking in her body.

"I wish to speak with Matthias Farraway." She achieved a calm tone between the spells and the danger from the 'kin. The Prime's son and, if her guess was correct, second-in-command, far more powerful than the 'kin gathered around her. They had met before, and he had not harmed her.

"Got an appointment?"

"Please tell him that Arrow is here." She ducked the obvious verbal trap.

"Con." The first 'kin did not raise his voice. One of the others in human form ducked his head, turned, and jogged into the building.

Arrow did not move, barely breathed as they waited. The two in front of her were motionless, a hunter's trick, eyes unblinking on her.

"He'll be along in a while." The 'kin reappeared at the door, voice pitched loud enough that Arrow could hear.

"A while." The first smiled, showing too many white teeth. "Well, let's see." Before she could react, his hand shot out, curled around her upper arm, and dragged her away from her vehicle, spinning her about into open space. She stumbled, righted herself, and stilled as soon as she could. Surrounded.

The 'kin who had grabbed her was shaking his hand, brows drawn together in confusion for a moment before his jaw tightened in annoyance. Stung by her wards. Not enough to truly hurt.

"Magic bitch," he sneered, and the others copied the gesture, a barricade of teeth and fangs. Bitch was not as foul a word among the 'kin as among humans. Arrow had borne worse.

"I have magic, yes," she confirmed. And dared not use it. If she used magic and harmed the 'kin, then she was dead. The 'kin would kill her before she could leave the mountain, and if by some miracle she escaped them, the Erith would execute her for disobeying them.

"This should be fun." A voice behind her.

A hard shove in the small of her back sent her stumbling forward against another shove that spun her sideways.

They were playing. Far more gently than many of the Erith had played with her. Hands only. No teeth. No claws. No steel. She was not bleeding, and no bones were broken. There would be bruises, surface only. That did not count as real damage as far as she was concerned. And despite the anger, there was a grin on more than one face as they passed her around the circle, a lifting of tension, the 'kin laughing as she tripped on her own feet.

"Stop."

Power rippled in the air, unfamiliar magic with the scent of earth and freshly cut pine trees. Shifkin's natural magic.

Everything stopped apart from Arrow, mid-flight from a hard shove. She tumbled to her knees, wincing at another bruise, then got to her feet, dizzy from the circles. She turned to look at the speaker, opening her senses a fraction to better understand him.

Matthias Farraway. With his inherent magic unleashed, he appeared larger for a moment until her eyes adjusted. Compact, solid with muscle, he was mid-sized among the 'kin and would be short among the Erith. Dressed in close-fitting, black combat clothing, arms crossed over his chest, there was no softness from the close-cropped auburn hair to his serviceable boots. He glared at her with green eyes that held no welcome, jaw tight.

"Leave." He tipped his head and the other 'kin vanished as abruptly as they had arrived. "Arrow." It could have been a greeting.

"Matthias Farraway. Greetings."

"What in the hell are you doing here?"

"The Erith sent me. They told me that ..." She stumbled as his eyes flared, bright green with 'kin power, swallowed, then went on, voice weaker. "... that Marianne Stillwater was dead. And asked me to lend aid to investigate."

Matthias growled. The sound raised hairs all over her body, picked up her heart rate, and made her wish, very much, to be elsewhere.

"The Erith killed her." His voice had dropped, fury clipping each word.

"What? No. No, that is ..." She paused as he growled again. "They sent me to lend aid," she repeated, heart hammering in her chest. The Erith would not have killed someone and sent her to investigate. That certainty held for a heartbeat, then slid away. Maybe. It was the sort of double-thinking the Chief Scribe and elder might well use to be rid of her. Send her on an impossible task. She closed her eyes a moment, hiding the hurt.

"Even so. Erith killed her."

"I ..." Arrow ran out of breath and words, bowing her head. He was certain. There was not a trace of doubt. The second of the 'kin nation believed that the Erith had killed the Prime's mate. It was a prelude to war.

A harsh snarl drew her eyes back up. He was several steps closer, just as angry.

"We asked the Erith to send representatives to explain their actions." His voice was still deep, vibrating through her. "They've said nothing. And send you. Why?"

"I am disposable," she answered, hearing the bitterness in her tone and, for once, not caring. Oh, yes, the Chief Scribe and elder, her very existence an offence to both of them, were quite capable of this.

There was a long, uncomfortable silence. Arrow blinked, trying to clear her eyes. Every time she was sent to complete a task for the Erith, there was a real risk to her life. This close to the end of her service, the remainder of it mere handfuls of days that had been counting down in her mind, she had allowed herself, for a stupid moment, to imagine that she might be free. That the years of service she had provided would result in the reward she had been promised at the start: her freedom. Fool. The Erith, Seggerat and Eshan in particular, did not mean for her to live. The 'kin had every reason to kill her to send a message to the Erith. On the certainty that an Erith had killed the Prime's mate, execution of a messenger would be an acceptable measure.

She wanted to live. Wanted to be free of the spells choking her blood. Wanted to explore the world outside the Taellaneth. Wanted to have a chance to think for herself, to decide her own fate, wanted a hundred other things that ran through her mind in a jumbled list. The wishes choked her breath, closed her throat, and set a hard, painful lump in her chest. Her eyes fell on the mangled wreck and she swallowed. Metal was far harder to tear apart than flesh.

"And you were ordered to provide aid?" Matthias' voice was calm, snapping her out of her melancholy. He was thinking, his emotions held in check. The anger had faded, shadow of grief rising. Marianne Stillwater had not been his mother, but she had been partnered with the Prime for many years.

"Yes," she said, throat still tight.

"What aid can you provide?"

"I have training." She saw the curl of his lip, a too-long incisor showing, and hastened on. "Death leaves an impression. I may be able to reconstruct her last moments. Show you what happened."

"Reconstruct? Twist for the Erith? Show them innocent?"

"The spell reveals what happened. It does not invent." Her spine straightened. Fifteen cycles of Academy training had taught her to wield magic, not to fabricate. And she was charged with finding the truth. She wondered if the elder knew the truth of what had happened and decided not to follow that line of thinking too far.

She had Matthias' attention. His shoulders relaxed fractionally.

"What do you need?"

"To be at the site where she died, and to have something that belonged to her. Something she wore next to her skin." She thought he might be listening, considering accepting her help. A flicker of hope lit inside even as her eyes strayed to the wreck again. Perhaps she would not end up like that after all.

"Bloody reporters." Matthias had followed her gaze. "Pa doesn't like them, best of times. Stuck a microphone in his face." Matthias' grim expression cracked into a gleaming white baring of teeth. "But Pa enjoyed the workout."

"Foolish reporter," Arrow said, surprised by the revelation and the idiocy demonstrated. Human, of course; the Erith did not possess journalists, and no 'kin would approach the Prime in that way. She wondered what had happened to the reporter's body.

Matthias gave a short laugh, "Ran all the way down the mountain. Don't think he'll be back."

"Most likely not," Arrow agreed and shivered lightly. She could all too easily imagine the fear that would lead someone to run that far.

"You're turning blue." His voice was utterly dispassionate. "Go wait in there." He pointed to the small cafe next to the municipal offices. "And I'll be back soon." He turned and stalked away, leaving Arrow to follow his direction.

She watched him go for a moment, lightheaded in relief. She was in one piece. She would live a little while longer. Now she had to deliver what she had promised.

Chapter Four

The site where Marianne Stillwater had died was not far from the township, Matthias had said. He may have regarded it as close, but it had taken a short journey in his rugged vehicle, weaving through trees, Arrow clutching on to her seat, and then a long walk through primitive forest before they had reached it.

The forest was another wonder to Arrow, so long used to the planned beauty of the Taellaneth. Farraway Mountain's forest was steeped in age, apparently uncultivated, trees growing where they would. The trees were a mix of species she did not recognise, some giant, their wide trunks rising high over her head, others smaller, looking like youngsters next to the mighty adults, while some were crowded together, others spaced out. In places, patches of bare earth showed under thick, evergreen canopies while elsewhere, light shone through bare branches, reflecting from snow-covered ground. Picking a path between the trees required concentration to navigate the roots and the snow, which fell where it could, at one moment hardly there, knee-deep at the next step.

Bare moments outside the vehicle, Arrow had realised how unprepared she was for this journey. Her heavy-soled boots, more than adequate for urban areas, slid on snow. Her messenger bag, so useful for quick access to her tools, kept slipping, threatening to unbalance her and more than once, she had sunk into the snow, trouser legs cold and wet.

Now she stood in the middle of shifkin territory, disoriented, cold seeping in through her layers of clothing.

The place where Marianne Stillwater had died was no different from the surroundings they had walked through, as far as she could tell. Another patch of woodland, a mix of evergreens and trees that had long since cast their leaves, bare branches reaching to the sky, heavy cover of snow thinning here under the evergreen trees, and a heavy scent of pine complementing the cold in the air. One of the old, tall trees had fallen a while before, letting in more snow and light, and it was in this bare patch that Matthias stood.

"She was found here." He indicated the space at his feet. "So, show me."

"I would like to look around a moment, then prepare. The spell takes a little while." That was an understatement. The reconstruction spell was fiendishly complex, one of the creations of Serran vo Liathius, generally regarded as the foremost magician the Erith had ever had. The whole thing took hours to prepare. Arrow had begun her preparations on the journey here, thinking it might be useful. The preparation had required another stop for food, magic burning through her energy, and had left her with a dull headache and dry, tired eyes. Now, already chilled, she was glad of the effort, the spell primed in a series of keywords, requiring only her will, power, and a little time to ignite.

"Very well. Here." Matthias handed her a paper-wrapped bundle. "One of Marianne's scarves." Something in what he said, or did not say, caught her attention. Some mystery that she did not have time to consider.

"Thank you." She took the bundle, tucked it carefully into a pocket, and walked around the space, opening her senses slowly to the world.

Winter still, the mountain was apparently serene and calm in the late afternoon. She had thought that the mountain and forest might be quiet, away from the township and 'kin, but there was wind in the trees, the far-off call of a bird, the crunch of snow underfoot and a dozen other small sounds she could not identify.

So far from everything that was familiar to her, Arrow thought it was beautiful, and would be a lonely place to die. A lump of pain caught in her throat at the thought that she might find out before too long, if Matthias was not happy with what the reconstruction spell showed.

Shaking off the useless speculation, senses open, she gathered impressions of the place. Echoes, fading with time. Distress. Grief. Shock. Loneliness. Rage. Murderous rage, in fact. Loss. Several different personalities, none of which she knew, and all within the past few days. No violence. Death left its mark, and violent death more so, and yet all the impressions here were reactions to death, not the cause.

Frowning a little at the anomaly, she dug further. Under the sound and feeling was the scent of something primitive, earthen, and ancient. For a moment she thought it was the 'kin, but as her senses settled, she realised it was the mountain itself. Not a fully formed sentience, but definitely aware, the land beneath her feet full of power. Arrow nearly fell again as she walked.

It called to her, seductively close. More power than any magician could use in a lifetime. Power enough to conquer the world. And only a fool would try to take it without permission. The mountain's awareness had stirred in response to her seeking, a sharpening of attention in the second world, the place of power beyond the plain reality of the here and now, where magicians trained in high magic could see the lines of power and work their spells. The mountain was responding to her presence, recognising a possible threat. The mountain's power could brush her aside with as much effort as a seed scattered in the wind.

The Erith would call it the mountain's spirit, that awareness, and accord it the same respect as any living thing. The spirits of the world could help or hinder a magician in their work. Arrow murmured a few words in Erith almost reflexively, reassuring the awareness she had no harmful intent. Settling a little, it watched closely.

When she was satisfied that there was nothing else to learn, she came back to the place Matthias was waiting, set her bag down in the snow and gave him a nod, letting him know she was about to begin. He did not reply, simply stepping back to allow her more room.

Kneeling in the snow, she tugged off her gloves and dug down to the earth, fingers icy cold, burns from the snake venom almost gone. When she had a small, bare patch of earth, she drew her *kri-syang*—a slender silver blade—from the sheath against her forearm and made a shallow slice at the base of her thumb with a practised move, letting some drops of blood fall into the earth, beginning the spellwork by asking for the mountain's aid.

The rush of power from the earth lifted her hair, escaping from her hat, warming her frozen face and singing through her being. So much power. The spirit's voice rang, depth and strength nearly overwhelming her, greater than anything she had ever encountered. Training, and the oath spells stirring, brought her focus back. There was work to do.

Connection made, she carefully unwrapped Marianne's scarf, a feather-light bundle of vivid red wool, and placed it on the earth, holding it with her bloody hand. Drawing on her own power and the power the mountain lent her, she spoke the prepared words to trigger the spell, setting her will behind each part.

The lines of the spell blazed in second sight, each part locking together to form a twisting, complex whole. She took a moment to check that everything was in order before rising to her feet.

Releasing the spell, she took a step back from Marianne's final resting place, and then promptly ducked and stumbled back again as a chocolate-coloured wolf leapt out of the trees beside her, mouth open, teeth and tongue showing.

Falling back against the fallen tree, giant trunk keeping her upright, Arrow felt heat surge up her neck, face, and ears. The wolf was translucent, and silent. Reconstruction. The wolf was not here. The power of the mountain made the images sharp and clear, full of colour in the winter landscape.

The wolf's leap was cut off abruptly, something causing her body to jerk mid-air, then fall. There was no sound, but none was needed. All life had gone before she landed. Thrown back to earth, the wolf returned to her human form in which Marianne Stillwater had been a tall woman with pale, flawless skin and waist-length brown hair, blue eyes staring sightlessly at the sky. Tall for a 'kin, Arrow noted.

Out of the trees, from the direction the wolf had been running, a shadowed, indistinct, man-shaped figure came into view, movements oddly uncoordinated, standing over Marianne's body for a long moment before flicking out one arm, dropping something on the ground beside her body, then turning and moving back the way it had come.

The scene froze, nothing else moving. Arrow looked down at the object beside Marianne's body, understanding at once why the 'kin were so convinced that the Erith had killed her.

"That wasn't White Guard."

The new voice startled her into a squeal of surprise, wards flaring, hand flexing, mouth opening to speak a spell as she whirled to face the newcomer.

Out of shadows near Matthias another shifkin had arrived. Slightly taller than Matthias, casually dressed in rumpled outdoor clothing, with dark auburn hair that tumbled wildly around his head and brilliant green eyes glittering with power and emotion. Against Arrow's open senses, the newcomer radiated authority and anger. On the surface, he appeared no older than Matthias, a mid-thirties male, but very little in the Erith or shifkin world was as it appeared. The most powerful shifkin she had ever encountered, it was only when he had spoken that she had become aware of his presence, catching the briefest sense of age and power, and the dangerous coil of tension and emotion.

She snapped her mouth shut, and carefully lowered her hand to her side, pulse racing, fright holding her still. She had never felt so insignificant next to a sentient being. He was ancient, the weight of his age pressing on her. Older, she thought, than any of the Erith suspected. Zachary Farraway, Prime of the shifkin nation.

He had arrived without escort, or any of the ceremony that accompanied senior Erith. Confident in his own territory, perhaps, but Arrow thought it was more likely that it was simply the shifkin way. Leadership was won in combat, not granted by bloodlines or negotiation.

"No, Prime," Arrow agreed, although she was not sure it had been a question.

"And what is that?" He waved a hand in the direction that the shadow had gone.

"I do not know, Prime, but I can try to find out."

She waited for his abrupt nod of assent before she turned her attention away. In this territory, courtesy to the Prime was basic survival. Heart still thumping from his abrupt arrival, it took some moments to achieve enough calm to open her second sight again and pick up the threads of the spell.

Moving the spell back to the point that the shadowy figure had arrived, she moved it forward again as slowly as she could, the power of the mountain holding the images clear. It was like watching a human-made film frame by frame. The spell obeyed, showing the shadowy figure moving across the clearing until it stood next to Marianne's body, the heart of the spell and the clearest possible image. Holding the spell, Arrow called more power and focused her will on clearing the darkness. Nothing.

The mountain's power was vast, and Arrow was stubborn. In the daylight world, time ticked past. Despite the freezing cold, sweat broke on Arrow's face, trickling down her back, and a tremor of effort ran through her. And still the darkness would not clear.

"Enough." The gruff command came from Matthias, who had moved around the figure, examining it from all angles. "It's disguised. Doesn't want to be seen."

Arrow inclined her head in agreement, letting power seep back into the ground, gasping with the effort of staying upright and conscious as magic drained from her. The scene remained frozen, a film on pause.

"What is it?" A low growl from Zachary, moving forward until he was nose-to-nose with the shadow.

"No idea." Matthias was scowling, attention likewise on the shadow.

Arrow shook her head slightly. She could not break through the glamour, could not see the thing's true nature. The mountain was also frustrated, unable to aid her.

"The spell will hold a while longer. We can view it again, at normal speed," she offered. It seemed the least she could do. This thing, whatever it was, had killed one of their own, and that made it prey for the shifkin.

Zachary moved out of the way without comment. A nod from Matthias and she drew a breath, calling a little energy back, wrapping the magic to her will and rewinding the scene to the beginning.

Prepared for the sight, Arrow found time to admire the grace of the wolf as she sprang over an unseen obstacle. And noticed other details, too. The whites of the wolf's eyes were showing, teeth bared, sides heaving with effort, beautiful coat ragged in places with what looked like bits of twig and burrs, pads of her paws red and raw as she soared over the ground. The silent snap as something hit the wolf made Arrow flinch involuntarily. All that vitality and life disappeared instantly.

Eyes narrowed in concentration, Arrow examined the pale, lifeless body on the ground. Apart from the raw patches on her feet and hands and a few minor scratches on her body from the undergrowth, there was no obvious wound on Marianne's body. Whatever had hit her had killed her without leaving a mark.

"Magic," Matthias growled, too close to her ear. She was too tired and too curious to flinch.

"Not any magic that I know," Arrow replied almost absently, stomach unsettled.

"Not Erith, you're saying?"

"I do not know. Just that I do not recognise this magic that can kill without leaving a trace."

He made a low sound, unconvinced, and padded away, eyes on the shadowy figure now emerging from the trees.

Moving at normal speed, the shadow's awkward gait was obvious. Frowning again, Arrow wondered how such an ungainly thing had chased the powerful, fast wolf across the mountain, and for how far.

The sky was nearly fully dark overhead, edges of the reconstruction beginning to fade, and Arrow was trembling with effort when Zachary and Matthias were eventually satisfied that they had learned all they could. No one mentioned the damning object left next to Marianne's body.

"That will do," Matthias told her.

Trying not to sigh too obviously and reveal the depth of her relief, worried the 'kin might be as intolerant of weakness as the Erith, Arrow sank to her knees on the ground next to the bare patch where Marianne's scarf lay. Using some power, she carefully cleansed the scarf, removing all trace of blood and earth before wrapping it again, setting it aside.

Drawing her knife, she cut her finger, calling a little strength from the mountain to dissipate the spell and gave her thanks to the mountain for its aid. The mountain responded with another caress of warm air across her face and a trickle of warmth through her veins, making her aware of just how cold she had become.

Over her head, the images faded to nothing, leaving the space occupied only by two 'kin and a very weary magician.

Arrow closed her eyes a moment, keeping her head down, every part of her being aching with weariness. She hated this part. The dragging exhaustion. The vulnerability. The leaden weight in her centre where her seals were. Her wards were a memory, worn away with her magic, senses open to the world; there was nothing between her and the whirl of emotion that had passed through the place, the scrape of anger from the Prime and his son, the cold of winter, the depth of the mountain.

If she had been pure-blood Erith, there would be a full cadre of White Guard around her just now. Trained to work with Erith magicians, the warriors would have wards set to protect her raw senses, putting themselves, with their disciplined minds, between her and any danger. And whilst she was being fanciful, perhaps they would have some Erith tea for her, and a cloak to warm her.

Instead, she was in shifkin territory with two enormously powerful 'kin who had every reason to detest the Erith and not a single scrap of power left to defend herself.

Eventually, she regained some calm and pushed herself to her feet, a little surprised by the 'kin's patience. She returned the paper-wrapped bundle to Matthias who handed it straight to his father. Bending to pick up her bag, she hissed involuntarily at the effort, heat surging in her face at her weakness. When she had settled the bag over her shoulder, a dead weight against her, she turned to find them watching her with keen, bright eyes.

"The Taellan sent you," Zachary stated. She nodded. He moved closer, absolutely silent to her too-sensitive ears, whether through his natural magic or years of practice she could not tell. Predator. She stayed as still as possible, allowing him close, allowing him to take a few deep breaths, catching her personal scent to remember her. He hissed, an angry sound. Concentrating on not flinching, trying not to let her fear show, she kept her eyes down.

"You reek of Erith." His voice was dark. "But you don't smell like Erith."

"I live with the Erith," she said. Absolute truth.

"But you are not Erith."

"No, Prime."

"And not human. What are you?" From another being, at another time, that would be unforgivably rude. In this place, it was a question that required response.

"I am the Taellan's representative. Of mixed blood. My lineage is struck from the records."

She was mostly Erith, however much Seggerat might wish to deny it, yet she had enough other blood in her to mark her forever apart from a race that took pride in its heritage and purity. One non-Erith grandparent, a long-dead human woman, and she was shunned. Perhaps her parents would have protected her if they had lived more than a few months past her birth. Perhaps not. No one talked about her parents. Or her lineage. There was no record of her at all among the Erith.

That lack of record was an old shame and should not still hurt. The Erith loved records. Every Erith, or servant of the Erith, knew where they belonged, the lines of their heritage meticulously recorded. Apart from her. Should not still hurt, she reminded herself, even as her eyes stung.

The Prime absorbed that information in silence and took a few more deep, even breaths, testing her scent. His face, when she glanced across, gave nothing away.

"You did this thing on your own? Without aid?" He gestured around them, recalling the translucent shapes of the reconstruction.

"The mountain lent its aid," she clarified and saw that he understood that perfectly. She bowed her head. "Otherwise, yes, alone."

"And you don't think the Erith killed Marianne?" The Prime's control was excellent, but her senses were still open. There was a vein under the name. Not quite grief. Mostly anger. Not the new, raw anger of the recently bereaved but something older. Arrow had no time to follow her curiosity as to why the Prime might have been so angry, for so long, at his mate.

"I do not know, Prime," Arrow said quietly, "but no White Guard would leave something so personal behind."

"Personal?" Matthias' voice. She had been so intent on the Prime she had nearly forgotten his son.

"The medallion left next to the body," Arrow clarified. "It is…" Tongue clumsy with the common language, she had to search for the right words. "…Something sacred. Revered amongst the White Guard. No warrior would leave it." That was not quite right, just the closest she could manage just now.

"The White Guard were framed." Zachary's voice was dark again, old anger giving way to something newer, and a hint of satisfaction. Teeth flashed, bright in the dying light, as he grinned. Not pleasantly. "Someone thinks to fool us."

"Or it's a double bluff," Matthias speculated.

Brow furrowed, having to concentrate to follow the casual phrasing, a chill ran through Arrow that had nothing to do with the winter air. A double bluff, as Matthias put it, was something that the Erith were very capable of. Leave blatant evidence which was impossible for any White Guard to leave and disguise the fact that another Erith had killed Marianne Stillwater. From the Erith's point of view, believing the shifkin to be simple, violent beings, there was an obvious course after that. Provoke the Prime and the shifkin nation into outrage that could be coolly denied by the Erith, perhaps even pushing the 'kin into violence which the Erith would then return, the peace broken and the races spiralling down into another war.

And yet, even angry and full of hurt, both 'kin in front of her were thinking. Not the near-feral beasts some Erith judged them to be.

"Do you have the medallion?" Arrow asked, earning sharp, suspicious glares from them both. "I may be able to trace the owner."

"No need," Zachary growled. She kept her surprise to herself, wondering how the 'kin had managed to identify the carrier of a White Guard medallion. The precious metal disks, awarded at the successful completion of the warrior's trials, were imbued with magic unique to each individual. Never displayed, they were worn underneath clothing, next to a warrior's skin. They were for the living only, and went with the dead into their final journey, never left behind.

By a trick of the fading light, Arrow caught a clear glimpse of the Prime's face tight with emotion, cheeks hollow and eyes shadowed. He looked as worn out as she felt, as though carrying a heavy burden. Around him, first world overlaid with her second sight, she could see and sense thick tangles of shifkin magic, earthen colours almost invisible in the forest. Ties that vibrated with energy, tugging at him. Arrow had brushed against the invisible ties around 'kin before. Ties the Erith did not understand. Ties that bound each 'kin into its own collective unit, the muster. And from there bound them all together. Muster ties were tighter by far than the family and House connections that bound the Erith together.

Looking at that web, Arrow wondered if he could feel the emotions of his muster, all the grief and anger and loss that had filled this clearing at the discovery of Marianne's body. There was none of that grief in the Prime. Matthias, too, had damped down whatever loss he felt. The clearing was full of tight anger and determination, and suspicion. That last made her wish for her wards, although she was not sure how much use they would be against two determined 'kin.

There was no sense of Marianne here, not even an echo, personality erased along with her life.

In the quiet of her mind, Arrow remembered the vivid, silent images of the wolf that had sprung out of the forest, running for her life, so determined to keep moving forward she had run her feet bloody. Arrow stung with the loss of someone she had never known, a scrape against her soul, and made a silent promise to Marianne—and not the Erith or the shifkin—to find out who was responsible. The promise slid through her body, binding itself as surely as the oath spells.

"Is this all you can do?" Matthias asked, voice sharp, breaking into her thoughts.

Arrow held a bitter laugh behind her teeth. All? All her energy, and a good deal of help from the mountain to power a spell that fewer than one in twenty Academy graduates, an elite group of Erith magicians, could perform. It seemed the 'kin were as hard to please as the Erith.

"What do you need?"

"Can you track? Follow a trail?" She was no 'kin to read body language like a book, but both the question and his casual pose were subtly wrong. Too deliberate, she thought.

"Not in the way of your people." She gave him truth. "But there are spells that allow me to trace where a person has been."

"And?"

"I need to understand the person's essence to do so." A low sound from Matthias and she hastily added, "It is the magical equivalent of scent. It does not usually tell what a person was thinking or feeling, just that they were there."

"And?"

"And I cannot do that with what I know so far." She heard the exasperation in her own voice and swallowed before she continued. "As I do not understand Marianne Stillwater's essence."

"The scarf?"

Although Matthias was questioning her, the Prime was listening intently, pacing back and forth behind her. She checked an impulse to turn and follow his movement, caught between two predators, not wanting to draw any more of the Prime's close attention.

"The scarf allowed a connection with the earth, and a person's death leaves a clear mark on the world." For a moment, she wished she was speaking Erith to another magician. Trying to translate her innate understanding into Erith words and then the common tongue was frustrating. Matthias was glaring, arms folded over his chest.

"You need something she loved." The Prime's voice was quiet. Arrow's heart picked up pace, attention snagged on the understanding in those few words. Erith and 'kin magic had nothing in common. She had not known that any 'kin had tried to understand Erith magic.

"Yes, Prime. Something she wore regularly or had a close connection with." Or a space that she was happy in, she could have added, staying silent because of something she had understood from the way both 'kin had moved or behaved. Marianne had not been happy on the mountain.

The soft growl at the edge of her hearing made her twitch, an outward reaction she controlled as soon as she could. Stripped of her usual defences, wards useless, she wanted to run away, far away, from that sound. The low, involuntary noise of a master predator. But there was no safety to run to here. And on her shaking legs, exhausted from the day's efforts, the 'kin would run her down in moments.

"Marianne spent most of her time in Lix," Marianne's widower told her. The mostly human city that sat between the Taellaneth and Farraway Mountain. Arrow stilled. She was not an expert on 'kin but she knew that mate bonds were close. For a 'kin pair to live apart was unusual. "The house should be enough."

"We'll arrange access," Matthias added.

"Thank you." Arrow wanted to ask why the 'kin wanted her, an outsider, to follow Marianne's trail. The want was easily set aside; the 'kin had a use for her. They were allowing her to live, and she would not push them. Not yet anyway. Perhaps when she understood their tolerance of her better. Maybe then she would venture some questions, try to satisfy the curiosity that burned almost as strongly as her wish to live.

"Will you be armed there, too?" Matthias glared at her.

"Armed?" she queried, wondering if she had not understood.

"The knife," he bit out.

"The *kri-syang*." She lifted her arm, leaving the blade where it was at Matthias' low growl. "It is a tool used in magic. No Erith would think of it as a weapon. A tool only."

"Looks like a blade to me." He was not satisfied, but at least did not insist she hand over the blade. As personal to a mage as the medallion was to a warrior, Erith law forbade the use of the individually bonded blades as a weapon.

Behind Matthias, Zachary remained silent, watching the exchange with fever-bright eyes and no expression.

"I'll get you the address back in town," Matthias glanced up. "We should head back."

Arrow followed his look and realised that it was fully dark above the trees, the snow reflecting just enough light from the stars and moons for her to see.

When she looked back to Matthias, the Prime had disappeared silently into the trees, leaving no trace of his presence behind.

"This way." Matthias led them back along the trail to his vehicle, Arrow deeply grateful for the guidance as they made their way through the darkening forest. Her power gone, she would not have found her way out without his help.

Chapter Five

To her surprise, the 'kin had provided her with a comfortable room for the night at the Township's only hotel, managing to convey without saying so bluntly that she should leave in the morning and wait in Lix until the appointed time for her access to Marianne Stillwater's residence.

Refreshed from the first unbroken night's sleep in longer than she cared to remember, and with no duties until her appointment, Arrow had been looking forward to a complete day to herself. She could not remember the last time that had happened. All she had to do for that day was get to Lix. One, simple task. Within the Taellaneth, she was at the disposal of the Taellan, Eshan, Evellan and the Academy's teaching staff, frequently on the same day. Some time of her own was a rare luxury. She had the length of the journey to Lix to plan how to use it, fingers tapping an impatient rhythm on the steering wheel as she left Faraway Mountain.

A direct summons from the Chief Scribe as soon as she had left shifkin territory had cancelled her plans before they had been fully formed. She had managed curt civility for the scribe as he would tolerate nothing less, muttering a curse into the uncaring air when the connection was cut and the oath spells stirred, binding her to follow Eshan's directions.

She was back in the Taellaneth by early evening darkness.

Dealing with the mechanic who seemed convinced she had somehow harmed the vehicle, and the open sneer of the White Guard sentry at the gate—disgust equally divided between her return and human clothing—were familiar frustrations, as was having to force open the door to her residence, the untreated wood warped with winter cold.

She shed her human clothing, returning to the formal, Erith clothing that she was required to wear within the Taellaneth: a servant's knee-length coat, slit to hip-height at front, back and sides for ease of movement, with a series of small buttons that ran to her chin; plain breeches; and knee-length boots, all in dark, plain cloth. She tugged her sleeves to an even length as she walked. The Taellaneth Steward had high standards and while he was a great deal kinder than the Chief Scribe, his gentle disappointment was somehow worse than Eshan's sharp tongue. There was nothing she could do about her unruly hair, but everything else was as proper as she could manage. Her second-hand boots were a fraction too large, the soles parchment-thin from wear so that she could tell precisely where she was in the Taellaneth simply by the ground underfoot.

Passing around the back of the scribes' quadrangle, she breathed deeply as she entered the heart of the Taellaneth, the landscaped grounds that housed the Taellan's residences. She paused out of habit, struck by the contrast between the extraordinary, sculpted beauty of the Taellaneth and the uncoordinated, stripped-back simplicity of the shifkin territory. The 'kin had settled their living spaces into their territory with minimal change, while the Erith ordered the landscape to suit their will.

In the manner of the Erith, the residences provided for the Taellan were set apart from each other, half-hidden amongst mature trees and forming a gentle curve that mirrored the tables in the Taellaneth meeting rooms. The centre was occupied by an expertly crafted copse of trees with a water feature that burbled contentedly, the taste of fresh water in the air complementing the scent of growing, even in this season.

The residences were spaced five on each side and at the far end was the eleventh manor kept in readiness for their majesties. In the fifty years that the Taellaneth had been in operation, the Erith Queen and her Consort had visited fewer than half a dozen times that Arrow was aware of. Still, the manor was always staffed and glowed quietly in the night.

Apart from the Queen's residence, only a few of the manors were lit. Several Taellan would have returned to the heartland and one was never occupied as the Halsfeld lords resided in the same building.

Arrow drew a slow breath in, absorbing as much of the peace of the gardens into her as she could, knowing she would need it when she entered the elder's residence. No matter what she had done, he would be dissatisfied and find fault.

Shown into the elder's personal study, Arrow found that he had guests, other members of the Taellan. The two Halsfeld lords, Juinis and Kester, were seated with the elder, along with Gret vo Regresan and Eimille vel Falsen.

As Arrow made her bow her mind quickened. The closeness among this disparate group was a new development as far as she knew, and she wondered if the rest of the Taellan were aware.

They were a curious group, the three oldest Taellan and two of the youngest. Gret and Eimille could be brother and sister, elderly Erith with parchment-pale skin and black hair liberally streaked with grey. They, along with the elder, were clothed for their station, jewels and ornate cloth shimmering in the candlelight, the air scented from the candles and warm, spiced wine in delicate glasses at each of their elbows.

The Halsfeld lords were a study in contrast, Juinis, pale-skinned with rich brown hair, Kester with pitch-black hair and golden-bronze skin that blended well into shadow. Juinis was dressed for his station as elaborately as the older three, Kester dressed almost plainly. Not related by blood, Juinis had insisted that Kester surrender his House and join House Halsfeld on Juinis' marriage to Kester's sister, a ruthless piece of negotiation of the sort generally admired among the Erith ruling class. And it seemed Juinis continued to be ambitious, keeping such close company with the three eldest and most influential Taellan.

Arrow straightened from her bow and waited for their commands. If the Taellan were surprised, or disappointed, by her return, they hid it well behind their public faces, as she had expected.

"Tell us what you have learned," Seggerat vo Regersfel ordered.

"Was she killed?" Eimille vel Falsen followed the elder.

"Are the shifkin likely to declare war?" Juinis vo Halsfeld demanded.

"Who killed her?" Gret vo Regresan wanted to know.

"Elder, my lady, my lords." Arrow bowed slightly, politely, once the barrage of questions had calmed, the peace of the gardens outside remaining with her for now. "There are few answers at this moment. It is clear that Marianne Stillwater was killed—and killed by magic."

That sparked another round of questions. Arrow waited for a suitable pause before bowing slightly again and speaking.

"My lady, my lords, it is not clear who was responsible for the lady's death. She was chased for a while across the mountain and then brought down by something unseen. I performed a resurrection spell at the site where she was killed for the Prime and his elder son."

"Describe this scene," Gret vo Regresan instructed.

"Did you record it?" Seggerat asked, overriding the other lord.

"Yes, my lord." A simple twist of magic was built into the spell, a precaution in case the scene needed to be viewed again.

"Project it here." He gestured to the spell mirror on his desk, black and calm in its dormant state. A finely crafted magical tool, the square mirror was as long and high as the elder's forearm, set in an ornately carved wooden frame. Having used the mirror before, it took little effort to wake the mirror's spells. Once the mirror surface rippled, ready for use, Arrow released the images onto its surface. There was a momentary flicker then the surface settled, shimmering with a clear replication of the images.

Five of the most influential Erith alive gathered around Seggerat's mirror to get a better look. Arrow stepped back to allow them room, positioning herself behind the lady's shoulder where she could see the recording to ensure the images stayed sharp and clear. Watching the Erith crowd around the mirror, Arrow was reminded of a human television, even though none of the Taellan would ever admit to having seen one.

The Taellan were as curious as the shifkin had been, and as demanding in their viewing. They required different angles for the images, the scene played at different speeds, close-up detail of the point Marianne fell, the disposition of her body in the snow, and further clarity at various other points. The Taellan's formidable attention to the images reminded Arrow once more of television viewing, or possibly of human film directors wanting a different angle, a different lighting scheme, a different pace to the action.

The Taellan were neither as patient nor as silent as the Prime and his son had been. Arrow held her concentration, showing the images through the disjointed commentary and speculation from the viewers. At length, they seemed satisfied that they had seen enough different views of Marianne Stillwater's death and the elder commanded Arrow play the scene through again.

"What was that object?" Kester vo Halsfeld, youngest of the Taellan, asked, curiosity drawing his attention to Arrow for a moment. In the recording, the figure had just dropped the barely seen object next to Marianne's body.

"A White Guard's medallion, my lord." Arrow kept her voice even.

The room stilled, all attention on Arrow for the moment.

"Where is it?" the elder demanded, amber sparking in his eyes.

"With the shifkin, my lord."

"Did they know who it belonged to?" Kester asked, face a shade paler. He might be dressed in brocade and silk now, but he had been a member of the White Guard before his sister's marriage to Juinis.

"They did not say, my lord."

He looked as if he wanted to say more, holding back words with effort, lips thinned together. Perhaps wondering which of his fellow warriors had died without record, for no living warrior would allow their medallion to be taken.

"Now we know," the elder said quietly, setting aside Kester's concerns. The others agreed, clearly needing no explanation. Arrow tightened her jaw. Disposable, she had told the 'kin. She had been right. "I assume the Prime was informed that no warrior would leave that behind?"

"He was, my lord," Arrow confirmed.

"Good." It was not praise, simply satisfaction. Whether because his plans were unfolding as expected, or for some other reason, it was impossible to tell, and he would not share anything more with her even if she asked.

"She was remarkably graceful," Kester commented, dragging his attention away from the small, damning object in the snow.

"Hard to tell size without any scale to measure it by," Juinis noted.

"The scene looks primitive," Eimille vel Falsen said, her eyes narrowing slightly. "Completely untamed." It was hard to tell from the slight pinching of her expression if she disapproved or was envious of the untamed space that the shifkin claimed as their own.

"What is that creature?" The elder was irritated, leaning closer to the mirror to get a better look at the dark shape that had followed Marianne Stillwater across the mountain.

"Show us a larger image," Gret vo Regresan commanded, not taking his eyes off the mirror.

Arrow complied without comment, taking a breath against the sharp pain in her head. The image on the screen wavered a moment to the immediate protest of the gathered Taellan, then the mirror settled to a larger image of the dark form. The edges of the creature were indistinct, the dark shape filling the mirror's frame.

"What kind of camouflage is that?" Gret asked, fretting.

"Perhaps we could ask the Preceptor for his views," Kester speculated. "If anyone would know, then it is he."

"We do not wish the world to know," Gret objected.

"The Preceptor knows how to be discreet," Juinis commented quietly, supporting his vestrait brother.

"He is not of Family." Eimille, longest serving of the Taellan, voiced her objection, tradition winning over her own curiosity.

"Play it again, focusing on the creature," the elder commanded. Arrow silently changed the mirror's focus again, showing the first appearance of the unknown shape again.

The elder's attention was fixed on the images in the mirror as the dark shape moved awkwardly across the clearing.

"Is this at normal speed?" he asked.

"Yes, my lord." Arrow needed only the inflection of his voice to know she was being addressed.

"The creature has a strange gait," Kester said. "Did the Prime or his son make any comment on it?"

"No, my lord."

The elder wanted another replay. Arrow obeyed, ignoring the stab behind her left eye, focusing instead on making the image as clear as she could. Magic had recorded the images, and it required magic and concentration to retrieve them.

The Taellan had never cared if she was comfortable, so there was no point in mentioning her headache. She clenched her jaw slightly, observing them watching the recording, wondering how many of them would have made it through the wild of Farraway Mountain to the site. Kester would, she realised immediately. Former White Guard, he would likely regard the hike as little more than a stroll.

"It does not appear Erith," Juinis commented at the end of the review, breaking through Arrow's thoughts. The other Taellan agreed without hesitation, even the elder. That meant little. Juinis' observation had been carefully phrased. Arrow's opinion was not sought. She thought that the figure could be of any race as it was so heavily disguised.

"How could you not get a clear image?" Gret asked peevishly, peering at the blur. Arrow shook her head slightly. Holding the images was not as difficult as the actual spell had been, but her energy was not fully recovered, and she had had a long day's driving besides.

"I cannot be certain, my lord. I speculate that whatever being was on the mountain used a camouflage to hide their identity."

"But you should have been able to see through it," Eimille vel Falsen pointed out. None of the Erith were looking at her but Arrow still inclined her head slightly in respect.

"My lady, not necessarily. I did not detect any magic at the site before I began. The spell I used was simply designed to tell me what had been there. It was not designed to counter any magic that had been in the place."

"What spell did you use?" the elder asked.

"Serran vo Liathius' resurrection spell, my lord." That was the founding Preceptor of the Academy, one of the most powerful magicians in Erith history. The Taellan's natural reserve was broken for a moment as they glanced back at her with expressions of disbelief. Lord Liathius' spells were renowned as being among the most effective, and most complex of Erith magic working, requiring powerful magicians to wield them. The Taellan were strong in Erith magic, but not one of them was powerful enough to wield one of the former Preceptor's spells.

"The detail should be there, then," Eimille vel Falsen speculated. "Serran did nothing by halves." The oldest member of the Taellan, Eimille had served more than one monarch and was likely one of the few Taellan to have known Serran from his youth.

"We need a clear view of this creature," the elder agreed.

"Perhaps if we combined our wills," Gret said slowly, eyes on the blurred image. Eimille frowned at him for a moment before nodding her assent.

"Perhaps an unravelling spell," the lady suggested. The others agreed.

A moment later, the Taellan spoke the simple spell and combined and released their own magic. With singular purpose, the counsellors directed their magic and their will at the uncooperative spell mirror, trying to peel back the camouflage through sheer force.

Arrow had the bare space of a heartbeat to realise what was happening. In their rush to uncover the truth, the Taellan had forgotten that they were watching a recording. Their power found nothing in the mirror to latch on to, the mirror simply showing a reflection. The only active spell was Arrow's spell to show the scene on the mirror. The lash of power rebounded, seeking magic to unravel, and scorched through Arrow. She lost her concentration, her spell shattering. The mirror shivered before it fragmented, sending another backlash of magic into the air. She lost her balance, the recoil of the Taellan's power searing through her body, sending her falling first to her knees and then onto her side. Power ripped free into the air.

Above her head, every loose object in the room fell, toppled by the whirlwind. Unleashed with the simple purpose of stripping away the disguise over the shadow, the Taellan's power twisted into a vortex, seeking a target. Arrow drew a deep, shuddering breath, vision dimming as she focused her remaining strength, putting her trained will against the untamed power and binding it to do no harm. The words of the simplest binding spell rasped in her throat. The power twisted, railing against her hasty confinement, seeking to fulfil its purpose, testing the binding that Arrow had thrown up.

Lying on her side, Arrow scrabbled for a safe release for the checked bundle of energy. Seggerat's study had an open chimney with a fire lit. Tasting blood in her mouth, Arrow gathered her will, requiring every scrap of training to keep focus, and shoved the snarl of magic towards the chimney, adding a command for dispersal underneath her hastily-put-together binding Pushed towards an escape, the power danced up the chimney with the smoke, sending sparks into the air. The night air above that chimney would be brilliant with fireworks as the magic dispersed.

Arrow heaved a breath, lungs searing, shaking with the aftermath, holding herself to consciousness long enough to be certain that the power dispersed without harm to anyone. The last things she saw before blackness took her were the ornately embroidered toes of Seggerat's hand-sewn silk slippers.

She came back to her senses moments later, pulled out of her faint by a surge of Erith magic. There was a thump of displaced air against her exposed face, the by-product of a translocation spell. A rattle ensued as the loose objects in the room were shaken again, followed by voices raised in fury. Behind the loud voices were soft voices speaking with concern, and a keening sound of distress. No one was paying her attention, so she had a moment's grace to realise that the translocation spell was not dangerous magic and then to draw a careful breath before opening her eyes, vision blurred.

The first thing she was able to focus on as her eyes cleared was a pair of sturdy boots planted firmly not far from where she lay. Her stomach lurched and sank. She recognised those boots. She had thrown up on them on one memorable occasion during her Academy training. Something had called Preceptor Evellan from the Academy, something so dangerous to his mind that he had used a translocation spell straight into a Taellan's residence. It was a shocking breach of protocol, and one of the angry voices she could hear was of Seggerat vo Regersfel expressing his displeasure.

She slowly sat up, careful to avoid the various delicate objects that had fallen to the floor. Her body was trembling in reaction, the force of so much magic through her and the near-miss. Unconstrained, the magic would have killed her. Could have killed them all. Her chest tightened, and she had to force a breath. The air in the room was thick with the bitter aftertaste of burning magic and the scent of the spilled wine, soaking into the hand-woven floor covering.

"How dare you invade my home?" Seggerat was furious. It was not the first time he had said that, but this time, he paused to allow the Preceptor to answer.

"I came in response to rogue magic," the Preceptor responded, equally furious. "What has happened here?"

"The lady is injured." That was Gret, his voice high and petulant.

"A nosebleed." The Preceptor dismissed the injury.

"An injury that that lady should not have sustained," Seggerat intervened, voice now smooth and quiet. It was not the quiet of calm but of repressed anger. Arrow blinked and turned her head.

Eimille vel Falsen did indeed have a nosebleed. The elderly Erith was sitting in a chair, a slightly shocked expression on her normally impassive face, a delicate lace handkerchief held to her nose, and a few drops of bright Erith blood marking it. The House Regersfel healer was by her side, his bag open at his feet, and a maid from the House standing by holding fresh, fine cloths and a bowl of water for him.

Arrow tried to get her feet under her. She could taste copper in her mouth, and her ears were ringing from the aftermath of the magic. It was something of a miracle that she was still alive. She was not quite sure how, but she had managed to get the unused power out of the building without harm coming to anyone. Nausea rose; it had been close. Too close. She did not want to think about that. Another near miss to add to many. Her task was done. For now, she focused on getting herself to her knees and then, wobbling a bit, to her feet.

She found herself beside the Preceptor. He was still in his teaching robes, his hair in wild disarray around his aristocratic features, expression difficult to make out with his burnished skin and the poor light in the room. Most of the candles had been snuffed out, walls cast with uneven shadows.

"You," Seggerat snapped at Arrow.

"My lord." Arrow could not bow, sure she would topple over if she tried, but she could manage basic courtesy.

"Get out," Seggerat told her, voice clipped, eyes snapping.

Arrow made the tiniest of bows, movement slow and stiff. She was about to leave the room when the Preceptor waved a hand in front of her, cutting through her path. She froze.

"A moment."

"I have dismissed it." Seggerat informed the Preceptor, voice and face tight.

"No one will leave until matters have been explained to my satisfaction," the Preceptor said, maintaining a relatively calm voice with evident effort.

"I do not require to explain myself to you," Seggerat snapped.

"In matters of magic, you do." Evellan had been Preceptor of the Erith Academy for many years, since long before Arrow's birth, and was not daunted by one annoyed elder.

"Your pupil was deficient," Seggerat told the Preceptor. "A simple spell. And it caused all this." The elder's sweeping hand indicated the objects lying haphazardly over the room, and Eimille vel Falsen's bleeding nose.

The Preceptor's eyes narrowed, amber sparks glinting in his dark eyes. "Please tell me precisely what happened."

"A simple reconstruction spell." Seggerat waved his hand towards the shattered spell mirror on his desk. "My mirror is ruined."

"A reconstruction spell? Arrow performed a reconstruction spell here?"

Arrow held her ground as the Preceptor's rage was transferred to her.

"My lord, I performed a reconstruction spell on Farraway Mountain to seek the truth of Marianne Stillwater's death." Unlike the others present, she had faced the Preceptor's wrath more than once and knew he always listened to clear and honest answers.

"So, what happened here?"

"A recording of the reconstruction," Kester vo Halsfeld put in. He spread his hands, long fingers open wide. "I do not know what happened."

"So, Arrow played the recording of the reconstruction onto the mirror?" the Preceptor summarised. "Then what?"

"There was a blank in the recording," Kester added.

"A blank? How could that be?"

"Your pupil was incompetent," Gret said.

"Arrow?"

"My lord, a subject of the recording had used some camouflage. The reconstruction spell could not penetrate it. I encountered the same difficulty on Farraway Mountain."

"So, then what happened?" The magician glared at the younger Halsfeld lord.

Kester glanced sideways at the other Taellan. Even through the strange sensations in her head, Arrow could see his discomfort. The newest, youngest, Taellan,

Kester was torn between loyalty to his colleagues and the demand of the highest authority of Erith magic.

"We tried to penetrate the disguise," Seggerat informed the Preceptor, unwittingly rescuing Kester.

"Penetrate ..." The Preceptor's scowl transferred from the elder's face to the shattered mirror, to Arrow, then back to the elder. "Do you mean to tell me, my lord, that five Taellan attempted a reveal spell?"

"That is so."

"Upon a recording?"

"We believed we could uncover the truth."

Arrow watched, fascinated, as the Preceptor closed his eyes, his lips moving soundlessly. She thought she recognised the text. It was a favourite of his, an Erith warrior's prayer for courage and patience.

"My lord." The Preceptor opened his eyes at length, amber sparks of Erith magic strong in his gaze as he fixed the elder in his sights, "neither you nor any of the Taellan shall attempt the use of collective magic without my express permission or authority. Is that clearly understood?"

"You ..."

"I am appointed by their gracious majesties with the sacred task of ensuring the preservation and learning of Erith magic." There was power bound into the Preceptor's words, power that was his from birth, supplemented by the power granted by their majesties. The Taellan were bound by the Preceptor's voice just as surely as the new pupils at the Academy were bound.

"So be it." Seggerat was wise enough to know when he was defeated, displeasure plain in his pinched expression. He drew himself up. "You may be certain that their majesties will hear of this."

"You may make your own report if you wish, my lord," the Preceptor conceded. He glanced at Arrow, brows drawing together, mouth flattening. "Arrow, you are bleeding. Go and get cleaned up. Report to my study at noon tomorrow and we will look at this camouflage."

"My lord." Arrow managed a slightly deeper bow. She bowed slightly to the Taellan, the ringing in her ears worse as she moved her head, then very slowly made her way out of the room and back to her residence.

It was only when she returned to her residence that she caught sight of her reflection in the dark windows. She paused, startled. She looked feral, eyes wide, expression dazed. Her hair, normally wildly curling, was standing on end in all directions. There was a thick trail of blood running from her nose down her chin, and further tracks of blood along her neck from both ears. Not the first time she had bled in service of the Erith, or when she had used too much magic. Her head ached with the aftermath, a deep ache only several hours' sleep would cure.

Getting ready for sleep, she flinched slightly, realising that she must have bled over the elder's handmade heirloom rug, and all too easily picturing his wrath at the discovery. The rug was far more valuable to him than she was. Closing her eyes, she found her face wet, wondering what new punishment Eshan would think of for her and exhausted at the mere thought.

Chapter Six

Getting to the Preceptor's study required an all-too-familiar dance, avoiding the other Teaching Masters and Mistresses who might try and divert her, including Gesser vo Regresan who had positioned himself along the Academy's main corridor, the sour scowl on his face making the students tread carefully around him. Arrow took an alternate route, one the spoiled lord would not have thought of, through the concealed servants' passages that were built into every high-status Erith building.

She made it to the familiar territory of the Preceptor's study without incident, a little out of breath, soothed immediately by her surroundings. Fifteenth-cycle students spent a great deal of time in tutorials with the Academy's master, standing in a loose circle on the scarred wooden floor, trying to follow whatever task the Preceptor had set for them that day.

Some of Arrow's best memories of learning magic were in this room, with its one wall of spelled glass letting in as much light as possible, motes of chalk dust hanging in the air, the familiar creak of the wooden boards underfoot, and the thrill that was the unfolding of knowledge in her mind. Working her own magic, watching the spells she created come to life, brought back memories of the wonder Nassaran had shown her in early childhood when he would settle down with her and show her the beauty in the simplest objects around. A blade of grass. The fast-beating wings of a butterfly. Even the beetles that crawled on the earth.

Today, there were no students. The hum of activity in the Academy was kept at bay through the solid wooden door and the dampening spells the Preceptor had crafted into the room's surfaces.

She had arrived at the study at the appointed hour and stood in front of the Preceptor's enormous desk, waiting for his attention. He was scowling over what looked like a letter, elbow resting on a set of parchments; thirteenth-cycle student homework, she thought, reading some of the work upside down and wincing slightly at some of the runes drawn. At least one of the students would most likely have to repeat the cycle, as, despite their advanced place in the Academy's classes, they seemed incapable of drawing a straight line.

With Evellan's attention occupied, Arrow took a moment to study the room and the master magician. The piles of parchment and scrolls on his desk were higher than she remembered. The Academy's deputy, Teaching Mistress Seivella, was absent and had been for some time, which would explain the additional administration and perhaps a little of the tiredness betrayed by the dark smudges beneath his eyes. The lady's absence did not explain the faint lines of strain around the Preceptor's mouth, or the unease shown in the shadows. Usually coiled contentedly about his robes, wisps of shadow were curling about in tendrils from the dark cloth, constantly in motion.

"Blast the man. He seems to have written this on a hunt. Arrow, come, see what you make of it." He held the letter up. Accustomed to the request, Arrow accepted the letter, recognising the hand at once. Gilean vo Presien, a highly respected war mage and one of the Queen's closest advisors. Gilean and Evellan kept up an irregular correspondence, each complaining that the other's handwriting was impossible to read.

This letter was unusually bad. There were ink blots spattered across the surface and several crossed-out words as well as a dark stain on one side of the parchment that might have been blood. Gilean was usually on the move, travelling through the Erith heartlands, sometimes not heard from for months on end.

"From the third paragraph," the Preceptor prompted.

"Yes, my lord. Let me see ..." She frowned a moment more, piecing together the words, before beginning. "The testing ground for the young hunters has been ... recovered from the grasses. It is quite remarkable how quickly they grow. The grasses, I mean. The hunters seem to get younger with each passing turn ..."

She paused as there was a sharp knock at the door followed by another person entering the room, not waiting for the Preceptor's permission. It was someone expected, then, otherwise they would not have got past the room's wards. Evellan waved for Arrow to continue.

"Passing turn of the seasons ..." Arrow paused, trying to make out the next sentence. One of the most highly respected mages alive appeared to have written about red-spotted cows and she was sure that could not be right.

"A letter from my cousin?" Kester vo Halsfeld asked, joining Arrow beside the desk. He was dressed far more plainly than when she had seen him last in the elder's study, wearing an approximation of the White Guard's day uniform, charcoal-grey embellished, in place of braids of office and awards of merit, with a leaf pattern. He brought with him the scent of weapons oil and cardamom and did not seem disturbed that he stood on equal footing with her in front of the Preceptor's desk, giving her a nod as she glanced across. Stiffening, caught staring, Arrow returned her focus to the letter.

"Indeed. When you are next in touch, please tell him that his writing is growing worse with age. With the practice he has had over the years, the opposite should be true." Evellan held out a hand for the letter and Arrow returned it. He stared at the scrawl for a moment before shaking his head. "I will have someone else look at this. I cannot believe he means spotted cows, red or otherwise."

Arrow hid a smile, wishing she could be there when Gilean and Evellan had one of their rare meetings.

"The elder asked me to attend," Kester said.

"Yes, he sent a message to advise me." The Preceptor's eyes remained on the letter in his hands, voice as dry as the elder's usual tone, and Arrow saw a shallow, metal dish to one side of the desk with some burned fragments of parchment. Evellan had not liked the elder's message and Arrow wondered what the Chief Scribe had actually written.

Risking a quick, sideways glance, Arrow saw what might have been a smile cross the Taellan's face before it resumed a neutral expression of polite attention. She wondered how long the Preceptor and the former White Guard had been friends.

"Arrow, bring the spell mirror across and set up your record."

"My lord." She bowed slightly and moved to comply. The Preceptor's spell mirror was the largest she had ever seen, wider and taller than she was, held in a plain frame of black wood which had been set with wheels at some point in the past, making it easy to move.

By the time she had set up the record to run through the mirror, the Preceptor had risen and joined Kester.

"It should be possible to show this in three dimensions," Arrow suggested. She saw the Taellan's brows lift, perhaps in surprise at the idea, or perhaps at her speaking up without being asked.

"Very well. Take that side." Between them, she and Evellan lowered the mirror to lie on its back on the ground, and the images which had been flat—contained on the mirror's surface—sprang to full-sized life, the Preceptor merging with the shadowed figure for a moment as the recording ran on. Kester carefully removed his hand from a weapon hilt, a hint of colour in his face.

The afternoon passed with the Preceptor taking his time to inspect the recording for himself, firing questions to Arrow that she did her best to answer. When he was satisfied he had seen enough, he paused, standing opposite Arrow across Marianne's body.

"And you did this thing alone?" he asked. It was an echo of the question the Prime had asked, but with a more pointed slant. The images, sharp and vivid, lay between them.

"The mountain is very strong," Arrow told him. He was frowning, the coiling shadows settled into a series of tight curls around his robes, motionless for the first time that afternoon. She waited. A magician of her apparent level of ability and power should perhaps have struggled more with the spell. And he had no ability to test the strength of Farraway Mountain. He could only test her. A faint scent of burnt amber crossed the room, the sparks in the Preceptor's eyes growing as he stared at her. The familiar brush of his power, strong and certain, crossed hers. Testing. Probing. Not for the first time.

She endured, confident in her own wards and the seals deep inside, invisible to anyone but her. He would see what she wanted him and the rest of the Erith to see, which was a mage of middling power. It was rare for someone of average power to pass all of the Academy's classes but there was a precedent; some of the Teaching Masters and Mistresses in the building around them possessed less apparent power than Arrow and had graduated through hard work.

The oath spells in her blood stirred in response to their maker's power, stretching like a cat, then purring softly. Her temper rose in response, the despised magic turning contentedly in her body.

Satisfied that the oath spells were intact, and unable to find anything amiss, the Preceptor's expression did not lighten. His face was tight, intellect and instinct in conflict.

"My lord." Kester broke the silence. "Do you know what magic this shadow used?"

"No," he answered, not taking his attention from Arrow.

"Where might we learn?" the younger lord persisted. "Such abilities seem dangerous."

"They are." Evellan turned to Kester. Arrow was careful not to relax. Another dangerous moment had passed. There would be others. "The Archives might tell us more."

"The scribe's archives were destroyed," Kester said, confused.

"So I heard." The sour smile might have been satisfaction. The Chief Scribe was not well-liked and had shunned Evellan's assistance with the scriptorium wards. "The Academy has its own. Arrow, see what you can learn."

Dismissed, Arrow left, still more questions bottled up now laced with unease. Despite his flat denial, she thought Evellan did know something about the camouflage. There was a possibility, slim as it was, that Evellan had conspired with the Taellan in Marianne Stillwater's death. Arrow's lips thinned, brow creasing before she smoothed it quickly, frustration making her strides quicker than normal. There was so much hidden from her. Neither the White Guard nor Taellan would tell their secrets. That, she expected. But the Academy took pride, publicly declared, in teaching its students about all forms of magic. There was clearly at least one form missing if what she had seen on the mountain was anything to go by, and the Academy's Preceptor had not been surprised to find an unknown form of magic.

The highest authority on magic among the Erith, the Preceptor most certainly had the resources to find a White Guard medallion, and access to the knowledge and power to conceal himself from the mountain to kill Marianne, even if she could not understand, yet, how or why he might have done so.

Chapter Seven

The Academy Archives, a labyrinth of shielded tunnels under the Academy, yielded no answers and Arrow headed to her appointment at Marianne's residence in Lix with her silent promise to the dead woman to find her killer ringing in her mind, hoping that finding out more about Marianne would enable her to keep that promise. Even if no one else heard it, a magician's promise was as binding on her as the oath spells.

Lix was a sprawling city, crawling farther over the land each year, held back from the Taellaneth only by the treaties that bound the Erith and humans to peace. Even so, the city seemed larger every time Arrow visited, the humans greedily expanding into the land they held between the 'kin and the Erith. The territories which had seemed generous when they were recorded into the treaties now appeared small. Humans could never have enough land, it seemed.

Marianne Stillwater's residence and its surroundings were a sharp contrast to the simplicity of Farraway Township. The address was within a walled estate, one of a half-dozen or so former stretches of land claimed and bounded by long-dead human lords and ladies, the walls now warded, and the land now occupied by expensive, exclusive residences that rivalled the Taellan's manors in craftsmanship. Entrance to the estate was strictly monitored, gates manned by human magic users of mid-level power and skill, with only one road all the way through, winding in gentle curves through mature trees and high fences discreetly screening the buildings from the road and from each other.

It was a far cry from her usual visits to Lix, going to the business heart of the city surrounded by towering buildings and too many people, all so busy, noisy conversations, crowds smothering her, and the fresh scents of the Taellaneth replaced by the stench of exhaust fumes and the casually discarded waste humans seemed to generate. Or visits to tall apartment buildings, tracing people the Erith wanted found, too many people pressing about and not one single ward on half of the buildings.

This was beautiful. A stillness that reminded her of the Taellaneth gardens, though no Erith would admit the comparison. The wards were well-kept, the streets free of debris, and she could not hear a single voice. Peace. A place of harmony, free of the discordant politics of the Erith. The stillness reminded her of the cottage where she had lived with Nassaran, tucked away in a far corner of the vast grounds of the Taellaneth, away from other people. The cottage had long been abandoned, the one time she had been able to return to it offering no sign of the old man since he had left her at the Academy for training. Still, her soul eased at the reminder, her lips curving in a small smile.

Following the shifkin's directions, the residence she had stopped outside belied its age, a modern construction humming with electrical power that brushed her senses, designed to look as old as the original manor. The building was set back from the road, behind iron gates that opened with the smooth hum she associated with electric motors as she approached, boots crunching on the gravel as she made her way up the curved driveway.

The garden was stark in winter, only a light dusting of snow at Lix's lower altitude, the plants mostly bare twigs or cut back to clumps of dry spikes, trees bare of leaves. Here and there was a wild, sharp scent that Arrow associated with 'kin, hints that a human might not notice. Despite the leafy surroundings, the rest of the estate was almost exclusively occupied by humans and Arrow wondered how many of her neighbours had known what Marianne was.

The bright red front door, colour standing out among the dormant garden, opened as she approached, and she checked involuntarily in her stride.

Two people waited for her. A petite, immaculately groomed human female, blond hair shining gold from the artificial light behind her, and the Prime.

"Good day." Arrow made her feet move forward.

"Hello, Arrow." The Prime was self-contained, all the savage nature she had encountered on the mountain tamped down behind a polite facade. She did not trust the facade, or the fact that she could not pick up any of his feelings. "This is Lucy Steers."

"Miss Steers." Arrow nodded, and, after a small pause, took the hand offered to her in a brief, polite handshake.

Erith did not touch her, and Erith did not shake hands.

The sensation of another's skin against hers was odd, an unfamiliar assault on her senses, the human's hand smooth and well-maintained against her own roughened skin, her wards prickling at the proximity.

"Arrow? That's an unusual name." The woman meant nothing by it, simply making polite conversation, but Arrow felt her spine stiffen; the hated Erith word tripped through her mind before she squashed it.

"It is what I am called," she replied politely.

"And you work for the Erith." The woman's lip curled slightly. "What interest do the Erith have in Marianne's death?"

It was a good question, Arrow thought, and one she would also like to ask the Erith. She would not get a straight answer, so had to speculate. With the 'kin suspicious that there had been Erith involvement in the death, the Erith were using their most disposable servant to keep an eye on matters. A guess only. But she knew how most of the Taellan felt about her, and how most of the Erith felt about the 'kin.

"They did not tell me," Arrow answered honestly, "but have asked me to aid the shifkin in finding the truth."

Lucy was frowning, unhappy, and opened her mouth to say something, cut off by Zachary.

"The Erith don't share secrets," he commented, voice even. Lucy glared at him for a moment before turning back to Arrow.

"Zach said you need to get a sense of Marianne. What do you need?" There was a challenge under the words. This woman disliked her. Arrow was used to that. The dislike of the Erith was more unusual, but not unique.

Arrow tilted her head slightly, considering the question. She was outside the house yet could feel the energy of it brushing up against her skin. "A little time to meditate," she told Lucy.

"We'll go for a walk," Zachary said, ignoring the fact that Lucy was not dressed for walking. Lucy gave him a sharp glance, cast a look at her heeled shoes and gave a slight sigh.

"Let me get my coat." She disappeared into the house.

"Lucy shared the house with Marianne," Zachary offered. Arrow nodded, not sure what to say. "We won't be long." Perhaps he had noticed Lucy's glance at her feet.

"I should not need long, thank you."

The pair, an awkward match to Arrow's eyes even without all her senses engaged, made their way down the driveway, Lucy a little unsteady on her feet in her heels, Zachary making no move whatsoever to steady her. There was an odd undercurrent to that relationship that she could not pinpoint. Not the tension of secret lovers, which had a different texture to it. Something, though.

Shaking off distractions, Arrow stepped inside and shut the door quietly behind her, artificial light yellow to her eyes. She stood for a moment to absorb the energy, opening her senses a fraction. This was the first time she had been in a human's home, the unfamiliar hum of electrical current, human magic of the wards and the scent of artificial perfume all vying for her attention. Under that were the personalities of the residence's owners, vivid and bold. Satisfied there was enough here, she slid her messenger bag from her shoulder and sat cross-legged on the black-and-white stone-flagged entrance hall, slipping into a meditative trance.

The snick of the door closing, loud in her too-sensitive ears, snapped her out of the trance and back to the first world.

"You could have gone farther into the house." Zachary sounded almost amused. The back of her neck prickled at having him standing behind her.

"There was enough here, and I did not want to intrude," she answered, getting off the floor with slightly stiff limbs. She could not meet his eyes.

"Did you get what you needed?" Lucy asked, sharp undertone to her words, perhaps angry at the casual violation of her home.

"Yes, thank you. I have a clear sense of Marianne." And she still could not look at Marianne's widower.

"You would," he said darkly, that old anger back. "She had been living here for ten years."

"Ten years?" Arrow found herself holding the Prime's eyes. The residence had already told her that Lucy and Marianne were far from simply roommates. This place had been inhabited by a couple, both strong, passionate personalities. That Marianne had broken faith with her mate had shaken Arrow, as the Erith believed 'kin mated for life, something about the bonds they created making it impossible to break them. Arrow had always been a little sceptical of that, as most magic could be undone with enough effort. The sense of vibrancy in the building had felt immediate, fresh, and new, not ten years in the making.

Her understanding questioned, Arrow kept her senses open and looked again. Ten years was little time to a long-lived race like the 'kin. And the apparently human woman before her had had powerful magic grafted to her bones. A longevity spell, Arrow guessed. Somehow, Marianne and Lucy had kept their relationship fresh over the course of a decade. And apparently managed to hide the existence of the relationship from the Erith, given their concern about the effect Marianne's death would have on the Prime. With Erith relationships themselves sometimes being tortuously complex, no further enquiry had been made as far as Arrow knew.

"Yes." That sharpness was back in Lucy's tone, drawing Arrow's attention. For all that she appeared delicate and fragile, Arrow thought that Lucy Steers had a tough core. The human woman reminded Arrow forcibly of one of the very few Erith who had befriended Arrow at the Academy, another seemingly delicate female, ready to laugh and stubborn enough to stare down the stars. "Apparently, 'kin don't divorce."

Arrow had been right about the toughness, the human confident in her claim on the Prime's mate, standing her ground against him. Arrow could not help wondering how many times Zachary Farraway, the most powerful shifkin alive, had been spoken to in that way, with so little respect and biting hurt.

"I've explained." Zachary's voice was low, and underneath his words an almost subliminal hum lifted hairs along Arrow's neck. Shifkin anger. She had been right not to trust the facade. The anger was core-deep. She wondered if the Prime knew any magicians that could cloak themselves from discovery and kill with weapons that left no trace, and she realised that even if he did not personally know any, he had the resources to find them.

"Yes," Lucy said again, shoulders slumping, the fight draining from her. She rubbed her hands over her face, careless of her makeup, and Arrow saw that underneath the perfect grooming, Lucy's eyes were puffy and red-rimmed.

Arrow searched for something to say as the silence wore on. Her senses were closing slowly, tension grating her nerves.

"What now?" Lucy broke the silence, speaking to Zachary.

"Now Arrow will retrace Marianne's steps and we'll deal with her killer." The hard determination on Zachary's face said more clearly than any words that the killer would not survive the meeting. A chill ran through her, though it was nothing more than she had expected. The Erith were equally harsh on murderers. Lucy's head jerked, part denial, part acceptance, jaw set.

"Retrace?" Arrow's attention caught. She lifted her brows, something about the way he had said it grabbing her attention. "Marianne Stillwater was missing?"

"For four months," Zachary confirmed, his age showing for a fleeting moment. Arrow's breath hitched. He was the Prime, connected to his people in ways she did not fully understand, and he had not known where his mate was for four months. An eternity. "And I did not feel her die."

That admission was quiet, holding Arrow's attention.

Erith knowledge suggested that bonded 'kin were closely connected. He should certainly have felt Marianne's death.

"She disappeared." Lucy confirmed, hugging herself, arms wrapped around her middle, staring at nothing. "No note, no message. Nothing. Just gone."

"What was she doing before that?" Arrow asked, curiosity overriding manners.

"Her job." Lucy's tone was sharp, sharper than either the question or her grief warranted. She took a breath, shook her head, apparently realising that Arrow did not understand, tone still edged as she went on. "We ran a business together. Art gallery. I deal with the paperwork and accounts, mostly, and Marianne finds art to display and tracks down specific items for clients. Found." Her voice choked on the last word.

As interesting as that sounded, it did not appear inherently dangerous. Experience had taught Arrow not to dismiss minor details.

"Was she tracking down a particular piece when she went missing?"

"No." Lucy's tone was curt, and she did not look at Arrow. "She'd just finished a series of jobs for a new, well, new-ish, client. He'd had her running about a bit. Looking for paintings and some wooden carvings. She'd been to Hallveran and across to the north island, too."

A long journey. The north island was a human-only enclave involving at least two full days' travel each way, as both Erith and 'kin had forbidden human aircraft over their territories. Marianne would have needed a permit to go there, so there would be an official record of her visit.

"Was she successful?"

"Marianne was always successful in her hunts." Lucy's hostility slipped, mouth curving with a smile, pride in her partner evident.

"And she had not taken on any more tasks?" Arrow pressed, something snagging her attention in what Lucy had said or not said. Or perhaps it was that small smile which made the human woman seem almost familiar, although Arrow was quite sure that they had never met. Or perhaps it was the odd hostility, which had not lessened.

"No." Lucy's smile was gone.

"She hadn't been to the mountain in that time," Zachary offered, "though she usually visited about once a month." Arrow wondered how many of Zachary's immediate muster had known about Marianne's other life if her mate regarded her as a visitor to what had once been her home.

He had adopted a deliberately casual pose, hands shoved in his pockets, feet slightly apart, shoulders relaxed, as if he were taking part in an everyday pleasant conversation and not discussing his dead mate's last movements with his mate's mistress and an Erith agent. Another facade. Arrow wanted to give it more attention, but Lucy stiffened and tilted her head pointedly towards the door.

Not sure what more she could learn for the moment, Arrow decided to follow the woman's lead.

"Thank you for your time, Miss Steers." Arrow turned to the Prime and he waved her ahead of him through the door.

"Lucy." Zachary nodded in place of a goodbye and followed Arrow out of the house. She walked along the drive to the gates, Zachary keeping easy pace beside her, waiting for him to speak.

He remained quiet until the gates had shut behind them and he had glanced back to check that Lucy was not observing them.

"Marianne could be stubborn," he observed, although Arrow did not think that was what he wanted to say. Even with ten years to grow used to his mate's betrayal, he seemed overly calm. He turned a critical gaze to her. "We'll be hiking across the mountain after her trail." He took her compliance for granted. "And you'll need better gear. Go here." He produced a small piece of card from his pocket, a business card. "Speak to Peter. He's one of the local muster."

"Prime." Arrow took the card, skin heating. It was somehow humiliating that her lack of preparation had been so obviously noted. The Prime's mouth twitched, unexpected humour bringing further warmth to her face. He said nothing directly, simply told her to meet him at the township hotel early the next morning and walked away.

With too much to think about and the unfamiliar road, she managed to take a wrong turn when leaving the estate, ending up on a narrower road that was definitely not the one she needed. Turning the car around was an exercise in concentration and she was about to leave, return to the city and find the outdoors shop that the Prime had recommended, when the faint trace of old wards caught her attention. The entire estate was bounded by old wards, human-made. These wards, though, had a taste of Erith magic about them. Old and not renewed for many years. Dormant and close-by. A glance at the vehicle's clock told her that there was no time to investigate and do everything else that needed to be done if she was to keep her appointment with the Prime the next day.

Marking the location in her mind, she drove away, finally finding something to smile about as she realised that buying new clothing would mean that she could avoid the Taellaneth's stern laundry mistress for a little while longer. And she would have new clothes without holes or worn patches, for the journey across Farraway Mountain. Anticipation and apprehension mixed together. A wholly new environment, unknown magic and companions who had every reason to hate her. It promised to be a challenging journey.

Chapter Eight

Arrow caught the edge of her borrowed snowshoes on an unseen obstacle yet again, stumbling and catching herself this time before she fell. The weight of her backpack shifted fractionally, again, just enough to be awkward, and she paused, face warming at the sideways glance from the nearby 'kin, adjusting the straps once more before forcing her feet to move on. The Prime himself had provided her with the snowshoes and given her brief instructions on how to use them. Easier to move across the mountain for the most part, he had said. Awkward was how Arrow would describe it, though she was grateful that they held her up and stopped her sinking into the snow with every second step.

A morning's walk had taken them past the site of Marianne's death, Arrow having no difficulty in finding the shifkin's trail now, and farther onto the mountain. The Prime had chosen a very small group to accompany him, only four other 'kin. Matthias and his mate Tamara were in their animal forms, running ahead. The other two, males that Arrow recognised from her encounter outside the municipal offices, were walking with loose, easy strides, not hampered by the packs they carried, the snowshoes, or the weaponry that she could see. They carried long knives strapped to their thighs, rifles in their packs and at least one handgun. Used to the White Guard's presence, Arrow still felt disturbed by the human-made weaponry, wondering what dangers the 'kin expected within their own territory.

The Prime himself carried a pack, no weapon visible, and was taking the lead at the moment, bright red jacket a vivid beacon for her to follow. He moved as easily as his companions and had not even looked back when she stumbled this time.

Silently thanking the Prime for sending her to the outdoors shop in Lix, Arrow found a moment to be grateful that at least she was warm. The shifkin shop owner had been quiet and efficient, sending Arrow away with what seemed to be a daunting pile of items, and doubtless delighted to part the Erith from some of their funds. As far as Arrow was concerned, it had been worth it. Despite the freezing air, her heavy breathing creating clouds, her fingers and toes were warm and mobile.

She was also, for the first time she could recall, wearing colour. The shop owner had insisted she needed a coloured jacket to stand out in the snow. Bypassing purple, the Erith colour for mourning, she had given in to a clear, rich blue, sombre enough that she did not feel foolish, like a servant playing dress-up, and vivid enough to satisfy both the shop owner and a secret part of her that she had not known existed, but which revelled in the wardrobe change. Seen first in the shop, the blue had reminded her of the velvet-soft flowers that had grown in the garden around Nassaran's cottage, and wearing the colour now felt like carrying a tiny piece of him with her. She thought she might need his patience and wisdom on this journey.

The silver thread that was Marianne's trail, clear in her second sight and direct since she had picked it up earlier, suddenly swerved, taking a loop that Arrow did not think was physically possible for any creature. A little farther ahead, the trail wound back on itself then dived into a huge knot, reminding Arrow of a ball of yarn with not one single thread leading out from the knot.

Focusing on the first world, it looked no different than the forest they had been walking through all morning. Giant trees poked up into the sky, bark black against the light, smaller trees huddled among them, thick covering of snow over every piece of ground, drifting in piles against wide tree trunks.

She must have made a sound as the Prime had stopped, too, the pair of 'kin in human form taking a few steps out to either side, relaxed and watchful.

"The trail has been compromised," Arrow told the Prime. He had known, she saw, and he was watching for her reaction.

Aware of his scrutiny, she looked again, opening her second sight more, and winced.

"There has been magic used. A lot. Someone has hidden Marianne Stillwater's trail."

"Can you follow it?"

"Not yet." She unfastened her pack and slid it off her shoulders, trying not to sigh in relief as she set it down. It had grown heavier with every step. "The trail has been wound up, and there is nothing beyond it." She hesitated before going on at the silent query from the Prime. "The spells used were designed to confuse a tracker hunting by sight or smell."

"We were unable to follow the trail," Zachary confirmed, voice even. One of the other 'kin gave a low growl, an unhappy sound that silenced quickly at a sideways glance from his leader. A little shiver ran through her. Shifkin did not easily admit defeat. Although the Prime appeared calm and confident, they needed her or another skilled magician to go farther. Being needed did not mean she was safe.

"Can you break through it?"

"I do not think that breaking it will be wise. There are ... traps laid in the spellwork." The 'kin growled again, and she realised her hand had lifted, unconsciously, one finger tracing the power lines that only she could see. She stopped, shoving her hands into her pockets.

"Traps? Booby-trapped spells?" The Prime was sceptical.

"Indeed. If the spells are tripped, then everything within twenty paces will vanish," she told him, wincing a little at the power coiled into the spells. Someone had spent a long time creating this web of spells.

The Prime's scepticism vanished and she remembered that he had been part of the last great battle fought between 'kin and Erith, so had seen first-hand the destructive power of battle magic. There were pockets of ground near the highway to Hallveran that were still devoid of life many years later, places where even people with no magic sensitivity at all avoided walking.

"What do you need?"

"A little space and some time," she told him, careful to keep her shoulders rounded and not to meet his eyes, avoiding any possible perception that she thought she was in charge. Somehow, from her few interactions with the Prime, she thought he was confident enough in his own abilities to not bother. He was a little like the elder in that respect. However, the two 'kin with him were prickly of their leader's dignity, lips curling to show glimpses of bright white teeth when they looked in her direction.

"Very well." Zachary glanced at the darkening sky. "We'll set up camp while you work."

"Prime," she acknowledged and fetched a groundsheet from her pack, laying it on the snow in the centre of the spells.

"How far away?" Zachary asked, picking up her pack to take with him.

"At least thirty paces," she told him. They should be safe at that distance if anything went wrong.

Settling cross-legged, awkward in hiking boots, she slowed her breathing, closing her eyes and dropping into the calm state that was most efficient for spellworking. The sounds of the first world, the 'kin's soft footfalls, the rustle of canvas, a soft murmur of conversation, the breeze in the trees, and the crunch of snow, all fell away.

Opening her eyes to the second world, she was met with a blinding knot of spells in a world flat and devoid of natural life. Here was only power, the lines of magic that a magic user had laid, the faint shades of shifkin natural magic just at the edge of her range.

The spellwork took some time to understand, a triple-layered concoction of different types of higher magic interlinked in a way that the Academy had declared impossible. The three circles of spellwork criss-crossed in a slowly turning perpetual spiral, dizzying to her eyes at first.

There was a dense pattern of crimson runes, a thick strand of destruction the colour of dried blood. Powered by forbidden blood magic. Somewhere nearby, under the snow, were the remains of whatever sacrifice had unwillingly surrendered its life to create this spell. Threaded into those runes were commands for wider dispersal. It was designed to destroy all trace of Marianne Stillwater, to prevent anyone from following her trail.

Twisted around the crimson runes were primitive black-and-white shapes, one of the earliest forms of Erith magic, still taught at the Academy. The apparently crude shapes protected the main spells held in the crimson runes.

And underneath all of that, sliding through the black, white and blood, was the sinuous shape of a destroyer worm. Creatures of spirit, these existed slightly out of phase with the first world, feeding on the power in the second world, normally harmless as they swam through the currents. They could be trapped, as this one had been, and bound closer to the first world, brought into phase with the second world which allowed them to feed directly from life in the first. Their preferred meals were Erith. Even the weakest Erith had magic enough to satisfy a worm. This one was bound, starved of the magic that was its normal food source. Any magician attempting to use their power to unravel either of the other spells would quickly find themselves eaten by the worm.

Arrow shivered, memories surfacing. This giant worm, barely there even in her second sight, had smaller cousins—the flickers of their life barely the size of her palm—which were trapped inside suppressor collars that the Academy occasionally used for troublesome students. Arrow had worn one of those collars for much of her Academy career, once the Erith had decided she needed training, and she had lived with the twisting sensation about her neck and the whispers in the dark, unable to use her magic while the collar was on, unable to block out the murmur.

More than one magician had died thinking that the little worms could be controlled, calling the things to them for experimentation, the worms latching on to power and draining them. And there were far greater threats, out of phase beyond the second world.

It was a deadly, masterful trap constructed with unparalleled skill. Not one of the Academy masters, even the Preceptor, would be able to build this trap.

Which raised the question as to who had made the trap?

The Academy masters were amongst the finest magicians trained by the Erith, and where they did not have knowledge, they called in other magicians who did. None of them could have done this. Another Erith could have done. Or a human. A chill worked down her spine. Humans rarely managed such complex magic as this. On the rare occasions where they had, it had proved deadly to the Erith.

There was a reason Arrow and members of the White Guard were sent to watch various humans. The Erith remembered.

With the blood sacrifice, the magician could be at any power level. The only thing that was certain was the consummate skill involved in creating this trap.

And she had to unpick it before they could move on and find out why Marianne Stillwater had been killed. And how a shifkin had come to the attention of such a skilled magician, when 'kin and magicians generally had as little to do with each other as possible.

Ignoring the crude shapes and shifting runes, Arrow opened her senses further, focusing on the worm. It had sensed the minimal power she was using to hold her second sight and thrashed in its bonds, wanting to be free, hungry enough to be reckless. Staying quiet and still for a while brought her its true name, the necessary key to sending it back to its own realm. Setting her will and a trickle of power behind her words, she forced her lips and vocal cords to shape the sounds of the thing's name, ears assaulted by the psychic shriek as it was banished.

Dispatching the worm had woken the protections in the other spells, the crimson runes quivering in readiness, black-and-white shapes tightening in readiness.

Standing in the second world, *kri-syang* in one hand, silver blade solid and real as the lines of power, Arrow cautiously touched the lines of crimson. The black-and-white shapes folded on themselves, wrapping around her arms, pressure forcing her hand to open and let go of the rune. Reversing her grip on the *kri-syang*, she sliced through one of the shapes, freeing her hand and arm only to have the shapes twist around her ankles, holding her in one place.

Satisfied that the shapes would not move, she went back to the crimson ones. The spell was shifting, slowing down in its motion, preparing to trigger. She had to work quickly and delicately.

Slicing one strand at a time and replacing it with lines of her own, she rewrote the spell's code to focus all its destruction on the spot where she was standing. The loose lines of the runes, freed without purpose, slid through the second world, and attached themselves to her body, acid of unclean magic burning against her skin and distracting her with pain, raising red welts.

The second world, she reminded herself when the pain made her hands shake. The second world, not the real, physical world.

The pain lessened a fraction and she continued, the world around her glowing with the silver of her own power, her body coated in crimson.

At last, it was done. She was on her knees, encased in the shapes and the fragments of runes, vision blurring, *kri-syang* trembling as she put its tip to the last spell fragment.

The crimson died, purpose defeated, the black-and-white shapes falling with the runes, and she was left in a world nearly dark apart from a slender, clear line. Marianne Stillwater's trail.

Coming back to the first world was a study in pain. Everything ached, skin under her clothes raw and burning from the runes, eyelids stupidly heavy, breathing a labour against the rocks on her chest. Fumbling, she managed to get the *kri-syang* back into its sheath—then the world tilted, spun, and the side of her head hit something hard.

A moment later, and a pair of boots that she did not recognise walked sideways into her line of sight followed by knees she did not know and a face she thought she should know.

"Arrow?"

"Mphmph."

"Arrow." There was an earthquake. Everything trembled. The voice which she thought she should know called some incomprehensible commands over her head and then the world was spinning again. No earthquake this time.

"Is she alright?" Another voice she should know.

"Frozen through," the first voice, the one belonging to the boots and knees, answered.

"Kettle's on," the second voice said.

"Good. Get her boots. Check her feet."

"Will do."

Fires were started at her hands and feet and she moaned, twisting away from the pain, burning almost as badly as the oath spells in her blood.

"Arrow." There was power behind that voice. Power and intent. She froze, blinked. Dangerous. "Stay still. We need to warm you up."

"N-n-not," she started, then bit off her words in a hiss as the fires dimmed down, replaced with itching tingling that made her want to scratch and wriggle away again.

"Stay still." There was more power in that voice. Predator. Danger. No, not danger. No threat. Surprise held her for a few moments. Long enough for the fires and tingling to die to something more bearable.

"Here." Something was presented to her mouth and she took a careful sip, moaning again. Burning. All the way down. Too hot. "Again." The second voice was not as strong as the first and she turned her head away. Tried to. Something held her, a hold she could not physically break. More burning liquid was forced between her teeth. Swallowed, coughed, choked. Scalding salt fell down her face. More drink.

Eventually, the burning faded. She had endured. Liquid was taken away and the hold relaxed. She sagged, boneless, against whatever was holding her up.

"You'll do," the first voice told her with utmost confidence. She believed him. Zachary.

"More chocolate?" The second voice. Matthias.

Chocolate? She loved chocolate. When had they given her chocolate?

"Not just now. Warmth and sleep, I think." Zachary moved her somehow, laying her down and pulling something light and oh-so-warm over her.

Her eyes were clearing a little and she could make out their faces, blurred, and the bright cascade of oranges beyond that must have been a fire.

"F-found it," she managed to say, sleep pulling her down.

"Marianne's trail?" Zachary's eyes glinted green in the gloom. The shadow at his shoulder that must be Matthias had stilled.

"Yes. Follow easily."

"Very good." The Prime's praise, deeply satisfied, sent her to sleep.

Chapter Nine

Arrow surfaced from sleep to suffocation, chest weighted. Worse, there was no ward about her. Not one scrap of magic. A wordless protest tore out as she tried to move, blinking rapidly, trying to see, reaching for power on instinct, needing defence. The barest trickle, the tiniest fizz in her veins. Useless. Not enough for even the simplest ward. Hollowed out in her centre, all her strength gone. She could not even feel the seals.

Wriggling, she tried to sit up. The weight on her moved. A soft rumbling sound that did not sound anything like a threat vibrated against her, something damp and rough scraping her cheek, bringing her fully awake. Eyes clearing, she found herself nose to nose with a 'kin in animal form.

Tamara. Matthias' mate. Deep, chestnut red in her animal form, a white stripe between her eyes and down her nose.

Even as Arrow's heart rate slowed, Tamara made another soft noise, part protest part comfort, and nosed Arrow's cheek, casual gesture leaving a cold, damp spot on her skin.

"Good day to you." Arrow managed, voice rough. She was still unable to move, Tamara's greater weight pinning down the covers. Beyond Tamara's shoulder she saw another 'kin in animal form. Matthias, of course. Smaller than his mate's animal form, compact and powerful as he was in human form, he was charcoal grey, blending into the shadows.

Matthias' eyes glinted, but he merely got to his feet, shook himself, nudged Tamara and left Arrow's sleeping space, Tamara following with her ears and tail up.

She was in some kind of makeshift shelter, a canvas stretched overhead, groundsheet underneath, lying under layers of blankets that were covered with animal hair and the scent of 'kin.

Whoever had put her to bed had left her in thermals from neck to toes, and someone, perhaps the same someone, had laid out outer clothes for her, now warm from the 'kin and covered in hair. Underneath the thermals, her skin still felt raw and she pushed up one sleeve, finding traces of red across her skin from the spell trap. The Academy's teaching to junior students was that nothing in the second world could do damage in the first, helping their students overcome their fear of the unknown. A lie. Magicians carried power in their veins, and power could most definitely damage. Making an assessment from head to toe, she was satisfied she was functional. Nothing too badly damaged. Just sore.

Getting dressed took far longer than she had imagined possible, fingers clumsy and limbs uncoordinated. Lacing her boots took the sort of focus usually reserved for the most complex high magic, and then her arms would not fit in jacket sleeves on the first few attempts. Leaving the jacket open, breathing hard, and with a strong wish to climb back under the blankets, she ducked out of the small shelter into the bright bite of a winter day.

She found herself facing the Prime, putting items into his pack with brisk efficiency.

"Chocolate," he said, rising to his feet with a fluid grace she envied.

"Good morning." Her voice was higher than normal. He held out an insulated, metal flask.

"Chocolate," he said again. "Or coffee, if you'd rather?"

"Chocolate would be welcome. Thank you." She accepted the flask. "Is there a cup?"

"Drink it all. Slowly."

She measured the size and weight of the flask with secret delight. Chocolate was only found in faraway human lands, one of the many foodstuffs forbidden in the Taellaneth, and a rare treat. There had been mention of chocolate the night before, but she had not been able to taste anything. At her first sip, she forgot where she was, forgot the Prime moving about the small camp, entire focus on the taste and texture.

When she had reached the end of the flask far too quickly, she found that the small camp had been packed up. Only the Prime was visible, and he was binding her backpack to one of the others.

"It is late," she realised, dismayed. Close to noon, judging by the angle of the sun through the surrounding trees.

"You needed sleep." He fastened the last straps.

"I should carry my own." There was no conviction in her words, torn between relief and embarrassment at her obvious weakness. The Prime simply lifted an eyebrow and held a hand out. She offered him the empty flask.

Moving too quickly for her to guess his intent, he grasped her wrist instead, turning the inner side up, pushing her sleeve back to expose her skin to light. The flask fell to the ground. The dark markings buried inside her wrist, in sharp contrast to pale skin, were vivid in the daylight.

"And the other?" His voice gave nothing away, at odds with his too-still body.

Skin prickling as the runes woke up, Arrow tugged her other sleeve back with her teeth and showed him the inner side of her other wrist with its different set of markings below the sheath for her *kri-syang*. The marks were still and stark to outside view. Inside, the tendrils of the spells they held, woven deep into Arrow's body, flexed, coiling in readiness.

"Erith slave markings." He was no longer calm, a thrum of anger making her shiver, a reaction he measured with hard eyes.

It had not been a question so she said nothing, markings becoming darker and sharper as the spells remained active.

"What do they signify?"

"Service." She raised her right wrist a fraction. "And obedience." Now, the left.

"And how did you come by these markings?" He had both her wrists now, grip firm, not cruel. There would be no outward bruises.

Her mouth opened, sound cut off, spells coursing to life, unseen lines of pain crawling up her arms, fingers clenching in response. Biting her lip held in a gasp.

Zachary watched with a cool stare. "Oath markings," he guessed, and she nodded, "which you are not permitted to discuss."

"Yes." Bare sound. If she had been stronger, if she had had a fraction of her magic, she could have given him more. As it was, she had to lock her knees to remain upright.

"To the Taellan?"

"Yes." Not just the Taellan, but it was the easiest explanation. Originally, the spells had bound her to the service of the Taellan and Preceptor, but the Taellan had also commanded her to obey Eshan as if he were one of them. She supposed she should be grateful that they had not thought to repeat that command with others. With the spells live in her blood, gratitude was taken over by more familiar fury.

"For your lifetime?"

"No."

"A set period, then." He lifted one wrist then the other, to inspect the markings more closely. Assessing, missing nothing. "I didn't think the Erith still used such things."

"Made an exception." She forced the words out, anger giving her a moment's strength, jaw clenching. While the pain had faded, the crawling sensation of foreign, live spellwork in her body was growing.

"You have to follow the Taellan's commands?"

"Yes." She wondered how Zachary had learned so much about Erith oath-markings. His questions were careful. Although he was demanding answers, she thought he had already known everything she had told him.

"And what do the Taellan require of you here?"

"To find the truth of Marianne Stillwater's death." The pain faded.

"What else?"

"I do not understand."

"No other mission? The Erith haven't sent you with other orders, too?"

"No. I may be required to report ..." The pain flared again, spells reacting to possible disobedience. She had been commanded, many years before, to never discuss the Taellan's business. Her knees gave out and she fell into the snow, wrists still held by Zachary, who followed her movement with ease, crouching before her, observing.

She hated the oath-magic. Had tried to carve it out of her flesh before now, the pain of the blade nothing compared to the pain of the magic. She had hated it before she had fully understood what it was, when the crawling sensation of the marks first bit into her skin, the Preceptor implacable as he spoke the spells, a few of the Taellan as stern-faced witnesses, expressions not changing no matter how much she screamed. They had offered her a choice that was no choice at all. Accept the possibility of life—or be killed then and there.

And she had wanted to live. Still did.

Wanting to live, she had learned outward compliance, and how to discipline her mind most of the time so that now the oath spells rarely woke, the first coiling of the spells in her body usually enough to ensure obedience. The Erith were confident in their hold on her.

"Do you have orders to harm my people? Or me?" The Prime had set his power free, a wash of wild, earth-scented energy that hummed against her skin and tangled with the Erith oath spell, seeking an answer. The force of the strongest 'kin alive, seeking truth. Oddly, she discovered that she did not need to obey him. Interesting.

"No."

"And this?" He turned her right hand over, crooked fingers ugly in the daylight.

"An annoyed classmate at the Academy," she answered easily. Gesser's work. He had wanted to test how much pressure was needed to break bones.

He snarled, clearly displeased, but let her go, turning away. "We should move."

"Prime." She called his attention back, still kneeling in the snow. "There is something I need to do first." She managed to get to her feet and looked across to the space where the knotted spells had been the day before. Her second sight was dim, showing her clean air above the ground, and a lingering darkness in the snow that needed to be dealt with.

Zachary was waiting.

"The magician left remains." She moved slowly across the snow, feet dragging.

"Will they identify him?" The words were spoken just behind her ear and she jumped. Silent and quick across the snow, she had not noticed him move.

"Unlikely." A quick glance across and she caught his frown, and impatience. "I cannot in conscience leave this." That caught his interest.

The dark blot under the snow was vivid purple and yellow. A bruise, in second sight. In first sight, it was a slightly darker patch in the snow under a fallen tree trunk. She knelt close by, hissing a little as her muscles protested, and extended a hand cautiously. Bile rose in her throat.

"There are remains here, and not anything clean."

"Dangerous?"

"No. Just ..." She hunted for the words. "Well, the Erith would say *urjusi*. The best translation in the human tongue is unholy."

"Erith religion?" His lip curled.

"Not as such. The best approximation. Something unclean, but worse than simply that."

She carefully scraped snow away, picking up the small bundle that lay there, skin crawling at the feel of it.

"What is it?"

"Left over from the spell creation." She opened her hand, showing him. "Residue only. No actual magic remains. Too degraded to follow the creator. But ..." She bit her lip, swallowing revulsion and carefully peeling back the leather covering, exposing a small pottery jar full of dark ash. And she chose to be angry. "The magician powered his spell with *urjusi*. Powered by sacrifice. Blood power. This is what is left."

"Ashes?" He crouched nearby, eyes intent on the bundle. She nodded. "You said remains. Something living? A person?"

"Probably." She chose anger again. "And probably a young one. They have greater potential."

Zachary's lip curled again, teeth gleaming, canines prominent. A low sound lifted the hair on her neck. He rose to his feet.

"You cleanse it. I'll bury it," he said tersely and stalked back to the packs.

Left with the remains, Arrow shivered, swallowing against nausea. The remains were pathetically small. A handful of ashes in the jar. The wrapper felt like leather, but she knew it was most likely skin of the victim.

The cleansing spell was a minor one, the only thing she had power for, vision blurring and fading at the edges by the time she finished. She could not see any change, second sight temporarily gone with her power, and she had to trust her work.

By the time her vision had cleared to something approaching normal, the Prime had dug a small, deep hole, black earth a sharp contrast to the snow. She shuffled forward on her knees, not trusting her strength, and placed the remains in the bottom.

"It is clean. There will be no more harm from it," she told him. He said nothing, filling in the hole with unnecessary care, patting the surface down then brushing snow back across to cover the spot. Arrow wobbled back to her feet.

"You've seen this magic before?" He also seemed to be struggling between revulsion and anger, and also choosing anger.

"Yes." She grimaced and explained, "Academy graduates must be able to recognise *urjusi*. The Academy keeps inert samples for teaching." In a triple-walled dark wood cabinet warded with the strongest protections that the teaching staff of the Erith's magic Academy could conjure. Even passing that cabinet, in an out-of-the-way part of the buildings, was unpleasant.

"Erith magic?"

"It is forbidden magic. Not necessarily Erith. Human mages are also forbidden from sacrifice. Regrettably, there are those who seek to use sacrifice for additional power."

Zachary was watching her with an unblinking stare that she thought probably intimidated most of his opponents. She was intimidated, just too worn to show it.

"There's nothing else to find here?"

"Nothing that I could sense. I do not know why the magician would leave that here. It seems a foolish risk. Perhaps he considered the spell impregnable. It would have destroyed everything if it had been triggered."

"Speculation?" There was a gleam in his eyes that she had not seen before. Humour. He found her amusing. It was not a reaction she was used to, leaving her unsettled and confused. "I thought such a thing was strictly forbidden by the Academy."

"Perhaps in the lower cycles, but the Academy encourages senior students to formulate hypotheses based on incomplete facts." She inclined her head slightly, faint smile pulling her mouth.

The lightness on his face grew to something that might have been a smile before he turned and went back to the packs. Tamara and Matthias were waiting, back in human form, the other two 'kin a little distance away in their animal forms. Arrow hid a frown. She had not noticed any of them returning. Careless to lose track of her surroundings so completely.

"You look worn out," Tamara remarked lightly, handing Arrow a brightly coloured plastic packet she identified after a moment as a human-made snack.

"I am quite tired," Arrow acknowledged.

"You have the trail?" Zachary asked.

"Yes." Her second sight was slowly returning, but the thread was clear. "Are you able to sense it, Prime?"

"No," he growled, and she quickly lowered her eyes. "We tried earlier. There's nothing. Not a single scent of Marianne for miles."

"I can make tracking stones to help you follow her." She focused inward a moment, testing her strength, and calling up a headache for her efforts. "Although not quite yet. I need some more energy. Later," she added, seeing the glint of interest in his eyes.

"We'll walk on a bit, find somewhere better to stop for the night." He nodded and lifted a brow at her. It took a moment for her sluggish brain to realise he was asking her for a direction.

"Sorry. The trail goes that way." She pointed.

"Con. Jace." The two 'kin in animal form bounded ahead, the Prime following.

Matthias and Tamara took the other packs and set off, Arrow plodding in their wake.

She was barely aware of her surroundings for the rest of the few daylight hours. Her body was impossibly heavy, and, despite the packets of food that Tamara kept handing to her and the extra flask of hot chocolate she was given, her body grew heavier until it required almost her entire concentration to put one foot in front of the other, her breathing harsh and laboured in her ears, entire focus on the snow in front of her feet and how she was going to achieve that next step.

From time to time, the 'kin would ask her for a direction and she would open her second sight a moment, wincing at the effort, and point the way.

She did not notice when the sky darkened, and only realised it was fully dark when Tamara gently tugged her arm, drawing her to a stop.

Matthias and Zachary had set up a fire, bright orange blinding in the dark, and were constructing some kind of shelter that was too haphazard to be called a tent but evidently something they had used before.

"Come and sit a moment," Tamara suggested, flashing a smile, white teeth bright against her dark skin, eyes warm in the firelight. "Matt's got some more chocolate heating for you."

"Thank you." Arrow did not know her own voice, that weak thread of sound. Work for the Erith was never easy and yet she could not remember ever being so tired before. Used to functioning with the constant heaviness from the seals inside, this was another thing entirely.

"You had a tough day yesterday," the 'kin added, settling Arrow on a blanket spread over a thick tree trunk, some ancient inhabitant of the forest long since toppled over, then tucking another blanket over her legs. "Food in a little while, then sleep."

Arrow's mouth twitched, and she managed an answering smile. Tamara was one of the few 'kin women she had met, and very different to her mate. Warm, open and friendly, she bustled about the small camp on a variety of tasks that Arrow's tired mind could not follow, dull ache in her chest as she wondered for a moment what it would have been like growing up with Tamara.

The hot chocolate warmed her through and she ate the meal they provided, feeling a bit of energy return to her stiff, stupid body. Enough to notice that the two other 'kin, Con and Jace, had not returned for the meal, and Matthias and Zachary were keeping a close watch on their surroundings.

"Is there trouble?" Arrow asked Tamara as the 'kin collected her bowl.

"Not expected. We're just being careful," Tamara said cheerfully. "Do you want to sleep now? We'll sleep in animal form as it's so much warmer, but we've blankets for you, and your sleeping bag."

Arrow's mind snagged for a moment on the notion that the 'kin had to be careful in their own territory, wondering what was out in the dark that would have five adult 'kin, one of them the Prime, staying alert at all times. She shook herself slightly, catching up with Tamara's question.

"Thank you. I should try to make a tracking stone first, though."

"What do you need?" Zachary asked from the other side of the fire, eyes still on the forest.

"Almost anything would do, but a smooth stone to fit in a palm works best," she told him, only then wondering how they were going to find smoothed stones, normally worn away in water, on a mountain.

"We passed a creek bed earlier." Tamara was back with a white handkerchief full of odd shapes. "And we collected a few."

"Did we?" Arrow had not noticed the creek at all. She turned over a few of the stones, selected five and picked up the first, closing her eyes.

Her power was sluggish, reluctant to stir even for the simple tracking spell. The words were easy and familiar, power bound into them.

She held out the first stone to Tamara, closest to her.

"It will hum against your skin when you are on the right path," she told her. Tamara took the stone carefully, wary, and passed it to Zachary, who had come to stand behind her. The Prime took a few steps away from the camp and turned a circle, nodding once as the stone reacted to Marianne's trail.

"Good. How many can you make?"

"I will try to make one each." She did not promise, and was glad she had not as she swayed, vision blurring, when she had completed three.

"Here." Zachary handed her a white cloth. Handkerchief. She took it, staring at the cloth in her hand. "You're bleeding," he told her, touching his own nose.

"Sorry." Heat scorched her face and she used the cloth to blot the bleeding.

"Three will do." He nodded. "Keep it," he said when she would have given back the handkerchief.

"Thank you." Her face was hot again. It was a casual gift, meaningless to him. She would add it to the small box of possessions tucked under the stone floor of her residence when she got back to the Taellaneth. A piece of the 'kin, a tiny scent of the wild.

"You need to sleep," Tamara told her, hand under her elbow.

Arrow allowed herself to be put to bed like a youngling. She could not remember ever having been put to bed before, even in her earliest memories, and fell asleep puzzling on that thought.

She woke mid of night to absolute stillness and cold all about, alarm flicking through her. Her wards were intact. Nothing had disturbed her companions, several 'kin in animal form lying around her, too dark for her to identify. But there had been something.

Warm and safe under covers, she shivered. Perhaps it was the memory of the *urjusi*. Perhaps she had recalled the feel of that cold leather against her skin in a dream and woken before it had become a nightmare.

Her fingers curled. Her hands were clean. They had been washed. Several times.

None of the 'kin stirred as she settled more comfortably, more alert than she had been all day, energy slowly recovering. Unable to sleep, she wondered again what Marianne Stillwater had done to attract the attention of a magician using *urjusi*. And not a simple magician, either. Whoever had killed Marianne had concealed themselves from the mountain and managed to bring a sacrifice with them, without attracting the attention of the 'kin. The mountain was the 'kin's territory and, however vast, they would keep a watch over it. Following 'kin onto their own territory sounded foolish to Arrow. And what could Marianne have known that would drive a magician to that desperation?

Chapter Ten

Arrow did not think she had got any more sleep until she was nudged awake by Tamara, the 'kin dressed for the day and still wearing her infectious smile. The rest of the 'kin were already up, Arrow the last to rise again.

She stumbled out of the shelter, dragging her hair back from her face and trying to remember where she had put her hairpins, only to stop mid-step.

Beyond the camp, there was silence. The forest held its breath. In the midst of it, something. Something that made her want to run.

"Arrow?" The Prime was alert, enquiring.

"Something," she answered, distracted, sending her senses out as far as possible, headache blooming behind her eyes. The range was pathetic. Her strength was better. Still a fraction of what it should be.

"What?" He was less patient.

"Predator." There was no doubt.

"Check with Con and Jace," Zachary told Matthias, who set off at an easy run through the forest, not hampered by his human form or snowshoes.

Tamara sent a concerned look after her mate but said nothing, moving quickly to finish packing up the camp. A few moments later, Zachary's eyes flared green and his head tilted, listening.

"Matt says there's nothing out there that they can sense. You're sure?" This last to Arrow.

"Yes." She was too shaken by whatever it was she had sensed to fully appreciate what she had just learned. Shifkin could use telepathy, a skill denied the Erith.

"Bear? Human? Erith?"

"I do not know, Prime." She dropped her eyes.

"Still there?"

"No." Whatever it was, the sensation had gone, nothing left for her to follow.

"What d'you want to do?" Tamara asked, packing finished.

"Keep moving. We'll stay closer together." Zachary glanced at Arrow, assessing, before collecting one of the packs.

Arrow had nothing to carry but her own weight again, and once more she struggled with that, falling behind the 'kin as they walked ahead, unaffected by the weather or the weight they carried. Matthias returned, stern expression softening as he joined Tamara, taking one of the packs from her. With each of them carrying a tracking stone, Arrow had nothing to do but follow them, increasingly aware that her limited use was fading and her presence an extra burden along with her pack.

The day wore on, time marked for Arrow by the changing shadows of the 'kin ahead of her and the trees all around. The 'kin were moving faster today, and it was more and more difficult to keep up.

At some point past noon, after Zachary had called a short halt for a break and food, Arrow's sight wavered and she paused, breathing hard, waiting for her sight to clear—a familiar sign that she was too tired to be useful to anyone. She could not even keep herself moving.

The 'kin moved ahead, bright colours of their jackets fading in the trees.

Breathing nearly back to normal, she lifted a foot for the next step as a crack echoed through the trees. A harsh shout. Alarm. Another crack. Gunfire.

Adrenaline gave her the strength to push forward, moving as quickly as she could, leaving great, dragging trails through the snow as she fought the unfamiliar snowshoes.

She rounded a clump of trees and skidded to a halt, unsettling more snow, unable to make sense of what she was seeing.

The bright jackets of the 'kin were caught up among huge creatures with dull grey hides, too many long limbs, and jagged, sharp teeth. Too tangled for more gunfire, the 'kin in human form were partially shifted, using their teeth and claws alongside those in animal form.

"*Baelthras.*" Unwanted memories rose up, holding her. Too many teeth. Long claws. Flat black merciless eyes. Carrion breath. Fire.

The ugly snap and crunch of breaking bone and cut-off cry of pain from one of the 'kin broke her stasis, brought her back to the here and now. Three creatures from her nightmares. Too many legs. Armoured hide that the 'kin could not grasp with teeth or claws.

She kicked off her snowshoes and opened her senses fully, no meditation, no preparation, everything rushing in at once, a maelstrom of sensation. Roar of wind. Quiet, furious sounds from the 'kin. Low, almost inaudible keening from the *baelthras*. Sharp scent of blood on the air. Sweet rotten scent of *baelthras*. Bittersweet taste of her own blood. Cold on her face and her hands as she stripped off her gloves. The fight moving quickly, almost too quickly for her to follow, except that she needed to.

The mountain's spirit shifted under her feet, restless at the invasion of alien creatures. She kicked some snow aside, slid the *kri-syang* across her palm, blood falling to the snow, no time to dig down for earth. Her blood seeped down, finding the soil. With her senses open wide, she requested the mountain's aid.

The flood of power the mountain sent back knocked her to her knees, snow cold and numbing.

Eyes pure silver, wards crackling silver lightning around her, she got back to her feet as a 'kin's furred body flew past her head, thrown by a *baelthras* that was turning towards her, recognising her for what she was. The enemy.

Mage fire sprang to her fingers at her spoken command. Too much power, too quickly. The seals inside protested, insides tearing. She ignored the pain. No time for that now.

Silver spears of mage fire snapped into the *baelthras'* toughened skin, burning through armoured hide, burrowing into the creature's lungs, setting it on fire. The smell was worse than she remembered.

"Get behind me." That did not sound like her voice, weighted with more power than she had ever dared use.

Not waiting for the 'kin to comply, careless of giving the Prime orders on his own mountain, she stepped forward to meet the next *baelthras*, more mage fire ready for it.

The creature screamed, holding her still for a moment in memories she did not want before she remembered who and what she was, and sent the fire out.

As the mage fire met the creature, the third *baeltoras* struck her from the side, darting in too quickly on its six awkward limbs, sending her flying through the air and thudding into a tree with a loud cracking that meant broken bones.

Sliding back to earth, the mountain's power fading as her grip on it was shaken, she could not breathe. Lungs full of liquid. Copper Pain. Drowning.

Her palm was still seeping blood. She pushed the open wound through the snow, searching for the soil, a connection to the mountain, asking for help. Each breath was a weight, shallower than the last, liquid frothing in her throat. There. Cold damp soil met her palm. She bled into the mountain and it answered. Power shoved into her, pushing broken ribs back into place, sending the liquid in her lungs and throat out in a spew of bright red on snow, shock of healing power through her body brutal enough that she screamed, something she had not done for years.

Over her head, the 'kin were tearing the last *baelthras* to pieces, bits of limb and hide ripping off in ungainly chunks, the creature fighting until one of the 'kin finally got its heart.

Arrow lay in the stained snow, breathing too fast, too shallow, blinking to clear her eyes, insides rearranging themselves, the mountain still offering her power that she was having difficulty refusing. So much power. Even with the solid ground underneath, she was spinning in circles.

"Arrow?" Zachary's voice. He did not sound angry. She blinked, curious, and turned her head to find him crouched beside her. One sleeve of his coat was almost completely gone, down spilling out, and there was a deep scratch running down his face that was healing itself as she watched. Shifkin power.

"Prime." Her voice rasped; even that one word hurt. There was still blood in her throat.

"Are you alright?"

"I will be. Are you? Your people?"

A shadow crossed his face and she sat up, following his gaze. Tamara, Matthias, and Con were gathered around something in the snow. Jace. She remembered the animal-form 'kin thrown past her.

Her limbs did not want to work but she made them. Got up. Unsteady, she staggered over the snow to where the 'kin lay.

He was a pale brown, short-haired wolf in his animal form, and dying. His chest was deformed, caved in, one leg lying at an impossible angle, coat matted with blood.

"Not long now," Tamara said soothingly, kneeling by his head, stroking back his ears. Jace made no sound, did not move. The other 'kin stood quietly by, heads bowed, waiting.

The solemn acceptance of loss made Arrow abruptly furious. Three *baelthras* where no Erith creature should ever walk. And loss of a muster member for lack of proper healing. The mountain's energy rose up to meet her, equally angry and wanting out.

"Stand aside." Arrow flopped to her knees as Tamara scrambled back, all the 'kin on high alert. There was a cry of protest from one or more of the standing 'kin and a swiftly checked move towards her as she put her hand on Jace's ribcage. He whimpered, a bare thread of sound, then howled as she took the offering from the mountain and put power into him.

She passed out before she had had time to do more than mend his ribs, clearing the pressure around his lungs and heart.

She woke to pain, aching, from her dull headache to a bruised ankle. Sitting up made her hiss involuntarily. Her ribs, barely healed, pulsed in counterpoint to her headache, and breathing hurt, chest raw.

The torn-off limb of the *baelthras* lay a few feet from her. She had not been unconscious long, then.

"So you're awake." Tamara's cheerful voice cut through memories that threatened to rise, bringing her back to the present.

"So it seems." She gathered herself, meaning to rise.

"Stay there a moment." Tamara handed her a flask. "Jace is getting there," she said, glancing across to where Jace lay, still in animal form, covered by blankets. "You saved his life."

Uncomfortable under the praise, not sure how to respond, Arrow ducked her head to peer into the flask. Soup. She was disappointed but knew it was a more sensible choice than more hot chocolate.

Matthias appeared, grim-faced and moving with care, one leg stiff, a piece of cloth tied around his thigh. He picked up the torn *baelthras* limb without a word and carried it away.

"Are you hurt?" Arrow asked once the soup was finished, standing up.

"Bruised. Nothing serious." Tamara's eyes were on her mate who was, along with Zachary, dragging the dismembered corpse back together. "We've never seen anything like them before."

"*Baelthras*." Arrow nodded.

"*Baelthras*?" Zachary's voice called her across.

"Erith creatures," she confirmed, moving stiffly across the churned-up snow to join them. They were re-assembling the corpse to study it, she realised, as she had burned the other two.

"Erith again." The Prime's eyes flashed.

"They are predators, normally living in the deep jungle. No natural enemies," Arrow told him, reciting what she knew. "Armoured hide. The vulnerable points are armpits, eyes, and there is a narrow spot under the chin." She indicated underneath her own jaw. They had not got the reassembly quite right, she saw, and pointed out the errors to Matthias, who moved silently to correct the positioning, handling the bloody bits of creature with no emotion on his face.

Assembled across snow turning pink under the pieces, the creature was vast. Taller at the shoulders than any Erith, longer than it was tall, built in lean lines, even dead it looked lethal.

"What are they doing here?" Zachary's voice was low, contained rage.

"I do not know," she answered honestly, as disturbed as he was angry. "The White Guard have some in captivity for the Trials, but those would be branded, and I do not remember seeing any brands."

"No brands. No scars or other markings," Matthias confirmed, equally angry.

"That is unusual." She tilted her head, considering the dead thing. "They will fight, and eat, anything that gets in their way, even each other. *Baelthras* do not reach adulthood without scars."

"These are juveniles?"

"From the size, no." She shook her head, then wished she had not as her head pounded. "Full-grown adults. Young, perhaps."

"Why would the White Guard hold some?" Tamara wanted to know, nose wrinkling in distaste.

"The Trials," Arrow repeated, and saw Tamara's confusion. "The White Guard, and the Academy. Tests for graduation."

"You have to fight these things?" Tamara was incredulous. Zachary was silent, not surprised.

"The Trials change but, yes, for some Trials, the candidates have to face *baelthras*." She clenched her jaw against a shudder and memory.

"What—"

Chapter Eleven

Arrow did not hear the rest of Tamara's question, her head whipping around as a distant echo—a wave of magic—caught her full attention. Familiar magic. High magic. A translocation spell.

"What is it?" the Prime's voice cut through.

"A magician has just transported himself to the mountain. A little distance from here."

"More bloody Erith?"

"I do not know. The residue is ... odd." Definitely high magic, not natural magic. Only Erith and humans used high magic, the 'kin more than capable with their own natural magic. And this residue was neither Erith nor human. She checked her wards and began walking in the direction of the magic wave.

"Just one magician?"

"I believe so."

"How many goddamned ..." The Prime's words were cut off by the snap of something fizzing past his head, thudding into the tree nearest to him, clumps of snow falling, shaken by the impact.

"Down!" Matthias called, dragging Tamara into the snow.

Arrow stood for a moment, staring at the spot where the whatever-it-was had hit the tree before something grabbed her ankle and pulled her off her feet. Her ribs protested, breath knocked out of her, all protests dying as another series of whatever-they-were thudded into the tree where she had been standing, near-miss leaving her breathless, heart racing in her throat.

"Can you come closer? I will try to ward us." She called up power, and spoke the command for a battle ward, silver shimmer rippling out to cover the 'kin as they drew closer on Zachary's snapped command. All but one. Jace's animal form lay still in the snow, no longer breathing, and as Arrow watched, he transformed back to human. Around her, the 'kin stiffened, and Tamara whimpered, low in her throat. A wash of anger burned through Arrow. He had fought to live. She had held his life in her hands only a short while ago.

The dome of silver sparked, calling Arrow's attention back as another series of invisible things struck it, melting harmlessly against the wards.

"What the hell are they?" Zachary growled close to her ear. Arrow shook her head, most of her attention on holding her ward in place.

"Something magical," she offered.

"I know that." He was not impressed with her analysis.

"I have not encountered this before," she added. His growl had no words this time. "And how is the magician targeting us so well?" This last as a cluster of invisible bolts struck her ward in almost precisely the same place. The wards bowed under the pressure, held, and sprang back to place.

The Prime stilled, head tilting as he looked around.

"No good line of sight," Matthias commented from Arrow's other side, words so faint she had to strain to hear them.

"Must be close," Zachary agreed, speaking as softly as his son.

The Prime drew in an audible breath that lasted several heartbeats, during which more bolts sparked against the wards, then let the breath out with equal slowness, a wave of power rippling out from him. Arrow stared, mouth opening. She had not known that 'kin could do that. The power collided with Arrow's wards, silver sparking in reaction.

"Arrow," he snarled.

"A moment." Adjusting wards on the move and under fire had been missed from the Academy's curriculum. A serious defect, as far as she was concerned, frantically reviewing the commands she knew as the Prime's power grated against the wards and her slender personal reserves dwindled further. After too long a pause, she shouted a quick command for lift.

The edges of the wards lifted from the ground, a hand's span at most, but enough for the Prime's energy to soar out, dancing across the snow and trees and invisible to the naked eye, felt rather than seen even in the second world as she adjusted her sight to follow.

At the very edge of her second sight, invisible in the first world, the barest outline of something vaguely human-shaped appeared.

With a snarl, the Prime leapt forward, shimmering into his animal form as he leapt, pitch black and lethal, landing on four paws and sprinting after the human shape. Matthias was a wolf-length behind his father, Con and Tamara quickly following. Jace remained in the snow.

Using the Prime's effort as an example, Arrow changed her ward, directing the silver shimmer outward to coat the huddled figure. Her vision wavered as she spent power to outline the shape as long as she could. The shape rose, throwing something at the Prime that he smacked aside with a paw, not pausing in his headlong run. The figure abruptly dropped its disguise, revealing the blocky, shadowy form from Marianne's death site, stumbling away into the forest, moving far more quickly than should be possible with its awkward gait.

The silver fizzed and died as the figure and 'kin moved out of sight. Arrow dropped her head into the snow for a moment, breathing hard, ribs aching. As she gathered herself to rise, the ripple of a translocation spell washed over her again, followed by distant snarls of the 'kin, frustrated in their hunt.

She stumbled to her feet and trudged ahead until she found the 'kin, their hackles raised, teeth showing. Soft sounds of fury vibrated the air, the 'kin sniffing around a bare patch of ground, snow melted away.

"He has gone. Another translocation spell," she told them between breaths, heart slowing down as she realised the immediate danger was gone.

The Prime snarled, wolf form shimmering back to human, long-sleeved dark t-shirt and trousers following a moment later, leaving him barely clothed and barefoot in the snow.

"Where?"

"I do not know." Her head was thumping with the mere effort of standing. Putting a hand up to her nose confirmed it was bleeding again and she dug out the Prime's handkerchief to blot the flow.

"Anything?"

"The same magic user as killed Marianne Stillwater," Arrow confirmed. "The gait was the same."

"But?"

"Too fast. He was too fast across the ground." Matthias' voice startled Arrow. He was dressed the same as his father, equally comfortable with the cold and snow under his feet.

"Much too fast," Zachary agreed, crouching next to the melted snow.

"You can't follow him?"

"I am sorry, no," she answered Matthias' back as he stood beside the Prime. "It is not a skill I possess."

"So, another Erith mage might?" Zachary's eyes glinted as he looked back at her.

"Perhaps." Arrow thought of the Preceptor, whose skill with translocation spells was unmatched as far as she knew.

"More Erith," he said in disgust, rising to his feet.

"I do not know if the magic user was Erith. He did not seem either Erith or human."

"My people don't use magic that way." The Prime was not arguing, simply stating a fact.

"He threw something." Arrow turned, back the way they had come.

"He did." The satisfaction in his voice chilled her as he strode past, unerringly headed for the thing in the snow.

―*ele*―

Arrow plodded behind them, finding Matthias and Zachary motionless, attention on something in the snow at their feet. Jace's body lay in view, unseeing eyes turned up to the sky. Arrow flinched. She had failed to protect him. The failure stung along with the loss, another life gone.

Coming to stand between Matthias and Zachary, she saw what held their attention and bit her lip to stop a useless exclamation.

The thing in the snow was a true abomination.

Bone glistened, a few sinews still attached. Bones from something human-shaped. Arrow had seen enough bones to know the difference. Shifkin or human. Fixed together in a basic shape.

"Crossbow." She forced her voice to calm, crouching beside it.

"More unclean magic." Zachary's voice was so low it was almost inaudible. She did not look at him.

"Yes."

"I hate magic." Matthias' voice was nearly as low as his father's.

"This magic is ..." Arrow could not find a word and did not think the 'kin required one. The thing repulsed her in first sight, and was worse in second sight, crawling with crimson red runes. "Human or 'kin bones." She spoke her conclusion aloud. Erith bones had no strength after their owner's death.

"Can you tell the maker?"

"I will try." She put a hand out, paused to reinforce her wards, and touched the thing.

Cold wet against her skin. Filth. Abomination. Crawling under her skin up her arm. Darkness. Fetid air. Heavy. Something dead and rotting. Shuffling sound that echoed. Bare earth underfoot. Low light. She could barely see. Odd shapes in shadows. Shuffling. Something coming forward.

The thing shifted, sinews stirring against her skin. Home.

The crossbow was in her hand, in front of her. Something was moving in the shadows. A twist of darkness Something that should not exist. Her finger was on the trigger. The trigger moved under her skin, loathsome sensation, and a near-invisible bolt snapped through the gloom.

And she was on her side in the snow, bright sunlight burning her eyes, heavy weight, no, weights, pressing her down, one wrist screaming pain.

"Arrow!" The Prime's voice, with his full authority behind it.

"Prime," she gasped. He and Matthias were on top of her, pinning her against the snow, Tamara and Con snarling nearby. The bone weapon lay in the snow not far from her hand "What happened?"

"You fired at me," he told her, relaxing his hold, elbowing the crossbow farther from her reach.

"Sorry," she said automatically, then blinked. "I was not here. I was ..." She wriggled out from under them and threw up, retching until her stomach was empty.

"Here." Matthias was crouching nearby, wary, holding out a flask of something. Tamara, back in human form, was behind him, watching intently, ready to defend her mate.

"Thank you." Arrow's face burned. She sipped the flask. Water. Rinsed her mouth, spat in the snow, and then drank, grimacing at her raw throat.

"You were somewhere else?" The Prime had found time to pull on boots and a wool sweater, eyes hard as he crouched nearby.

"Yes. The ... weapon showed me its ... home." A few shallow breaths, then she continued. "Somewhere dark. Smelled like death. Rotting. And there was something there in the dark. It was ... other. Unclean. That is what I fired at." Her face was glowing, she was sure. Academy graduates were trained to guard their minds against outside interference, yet she had been pulled somewhere else with no warning. And had shot at the Prime. Remembering the invisible bolts and the immediate death of Marianne Stillwater, she shuddered again. She had nearly killed the Prime. She swallowed hard, trembling, and took a careful sip of water, needing both hands to hold the flask.

"Where?"

"I do not know. Inside. Earth floor. No identifying marks."

A snapped-off sound told Zachary's feelings on that. He rose, paced restlessly, the other 'kin careful to avoid his gaze. Arrow remained still in the snow, sipping more water, and ignoring the growing damp at her knees as the snow melted.

"This is what killed Marianne," Matthias commented after a while. He was now fully clothed, Tamara just behind him, her hand resting lightly on his arm.

"Yes," Arrow agreed, though it had not been a question. She gripped the flask hard enough that her knuckles turned white. "I do not think I should examine that thing further." She could not even look at the crossbow.

"No," Matthias agreed with a soft, unexpected laugh. "Not a good idea."

"Destroy it." Zachary was back.

"Burning will work. Mage fire," Arrow clarified. "I will need a branch or something to light."

A few moments later, Tamara brought a short, thick branch, still damp from snow. Exchanging the flask for the branch, Arrow dug deep for some power and called mage fire to the end of the branch. When the branch's tip was white hot, she shuffled forward and dropped the branch over the bone weapon, speaking the commands to extend the fire. Her nose was bleeding again, and she was unsteady as she got back to her feet, the bone weapon reduced to ash.

"Bury it," Zachary told Con, who nodded and set about his task. "Burn the *baelthras* and bury that too." Tamara took a small flask of something with a hazard label on its side and tramped across the snow to where the remains of the *baelthras* lay.

Arrow followed the Prime as he paced a short distance from the remains of the weapon, guessing he had more to say to her.

"Mage fire." Voice flat, eyes glittering with power. And she had nothing to defend herself with. Mage fire had often been used against the shifkin by the Erith in their shared, bloody, history. Wielded only by battle mages, who the 'kin generally killed on sight.

"She's a war mage." Matthias was equally unhappy. In name only, Arrow thought. She had all the necessary qualifications, but the Erith would never deploy her in battle. Had not even allowed her a cloak. The Erith were not concerned that the thought of battle made her stomach churn; they were only concerned with her impure bloodline and discordant power.

"Why have the Erith sent you?" the Prime asked. His question was underpinned by his power, unleashed to curl around her, trying to hold her still and compel answers from her. She almost told him that, in spite of her current weakness, it did not work on her, keeping that information back, a possible, slender advantage for a future date.

"I am disposable to the Erith." The old bitterness in her voice apparently convinced him, his face relaxing a fraction. It was the truth, too, which helped.

"It takes at least fifteen years to train a war mage, and they would just dispose of you?"

Her laugh was a sharp sound that took her by surprise. "Most easily, Prime, I assure you."

Fifteen years was a long time in human terms, but 'kin and Erith lived long lives. Fifteen years was a blink to Seggerat vo Regersfel or Eimille vel Falsen, or the Preceptor. It had felt like a long time to Arrow, the longest part of her life that she could remember, most of it under oath-spells and collared.

"Foolish." A damning assessment, but whether of her or the Erith, she could not tell. "They didn't give you a cloak, did they?"

Her eyes flew up and she met his gaze full on, she startled, he assessing. The Prime knew far too much about the Erith and their ways. No, she did not have a war mage's cloak. Fabric woven with additional protections to guard a mage at his work, the cloaks were crafted in secrecy somewhere in the Erith heartland and given to every war mage on their graduation. Every mage but one.

She could not speak to answer him, but he did not need an answer, tipping his chin in acknowledgement. A blush coursed across her face, another small humiliation among the others from the Erith. She looked down and away.

"She could harm us." Matthias spoke past her. She held herself still, wishing she were not there, at the mercy of the 'kin who had less reason than the Erith to keep her alive.

Zachary's face had no softness as he looked at her. She set her jaw, stubbornly silent. She wanted to live, the wish a burn in her veins. But she had not begged the Erith, had not given them a weakness to exploit. She would not beg the shifkin.

"No." Zachary's voice was cool. "We need her a while longer."

Matthias nodded, accepting the Prime's order. Arrow did not relax. A while longer could mean anything from a day to a year, or just until they tracked down Marianne's killer.

Chapter Twelve

The 'kin were letting her live but had their own dead to deal with. Arrow stood as still and quiet as she could whilst Tamara and Con, their grim tasks complete, wrapped Jace's body in a groundsheet. As they were doing that, Matthias had a low-voiced conversation with his father, then made a series of calls on a compact radio telephone that he had retrieved from one of the packs, the antenna extending so that it rose high above his head. No mobile phone towers on Faraway Mountain, Arrow remembered.

Zachary crouched in a patch of darkness between trees, hunter-still, even his face in shadow, giving away none of his thoughts. Peeking into second sight, Arrow could see the muster ties quivering, distress clear. The entire muster had felt Jace die, and all that distress was coursing back towards Zachary. A rare glimpse into the working of muster magic and she was fascinated, despite the circumstances.

When Jace was ready, the Prime rose silently, went forward and lifted the body carefully across his shoulders, movements controlled and oddly gentle. Once he had Jace settled, he walked away from the site. Tamara and Con took up the packs without comment, Con holding one of his arms tight across his front, fist clenched as they followed the Prime, leaving Matthias to limp in their wake. They were all damaged.

Arrow followed them at a careful distance, not wanting to interfere. She was shaky from the aftermath of battle, her mind skipping over a hundred details, most of them unimportant. The curl of Tamara's hair in the wind. The slit in the sleeve of the Prime's coat, white foam a sharp contrast to the red. The growing damp along Matthias' leg below the makeshift bandage, the square set of Con's shoulders, the absolute limpness of Jace's body, so carefully carried. And her inability to shape the words for the simplest condolence.

Her body tired as they walked, her mind slowed, and her brain woke up. The magician had hidden from her senses, only the dislocation from his transportation spell alerting her. Without that alert, he could have walked beside them, close enough to touch, and she would not have sensed him. Could have killed them all with the crossbow and its invisible ammunition. The near-miss made her lightheaded and shaky again.

She would not name the likely sources of its power even in her own mind, skin crawling at the possibilities. The Erith forbade unclean magic. The Academy recognised that it was too much temptation for some, the possibility of near-endless power, and armed their war mages accordingly. War mages were expected to stand against horror and had far too much knowledge of it. Something unspeakable had been done to create that weapon. And the home the weapon had dragged her to. Even now, walking among the fresh bite of winter air, her lungs remembered the heavy fetid air and the stench of rot. Clamping her jaw shut as her teeth rattled, she blinked, clearing her eyes.

The magician could be any race, powered by sacrifice and the unclean practice that made things like that crossbow. And that meant that anyone could be responsible for Marianne's death. Anyone. Erith. Zachary. Other 'kin. Humans. There were lesser races, too.

And she was no closer to understanding why. There had been not one clue so far as to what Marianne had been doing on the mountain, or how she had got here when she lived in Lix.

Arrow's toe caught on something under the surface of the snow and she stumbled, unable to stop a short sound of pain as her still-healing ribs jolted. Eyes watering, she kept walking.

The silence was interrupted by a high-pitched tone and Matthias answered the telephone, carried in a sling across his body, expression lightening fractionally.

"Backup is at the bottom of the hunter's trail, Pa. Should be here soon."

"Good." The Prime's voice was muffled by Jace's body.

"Hunter's trail?" The question was out before Arrow was aware she had spoken.

"We're going to regroup," Matthias told her, glancing across, shadows under his eyes. His leg wound must be worse than he was showing, she realised, seeing the pinch around his mouth.

"I am sorry about Jace," she managed to say, finally, voice catching.

"As are we." Matthias nodded acceptance. "He was a good soldier." High praise, from the 'kin's enforcer.

"Here," Tamara interrupted them, handing out packets of snacks. She was more subdued than Arrow had ever seen her, shadows of her own across her face. Not wounded, Arrow thought, at least not in body. Another loss to add to the day's total.

"Trail's just ahead," Matthias noted.

If she had not spent several days hiking across wild land, Arrow would never have noticed the trail, but the narrow, flattish strip of land that wound down the slope in front of them was almost definitely a trail and was already occupied.

"That belonged to Marianne," Arrow said in surprise, second sight showing her the trail leading right to the awkward snow-covered shape.

"Tamara, Matt, see what it is," Zachary ordered, moving a little away and setting Jace's body down with as much care as he had used to gather him up.

Shedding her pack, Tamara went to help Matthias brushing snow off the shape, revealing an odd, squat vehicle which looked, to Arrow, to be little more than four fat tyres, an engine, and a seat.

"ATV. Well, it seems she didn't run across the whole mountain," Zachary noted.

"Your pardon. ATV?" Arrow framed the letters carefully.

"All-terrain vehicle," he answered, to her surprise. "That's not one of ours, is it?" This last directed at Matthias.

"No. It's got a rental tag on it. From that waystation on the Hallveran road."

Arrow's mind snagged on that but before she could ask any of the half-dozen questions in her mind, a noise drew her attention. The quiet rumble of vehicle engines, coming towards them. From the way the 'kin were standing, it was clear that they had already heard them, their hearing—like their sight—far better than her own.

She kept quiet and still as the convoy of large, sleek vehicles arrived and produced a dozen 'kin, male and female, all dressed for combat rather than a winter hike, each of whom paused a moment in front of Jace to bow their heads in a quiet moment of respect, before moving to obey commands from Matthias and the Prime.

In short order, the vehicles were turned about to head down the mountain, filling the clean mountain air with exhaust fumes, tyres churning up the once-pristine snow, and the ATV attached to the back of one. Con's arm bound, Matthias' leg more carefully bandaged, and Jace's body wrapped in sheets brought for that purpose, the whole group gathered into the vehicles and headed down the mountain.

Arrow sank back into the cushioned seat with a small sigh, not caring who heard. She was wedged between two heavily armed 'kin in the back of a vehicle with the Prime in the front passenger seat, another unfamiliar 'kin driving. The Prime had taken a call on the radio phone and from the little Arrow could gather between the bouncing of the vehicle and the prickling hostility of the 'kin, Zachary was not happy with whatever he was being told.

Chapter Thirteen

Whatever the detail of the conversation had been, when Zachary had ended his call yesterday, he had simply told her that one of the Taellan was coming to visit the Hall the next day. They had finished the journey to the Hall in silence, Arrow not daring any question under the glares of the 'kin guarding her.

They had arrived in darkness, so Arrow had not been able to see much of the Hall. It was a huge building at least two storeys tall and several times as wide, built entirely from wood and clad in timber strips from giant trees, windows at irregular intervals glinting in the limited light. Typical of the 'kin, Arrow had thought, at the few glimpses of the building she had managed when she arrived. It looked quite plain, yet the craftsmanship was masterful, each part joined perfectly to the next. The oddly placed windows were in fact a strategic advantage, blocking an outsider from a clear view of the interior while allowing the inhabitants to see out. The Hall had stood for many years before Zachary had been Prime, originally a neutral point for different musters to meet and now the official meeting place for the 'kin, and the place where they received outside visitors.

Thanks to the human news media, Arrow knew that Marianne Stillwater's funeral had been held here, and she was now buried in the large cemetery that stretched along the hillside above the Hall. Unseen in the dark, Arrow could still feel the pull of the wards that guarded the cemetery and kept the dead safe and sleeping. There had been no time to do more than glance about, getting an impression of other buildings around and many armed 'kin before she was bundled into the Hall and along a seemingly endless corridor.

Even the hostility could not stop her falling dead asleep after she had been shown to a small, plainly furnished bedroom in the old wooden building that, however masterfully built, still creaked with every step, its old wards a reassuring presence that sent her to sleep without dreams.

It was only stumbling awake at the knock at the door that she had been given her pack back and had dug out the Erith clothing she had included as an afterthought. Seeing the creases had made her wonder if she would be better dressing in human clothes, that thought dismissed as soon as it had occurred. She did not know which of the Taellan was on their way to visit the Prime and did not wish to incur additional punishment. So, she straightened her Erith clothing as best she could, further dismayed to find that she had somehow misplaced about a dozen hairpins, leaving her unruly hair in danger of falling out of the few pins she had found.

She waited outside the Hall for the Taellan to arrive, stomach churning, shifting as discreetly as she could from foot to foot in a useless effort to warm her toes. One foot was wet from a newly discovered hole in her boot. The Erith servants' wear was inadequate protection both from the cold and the sharp breeze that ran around the Hall. And she was not prepared for whatever might happen next.

No explanation for why the Taellan was here, and no message for her with any additional commands. Something had happened since she had left the Taellaneth, serious enough that they had sent one of their own number. Someone who was not disposable to the Erith, she thought, bitterness sour in her own mind. Thinking back to the attacks of the day before, she wondered if the magician had come to the notice of the Taellan elsewhere, and how long it would be before the Chief Scribe decided that she was responsible for that, too.

The 'kin around her tensed, coming alert, snapping her attention back to the here and now. A few moments later, she saw the gleam of metal along the straight road that led to the Hall and the surrounding buildings. It was a good-sized village, in fact, complete with a small general store and chapel, laid out with no design and all built with the understated plainness that characterised most 'kin buildings.

The gleam of metal grew larger, resolving into a long convoy of vehicles, very like the ones that the 'kin had used on the mountain the day before. Sleek, black, with no insignia or any markers that would identify them as Erith in the first world, the vehicles bristled with wards in the second world, a swirl of familiar Erith magic.

The vehicles drew to a precise, coordinated stop and doors opened, White Guard in dress uniforms stepping out in smooth movements that spoke of much practice.

Hidden among the 'kin for the moment, Arrow could not help admiring the sight. The White Guard's dress uniform was a soft grey sewn with silver threads of rank and merit, the warriors' hair worn long and loose in deference to the ceremonial occasion. Their coats might look decorative, but Arrow had held one once and knew they were weighted with armour, and ward spells. Her brows lifted as she assessed the braids the cadre displayed. One of the highest-ranked cadres available, she would guess, their leader a tall female warrior with a reputation for fairness.

With the White Guard out, the final doors were opened in the middle of the convoy just as the double doors of the Hall behind her were opened; Lord Juinis vo Halsfeld stepped out into the winter, dressed sombrely, for him, in a velvet burgundy coat with matching breeches, his knee length boots polished to a mirror shine and a froth of white lace at his throat and wrists. He was accompanied by a pair from his House, servants dressed in a similar manner to Arrow, with much less creasing, and displaying their House colour, a pale lilac, as a sash. Arrow frowned slightly. One of the servants was a scribe, perhaps here to record his master's adventures. The other she did not know.

As Lord Juinis stepped towards the Hall, Zachary appeared at the open doors, dressed more formally than she had ever seen him in a dark navy suit that would have looked at home in any Lix boardroom. No tie, of course, a human device that the 'kin disliked. He was flanked by Matthias and Tamara, both dressed for combat rather than boardrooms.

The occasion was one for the history books. Juinis' scribe was looking about herself with wide eyes while trying to keep a solemn expression, no doubt taking everything in and already imagining the description she would write. The human media would be in a frenzy if they had been here, Arrow thought sourly. The Taellan had been represented at Marianne's funeral, of course, but as far as she knew, this was the first face-to-face private meeting of any member of the Taellan and the Prime—at least since the peace treaties had been signed. There had been several truly disastrous meetings of high-ranking Erith and high-ranking 'kin before the peace, which had simply led to more conflict. Here, despite the weapons on display, both 'kin and Erith were keeping calm, with the relaxed alertness she associated with warriors on duty.

Arrow wished that she could be more in awe of the momentous occasion. She ought to feel something, but a sodden, half-frozen foot and a bone-deep chill made her wish more strongly for an open fire than any pomp and ceremony. Erith formal greetings could take an age to complete.

"Lord Juinis vo Halsfeld, be welcome." Zachary's voice was cool.

There was an awkward pause and Arrow stepped forward to the lord's peripheral vision, making her bow.

"Would you like me to translate, my lord?" she asked in Erith.

"No." His voice was icy. He flicked a glance in her direction, face tightening despite the public setting. "Your presence is not required."

"My lord." She bowed again and stepped back, hoping her face was not as red as she thought it was. She should be used to such casual dismissal. The sting took time to fade, though.

The House retainer she had not recognised stepped forward instead, made a low bow to Zachary and an introduction in passable common tongue, then continued to translate for both the lord and Prime as they exchanged pleasantries; Lord Juinis stood at the bottom of the Hall's shallow steps, Zachary deliberately casual, hands in pockets, at the head. Arrow did not catch all of the words, judging by the quickly suppressed smile on Tamara's face that although the translation was understandable, the translator was stumbling occasionally.

At length, when she had lost all feeling in both sets of toes, Zachary invited the lord inside for tea. Arrow waited for a signal to follow, hiding another frown when none came. Juinis was quite serious about not needing her presence. The lord's personal retainers followed him along with a pair of White Guard, mid-ranked in the cadre. That had been pre-arranged, she thought, trying to puzzle through the meaning as normally the most senior warrior would accompany the Taellan.

With the absence of the Prime, the armed 'kin relaxed fractionally, and began a casual patrol of the area, careful to keep themselves between the White Guard and the Hall. Weapons were on display, pointed to the ground.

Standing unwanted by the Hall's wooden boards, Arrow waited a moment for someone to require her attention, certain that the White Guard would want to question her about her journey with the Prime. The warriors took justifiable pride in their intelligence and she had been in close company with the 'kin for several days. Her brow creased as no summons came. There were things the warriors should know if they were to do their jobs, protecting the Taellan. The oath spells prickled, reminding her of her obligations too. Her jaw clenched in irritation. She could not let the warriors and the Taellan proceed without some warning, even without the spells in her blood. She squared her shoulders and went looking for the leader of the cadre.

Kallish nuin Falsen was exchanging pleasantries with two other warriors Arrow guessed to be the remainder of her third, with the other pair inside with the Taellan.

"*Svegraen*." She made her bow and waited.

"Yes?" The warrior's voice was cool, dark eyes assessing.

"This visit seems arranged in haste. Is there something wrong?" Erith conversation generally tracked about in circles, so when something was truly urgent, directness tended to get attention.

The warrior watched her for a long moment, ageless face giving nothing away before giving one, sharp nod.

"There was an attack on the heartland."

"On the heartland?" Arrow repeated stupidly, pulse skipping. "Were there injuries?" It seemed to be the right question, the warrior's stiffness easing slightly.

"Several dead. More injured."

"I am sorry to hear that." Arrow made an instinctive half-bow, an expression of dismay and regret, sorrow weighing her. The Erith were proud, difficult, and stubborn. They were also living beings, and careful guardians of their lands. "On a particular target, *svegraen*?"

"House Falsen," Kallish nuin Falsen answered, voice cool. White Guard were supposed to give up their House allegiances on completion of their Trials, a rule commonly broken in practice. Adopted into the House rather than of the Family's blood, the cool tone told Arrow that the warrior felt strongly about the attack.

"I do hope the Taellan was not injured?"

"Lady Eimille was at the Taellaneth. The youngest, Vailla, seems to have been the target." The warrior's face tightened again, and she relented enough to tell Arrow bare details of the attack. A camouflaged attacker who walked with an odd gait and killed with an invisible weapon. None of the House retainers had been able to withstand the attacker, guarding the Lady Vailla with their bodies before the White Guard arrived. The White Guard had managed to repel the attacker, though from what the warrior said, it was not clear how.

Arrow swallowed her questions and exclamations and her dismay, holding back queries about Vailla's health that would bring her instant reprimand. Vailla had been a source of kindness and friendship at the Academy, bustled back to the heartlands as soon as her basic magical learning was complete.

The warrior had told her far more than she had hoped for, none of it good. The same attacker. The Falsen lands were deep within Erith territory; there was no border for him to have crossed. Possibly, translocation had been used. Yet translocation required the magician to have either an anchor point to travel to, or to have been to that place before and have a clear picture of where he was going. There were no non-Erith in the heartland, according to the Erith. He could be Erith. Or he could simply have walked in, cloaked in whatever spells he used to hide his identity.

The target was also a mystery. Eimille vel Falsen might be the longest-serving member of the Taellan, ruthless when she had to be, yet she had held her position for so long and for different monarchs through her own abilities and respect of those monarchs and her fellow Taellan. House Falsen itself was quiet, the blood family tending to artistry and studying rather than bloodshed and argument. There were other Taellan who were a more natural target for attack. Several faces crossed Arrow's mind, Seggerat and Gret among them.

From what the warrior said, and did not say, she guessed that the Erith thought the 'kin were behind the heartland breach. Juinis was here to make that assessment for himself. Nothing she could say would influence him. Juinis and his escort had no prior knowledge of the 'kin, and certainly not the close company that she had had. With that experience behind her, she doubted the 'kin had anything to do with the attack. Shifkin preferred to tackle their enemies head-on, face-to-face. Not hide under disguises and misdirection. Those were Erith tactics. And used by humans. Weaker in magic and physical strength than either Erith or shifkin, humans found ways to compensate.

Something else was at play. Some design she could not see. More information was needed, which she would not get from the Erith directly.

She opened her mouth to tell the warriors about the *baelthras* and magician, interrupted as the Hall door opened a fraction to admit one of the House retainers, the scribe, face flushed with excitement.

"We are going to Hallveran," she announced, voice high-pitched, "in pursuit of the shifkin female's trail."

"The lord has decreed this?" Kallish did not look excited. Arrow sympathised. So abrupt a change of plans, and to Hallveran of all places, made the warrior's task far more difficult.

"Indeed, he has. He wishes to aid the Prime in pursuit of his wife's murderer. We are to coordinate with the shifkin and travel in convoy."

Even as Arrow was wondering who had come up with that plan, which required two normally hostile groups of warriors to work together, the door opened again and Matthias came out, apparently relaxed, speaking commands into his shoulder. He must have a radio there, she realised, seeing small groups of 'kin coming to attention as he spoke, and 'kin moving purposefully in the direction of some of the other buildings.

"Arrow." Matthias nodded a greeting, then inclined his head to Kallish. "Will you translate for me, please? Pa wants us to get organised to move as soon as possible."

"Of course. May I ask?" She waited for his lifted brow before going on, "why Hallveran?"

"We returned the ATV and found a car Marianne had rented in Hallveran, about four months ago. Seems the next best lead."

"Thank you." Arrow filed that piece of information along with the other jumbled bits and pieces gathering and made the introduction between Matthias and Kallish.

Welcoming the distraction from her cold, wet foot and too much speculation in her mind, Arrow was amused—as she provided a rapid-fire translation between Matthias and Kallish—to see that despite their outward differences, they had a similar gleam in their eye as they planned the convoy and the weaponry they would need, and demurred, politely, over who should go first and who last. Amused, too, to see them each recognise a kindred spirit. If there had been more time, Arrow was quite sure they would have begun comparing weapons.

In short order, the Erith had their human-made, heavy-duty weapons ready, mounted on their vehicles' roofs, and the 'kin had their vehicles out and ready, with similar roof-mounted weaponry. Over a dozen vehicles, and about thirty warriors, 'kin and Erith, but Arrow was still uneasy. The road to Hallveran was a lawless stretch, a no-man's land of unclaimed territory between the Erith borders, the 'kin's borders, and territory claimed by humans. Outlaws from every race called it home, making their livings by capturing travellers along the road. Kidnap for ransom was common, as was simple theft. The outlaws had, over the years, got very good at making travel on the road difficult. And, thanks to ransoms and theft, they had the resources to provision themselves with human-made weaponry.

Any journey to Hallveran was fraught with danger, generally undertaken only in heavily-armed giant convoys protected by highly paid mercenaries. Or as once when she had not been able to join a convoy, by one terrified magician driving as fast as she could in a vehicle so heavily warded, she could barely see the road.

The only thing that generally remained was the road itself because all races depended on it for trade and any damage brought swift, bloody reprisal.

Chapter Fourteen

With most of the warriors on the roofs of the vehicles manning the weaponry, and Lord Juinis' retainer taking over what translation was required, Arrow was redundant. She also had the luxury of an entire backseat of one of the vehicles to herself for the journey. The vehicle's driver would not speak with her, concentrating on the road and his place to the rear of the convoy. With the fizz of familiar magic all around, a comfortable seat and nothing to do no matter the danger outside, she fell asleep to the sound of gunfire as the outlaws began their assault on the convoy.

The quiet woke her. The guns had fallen silent overhead. As she sat up blurry with sleep, she felt the familiar hum of Hallveran's city wards. It was fully dark outside, the desolate city showing only sporadic signs of life on its outskirts. The odd shapes that loomed out of the darkness around the vehicles were abandoned buildings, Arrow knew, and looked worse in daylight; some were partially destroyed, some little more than concrete footprints where the buildings had stood, and all stripped of useful materials to help rebuild the buildings closer to the city's heart.

Alone in the dark, she murmured an Erith blessing, a wish for peace and health for the city's inhabitants. Hallveran had been established by humans seeking a place not claimed by the Erith or shifkin when they moved to this land, and it was now mostly human with a small 'kin muster. The city was still healing and a long way from whole. A virulent plague, suspected by many to be magical in origin, had claimed more than half the city's population with little aid provided by other cities, themselves worried that the plague might spread. With a shortage of clean water, food, and basic supplies, the remaining population, perhaps affected by the plague, had taken to the streets in rioting that had lasted months.

Arrow had lived through most of it, sent to exile in Hallveran when she had been expelled from the Academy. The Preceptor claimed, when they seized her and brought her back, that the Erith had not known the true extent of the situation in Hallveran when they chose it for her exile. For the first time in her life, Arrow had not believed him.

The signs of ruin gradually reduced the farther in the convoy travelled, until to a magic-blind person, the vehicles might have been travelling through parts of Lix, the streets smooth and well-maintained, the buildings whole. For anyone with magic, the city was still devastated, the normal currents of underlying power twisted and deformed in unnatural patterns. Arrow closed her second sight firmly after one look, not wanting to see. There had been magic users in the midst of the riots, many of them not caring what damage they did.

At length, the convoy slowed and stopped. Outside the most exclusive hotel in the city, naturally, for the White Guard would not permit their charge to be housed anywhere less. Arrow wondered if they had taken over the entire hotel, and if anyone had factored in the human journalists who spent time lingering outside the hotel, hoping for a story. She spotted at least one long-lens camera in the shadows on the other side of the street from the hotel and sighed as she imagined the headlines. *Erith lord and Prime travel to Hallveran in secret.* The human news had vivid imaginations, and the presence of any Erith in Hallveran was unusual enough that this would keep them busy for months.

It would not take Eshan that long to blame her, though, she reflected, gathering her pack and following the White Guard and 'kin into the hotel, Juinis and Zachary closely surrounded by their own people.

"That was an adventure," Lord Juinis was saying, face alight, to Kallish, a few paces ahead of Arrow. Arrow blinked, startled for a moment, before she nearly missed a step, realising that he had probably never been under fire in his life before.

Protected by the ring of White Guard, the lord had never been in danger. He had probably passed the journey while she had slept, watching in fascination as outlaws fired at him from shadows, and the warriors around him returned fire. For him, it most likely had been a great adventure.

In Erith lands, his status and his House retainers protected him. Here, it was the task of the White Guard. He had apparently failed to notice, or perhaps did not care, that several of the warriors and 'kin bore the tell-tale traces of bullet strikes. The 'kin's body armour and the White Guard's warded uniforms had provided them with protection against most of the bullets that had made it through the convoy's wards. Still, there was blood on more than one face, and several hastily applied bandages on arms and legs. No one was seriously injured, making the price of the Taellan's adventure one he would doubtless think worthwhile. If he noticed.

Arrow watched, impressed, as Kallish kept her face admirably neutral as she made a non-committal answer to the Taellan.

Some trick of the light, some unhappy accident as they entered the hotel's foyer and he turned to take in his surroundings, put Arrow in the lord's line of sight—and he paused, face pinching in displeasure.

"You are still here?"

"My lord." She made an awkward half-bow, the weight of her pack threatening to unbalance her.

"I have no use for you." She was dismissed as easily as an unwanted object. He turned away without waiting for her compliance, taking it for granted.

"My lord." She still made a shallow bow, stepping back until she was against the wall, tucked in between a pair of giant plants in knee-high ceramic pots, stalks rising over her head, massive, glossy dark green leaves longer than her arm. Hidden by the plants, she was out of his sight. She set her pack down with a slight sigh and cast a quick protective ward over it.

Excluded from the group, she watched as 'kin and Erith exchanged silent glances and nods across the hotel's foyer, warrior to warrior, the luxurious surroundings an odd counterpoint, the gleaming gold-framed mirrors, comfortable chairs and thick carpet underfoot not meant to host so much weaponry. Her throat closed for a moment. The first time that she was aware that 'kin and Erith had aided each other in combat. It was a far more momentous occasion than the Taellan meeting the Prime at the Hall, and the Taellan seemed entirely oblivious. In the centre of the group, Juinis and Zachary exchanged a few words via the House Halsfeld retainer, and parted on seemingly good terms, heading in different directions out of the foyer. The lord and White Guard ascended the wide staircase, the 'kin disappearing along a ground-floor corridor.

Arrow hesitated, waiting until the foyer was empty of all warriors. She had been dismissed. And yet she had information that could be of use to the warriors, that they would need in defence of the lord. The oath spells prickled at her wrists. She muttered a curse and headed up the stairs, leaving her warded pack. She attempted to straighten her clothing as she went, creases horribly highlighted by the hotel's excellent, discreet lighting. Appearances mattered to the Erith.

A pair of White Guard wearing near-identical scowls blocked the entry to the hotel's upper floor.

"Greetings, *svegraen*."

"Go away."

"I need to ..."

"Go. Away."

She had a momentary sense of dislocation, reminded of her arrival at Farraway Mountain. The White Guard would not be so gentle in their handling of her, though. She took a prudent step back from them, making a small bow.

"There are things Kallish nuin Falsen should know. May I speak with her?"

"Tell us."

"That is for her to decide." Arrow held her ground. The White Guard had no power to command her, though they were doing their best to intimidate. They needed to see the Prime in action, she thought, for a real lesson in intimidation.

"Wait."

One of the pair stalked along the corridor, another pair of guard arriving at an invisible signal to take up position a few paces behind the solitary sentry. Arrow bit the inside of her mouth to hide a smile, wondering if she should be flattered that they clearly saw her as a threat when she was usually dismissed by the Erith.

After a few moments during which she found that a curl of hair had come loose and was brushing her cheek, the guard returned, face set with displeasure.

"Third door on the left," he told her, and waved her through with a curt gesture.

"My thanks, *svegraen*." She tucked her hair behind her ear, hoping that was the only loose strand, and went past him.

The door was shut but opened immediately at Arrow's knock, to reveal not Kallish but her second, a mid-ranked guard that Arrow had encountered before.

"Inside."

Wondering if she was facing a punishment for her daring, Arrow stepped into the room, forearm pulsing with a phantom ache. A clean break, a mark of the warrior's skill, the healers told her, the bone had healed without any impairment. The healers had been pleased not to have to spend too long with her. Still, she did not want to repeat the experience.

To her relief, Kallish nuin Falsen was there, stripped of her coat and finishing tying off a bandage on one of her arms, shirt sleeve rolled up to reveal forearms corded with muscle and at least one thin, silvered scar. Whatever it was must have been sharp to get through the coat's armour. Another scar to add to her coat, for the warriors had a tradition of mending rather than replacing.

"Well?"

"In private, if you please, *svegraen*." Arrow resisted the impulse to bow, facing the warrior as an equal. The warrior assessed her for a moment then nodded to her second, who scowled but ducked out of the room as requested. Arrow chalked a rune on the door, blocking their conversation from the outside. When she turned back, she had Kallish's full attention, the warrior standing apparently at ease, but with one hand on a weapon hilt.

"Well?" the warrior repeated.

"There are things you should know, *svegraen*. Which may concern the lord's safety."

"Go on."

It was not encouraging, but Arrow briefly told the warrior about the evidence of *urjusi* on the mountain, the *baelthras* and the magician's attack. She omitted some details, such as the crossbow's ability to haul her into its world, judging it would seem too fanciful to the warrior. She also kept her own darkest suspicions tightly locked away, the possibility that the Erith's worst fears were realised. The warrior's face was grim when she finished, and her hands were clasped behind her back.

"Your assessment?" the warrior asked. Arrow drew a breath, pulse skipping, eyes widening slightly despite her attempt to remain calm. It was the first time, the very first time, that a warrior had ever asked her for her views, and Kallish had done so as warrior to war mage.

"There is a very powerful, very dangerous magician skilled in forbidden magic somehow connected to the death of Marianne Stillwater. We are still following the lady's trail. We are likely to encounter him again."

"Erith?"

"I do not know."

That earned her a sharp look and she blew out a breath, frustration mingling with relief that she was being heard and believed.

"*Svegraen*, I have never seen the magic that this person uses to conceal themselves. Or the magic that created the crossbow."

"So, the lord may be in danger," the warrior summarised, her primary concern. "Should we leave?"

Arrow caught her breath, pausing a moment to gather some diplomacy before she answered.

"*Svegraen*, leaving would be prudent, if you were able to persuade the lord of that."

The immediate tightening of Kallish's face told her that the warrior's assessment of the Taellan matched her own.

"If not leaving, what do you advise?"

"Maintain vigilance, and a ward across the lord at all times."

"Does the Taellan know?"

"They have not asked me for a report, *svegraen*." Arrow kept her voice as neutral as she could. The warrior had listened, and believed her, which was more than she had hoped.

"Very well." The warrior nodded and turned her attention to unfolding her shirtsleeves, setting her appearance to rights.

Taking that as dismissal, Arrow left the room.

Outside the room, she found the second pacing short lengths, eyes sparking fury at being excluded. A quick glance at the door and Arrow saw the faded chalk mark of a listening rune. He had tried to wipe it away, but the shape of it was still there in second sight.

"Well?" he demanded.

"I have made my report, *svegraen*." And she gave a small bow.

The extra courtesy did nothing to calm him. "There is no place for you here. The lord has dismissed you. Get out."

She swallowed her irritation, mind supplying a few choice words for the warrior, and left, going back down to the hotel's lobby to find both the Prime and Matthias lounging in chairs near where she had left her pack. There was a delicate tea service in front of them, dainty human-made china perfectly in keeping with the hotel.

Matthias spotted her and waved her over, not bothering to rise. There were shadows under his eyes, and she wondered if he had been injured again on the road. The Prime was apparently relaxed, all his authority dampened down.

"Prime. Matthias." She remained standing.

"It's too late to do anything tonight," Matthias said, "but we'll meet here tomorrow morning and pick up Marianne's trail. Try to find out what she was doing here."

"Very well," Arrow agreed. Matthias would have said more, but something in his pocket started making an odd noise. He sighed and pulled out a mobile phone, glancing at the number.

"Tamara's looking for me." He glanced at his father who nodded. Matthias answered the call and left, movements stiff and careful.

"You are still free to aid us?" the Prime asked.

"Yes, Prime."

"Good. Your assistance has been helpful." The Prime rose, stretched and wandered out of the foyer, leaving Arrow speechless. The most praise she had ever had. She dug her fingernails into her palm, reassured by the slight prick of pain that she was in fact awake and not in a wild dream, warmth coursing through her as she fought to control the smile that threatened to break out across her face.

There was no time to linger. There was work to be done, preparations that she hoped would not be needed. Excluded from the hotel, she needed a quiet, warded place to work. The Erith maintained properties in Hallveran for their use, all of them some distance from the hotel.

With a sigh, she settled the pack on her shoulders and left the hotel by a side entrance, boots slipping on the slush-covered cobblestones, damp creeping in again, and trudged on into the night.

Chapter Fifteen

Eyes gritty from lack of sleep, stomach hollow with hunger, head thick with a hangover from magic use, Arrow waited for Matthias the next morning, standing in the hotel's foyer between the plants she had used the day before. Around her, the hotel's human staff bustled to and fro, cheerfully going about their daily tasks. Arrow envied them their innocence at the same time as wanting to shut out their good moods. She had a bone-deep conviction that today was not going to be a good day. Perhaps it was the lack of sleep, perhaps being in Hallveran again. More likely the cold fear of what they might find. Whatever it was, she could not shake the feeling and had long ago learned to pay attention to those deep-down instincts.

Those instincts had led to the new, unfamiliar, weight at her back. A weight of spirit, crafted through the sleepless night using every scrap of power she had, the seals inside heavier than ever this morning. One of the last spells the Academy taught its graduates, one of the few defences the Erith had against their fears. A spell she had never thought she would use, and a weight she had never thought she would need to carry.

The only good point to the day was that she was back in her human clothing, feet dry, warm from head to toe, messenger bag a familiar and welcome weight at her side. Not even Eshan would expect her to wander about a human city in Erith garb.

Matthias arrived through the hotel's front doors, not from the downstairs corridor as she had expected, and she moved forward to meet him. He was wearing the same clothes as the day before and looked as shadowed and weary as she felt. He was also carrying a large paper bag from the city's foremost bakery and a cardboard holder with two giant takeaway coffee cups.

"Good morning," Arrow said politely, almost her entire attention on the bakery bag.

"Is it?" Matthias grunted, drawing her attention. As well as being shadowed and weary, he was also grieving, a fresh wound.

"There has been trouble?"

"You might say that. Muster squabbles." He closed his bloodshot eyes briefly, and they were damp when he opened them. "We lost a young one overnight."

"I am sorry," Arrow said, voice quiet. Like the Erith, the 'kin treasured their young. And, like the Erith, 'kin young were a rare gift.

"Yes. Come, we've a long day ahead and not likely a pleasant one."

Uneasy at hearing her own thoughts so clearly echoed, Arrow followed him into the fading darkness of a winter morning, finding two muster vehicles along with Con and an unfamiliar 'kin ready to act as drivers. Marianne's rental car was towed behind the second muster vehicle. The pair of 'kin were holding coffee cups like the ones Matthias carried.

"We'll start at the car rental place, work back from there," Matthias told her, settling beside her in the back of the vehicle, and opening the bakery bag. "Help yourself. There's plenty. And here." He passed across one of the coffee cups.

Pastries and caffeine had cured her headache by the time they reached the car rental offices. Leaving Con to deal with the return of Marianne's car, Matthias ordered the other 'kin to drive them through the city at Arrow's order.

Despite Hallveran's twisted power lines, Marianne's trail was clear through the city, no effort having been made to conceal it here; it led them to a squat apartment building a few blocks from the hotel, with apartments for short-term let. The concierge, a young human magic-user, would not provide them with any information without an order from the human authorities.

They left the building and paused on the pavement outside, Matthias frustrated by the delay to wait for a suitable order, discussing what was required with the other 'kin. Arrow listened with half her attention, focusing on the trails she could see. Marianne had used this apartment building as a base, various traces of her presence showing that she had spent time going out and about in the city.

Arrow took a step forward, drawing the attention of both 'kin.

"I do not think we will find anything useful in the apartment. A feeling. It may be more helpful to follow where Marianne had been."

"Keep retracing her steps? She was here a while?" She had Matthias' full attention.

"Long enough to travel in several directions, yes."

"Any one of them stand out?"

"One..." Arrow turned her head in the direction and hesitated again. "...very strong emotion. Not pleasant. I cannot read more than that at the moment."

"We'll walk," Matthias told the driver. "Let the Prime know." The driver acknowledged the order and got back into the vehicle.

"After you." Matthias nodded to Arrow. His eyes drifted to a point just above her shoulder, as they had on occasion that morning, frowning as he tried to focus on something. "Something different?" he asked finally.

"Hallveran." She evaded his question. The city was damaged enough to serve as an explanation for all sorts of odd matters. She was just grateful that he was not as well-versed in Erith magic as the Prime appeared to be. Zachary would not have accepted that explanation for a moment. Zachary's son gave a non-committal grunt, stared at the point above her shoulder again, and followed her along the street.

Marianne's trail took them out of the inhabited area to the end of a deserted street, one of many in the city. Arrow hissed a little at the tangle in the second world.

"Something wrong?"

"Hallveran," she said again and stopped. Impossible to fully explain what she saw to someone magic-blind. A quick glance at Matthias told her that he understood enough.

"City's a bitch to track in. False trails, disappearing scents. And worse." His face closed in. Like him, she did not need any more explanation. The city was full of ghosts.

"This is the place," she told him. Whatever had sent Marianne running across a mountain, it had started here. Matthias snapped to full focus.

Barely a few streets from the apartment building, this had once been a prosperous residential area with a wide road, mature trees lining it and residences set back in modest, individual gardens. Houses, she reminded herself. Humans called them houses. In the morning light, the road surface was cracked, gradually being taken over by plants, many of the trees dead, houses derelict.

A few paces in and she realised that there was no animal life. Not one bird overhead, no rustling in the long grass.

And the air was warmer than it had been, no trace of winter here.

"City improvement project." Matthias interrupted her thoughts, dark humour imperfectly concealing his own unease. Doubtless he had spotted the same things she had.

Arrow shivered, opening her second sight a fraction more, looking beyond the tangle that was Hallveran. Marianne's trail was clear. A slightly meandering path led along the street, as though she had not been quite sure what she had been looking for. Unlike the mountain, the path was overlaid with emotion. Marianne had been uneasy walking into the street. Her trail out of the street was absolutely straight, coated with the bitter taste of terror.

"This is the place," Arrow said again, mostly to herself. "Marianne came here in unease and left at a run. Terrified."

"Marianne didn't run," Matthias stated, "not from anything."

"She did here," Arrow said flatly.

She slowed her pace, wards humming against her skin. There was a depression in the air. Pressure of a thunderstorm about to break. And the heavy, static charge of gathered magical power, sparking against her face, tangling in her hair.

She stopped, planting her feet, opening her second sight further so she was half in and half out, sights overlaid. The point at which Marianne's trail converged in the street was a house, unremarkable at first sight. Second sight was far different. Across the split and battered road surface and pavement outside the building, in intertwined lines, was a series of runes, lines continuing around the side of the house. Not the blood red runes from the mountain, but drawn by the same hand, with the same mastery. The runes gleamed dully in second sight, eroded by time and something else. A waiting black that had all her wards sparking to life. Behind the runes, the house watched them, grating her senses like chalk on a blackboard.

"It's getting darker," Matthias noted, cutting through her fear. She flicked a glance up to the sky, first and second sight overlaid, and fought the impulse to run. It was darker in the first world, that watcher gathering in the second.

"Back," Arrow commanded. "Walk back slowly, do not run."

"Back?" Matthias' eyes flickered, predator reacting to being given an order.

"Back. Now."

"Explain." He had not moved.

"At the end of the street. Something is listening." Her wards crackled, silver flaring.

"Where?"

"Matthias, please."

He snarled at her, a harsh sound that cut through all her defences, reminding her that she was mostly meat, incisors lengthening, eyes shimmering with 'kin power. Close to change.

"Matthias. There is something here that is affecting our judgement," she told him, keeping her voice as calm as possible, unease twisting her insides. "We should regroup at the end of the street."

He snarled again, but his eyes shivered back to mostly human and he began walking carefully, one deliberate step at a time, back to the end of the street.

When they were back at the junction to the street, the ground underfoot smooth and well-maintained, he shook himself head to toe, and made a sound somewhere between a hiss and a snarl. The morning had returned to something like normal, pressure lifting.

"What in hell was that? What was watching? All I got was static."

"Something that should not be here," she began, attention going past his shoulder. "Oh, no." The dismay was out before she could check it. He turned and saw the convoy of vehicles arriving, Erith and 'kin.

"What are you hiding, Arrow?"

She blew out a breath, shoulders bowing a moment, avoiding the question. Too many things, was the honest answer. "It is just. Juinis," she began instead, gritting her teeth when the oath-spells woke. She was not allowed to openly criticise the Taellan.

"Got a taste for adventure, but no experience of it." Matthias' bleak humour saved her additional pain.

"Quite so." The spells quieted. Agreeing with the 'kin was allowed, it seemed.

"So, you don't want him here?"

"It does not matter what I want." Something of a miracle her voice came out even, bitterness tucked away.

"What is the meaning of this?" Kallish nuin Falsen was out of the vehicles first, her cadre losing a fraction of their coordination as they tried to keep up and maintain discipline around the lord. Kallish ignored them, stalking ahead of the rest of the group, eyes on the point at Arrow's shoulder. She was speaking Erith, eyes sparking amber.

"*Svegraen*," Arrow began, interrupted again as the rest of the group arrived. Every pair of Erith eyes, including Juinis', was trained on the point above her shoulder.

"What's going on, Arrow?" the Prime asked, grim.

"Nothing good," she answered, choosing to misunderstand his question. His face tightened, inherent power gathering in his eyes.

"Why are the Erith so worried about you?" he asked bluntly.

"Because of this." A long breath out, shoulders bowing under the invisible weight again before she put her hand up to the empty space over her shoulder, closing her hand into a fist. Under her skin a stream of silver light bloomed, resolving into the long hilt of a sword in her hand.

"A sword? You've had a sword this whole time?" Matthias growled, angry.

"Just this morning," she told him, sword pressing on her, an enormous burden for something that had no physical weight, exhaustion of the spell-crafting and the purpose of the sword adding to the strain.

"Is that necessary?" Kallish was asking, urgent tone catching the 'kin's attention.

"I fear so, *svegraen*. I hope that it will not be necessary."

"Where did you get a war mage's spirit sword?" Juinis snapped the demand.

"I made it, my lord," she told him, watching the disbelief and denial cross his face. The Taellan knew that she had graduated. Many of them had been at her Trials. Yet they never seemed to consider what that meant. Trials were held only for White Guard and war mages. And she was no warrior.

She could hardly blame them their disbelief. War mages were rare. Trained in lethal magic, they were generally accorded utmost respect, even by the Queen, and granted a great deal of freedom. Not one had ever been shackled as she was. Every other war mage had their cloak. And the honour of their House.

She had no cloak, and no House to grant her honour. Her graduation had sent ripples of unease around the Erith, not celebration. The only recognition of her graduation was a rare gift, an old, worn harness, leather sewn with beautifully crafted spells to hold a war mage's sword. A treasured possession, the only outward sign of her graduation, it had been unexpectedly provided by one of the Teaching Masters, a former training aid uncovered at the back of one of the Academy's storage cupboards. Without that, she would have been carrying a war mage's sword wrapped in a scarf or haphazardly tucked into her bag.

"Arrow, explain," the Prime requested.

"This is a spirit sword, not something designed to cut flesh and bone."

"Explain," he snapped.

"I do not have the proper words," she told him honestly, trying to think of a better explanation that would translate. War mages' swords were not something the Erith talked about. And there had been no time to get used to the enormous presence of spellwork at her back, the thing alert in a similar way to her wards, only far more complex.

"There has not been an incursion in over a hundred years," Kallish interrupted, tense. Arrow remembered the sculpture outside the Taellaneth main building.

The six who had sealed the last breach at the cost of their lives. Fallen not Forgotten. A chill ran through her.

"I know," Arrow answered in Erith, "but there is something here. I judge the danger to be critical." Something less than an incursion. Some fool playing with power in the second world. She hoped.

"We should remove the lord," Kallish said, unguarded for a moment.

"Remove me?" Juinis stepped forward, colour rising in his cheeks. "I am come to discover more of the truth of Marianne Stillwater's death. It would be a grievous insult to the Prime were I simply to leave."

"My lord," Kallish bowed, discomfort evident, and Arrow wondered if the warrior would truly defy the Taellan's wishes. "Your safety is my primary concern."

"What's the problem?" the Prime asked, tone edged. Although no one was translating for him, 'kin were masters at reading body language and tone and, more than that, Arrow suspected the Prime understood at least some Erith. He was too wise in the ways of the Erith. "What have you found?"

"Nothing good." Matthias was grim, echoing Arrow's words. "Arrow and I walked a little along the street. It's got a really bad feeling. My skin is still crawling."

The Prime absorbed that information with a serious expression, assessing both his son and what he could see of the street which looked harmless at this distance, only the shaded sky showing anything wrong.

"A feeling?" Juinis, to Arrow's relief, was enquiring rather than scornful, words relayed by the House retainer.

"The spirits of this place have been violated, my lord." Arrow put the explanation into terms the Erith would appreciate.

"By what?" he demanded.

"That I do not yet know." Arrow exchanged a glance with Kallish, who was frowning. "My lord, I fear the worst. Marianne Stillwater was a confident, capable woman. She came here in apprehension and left in terror." And Arrow wished she had been able to give that information privately to Marianne's widower, however estranged. Zachary did not look insulted. His focus sharpened.

"She did not scare easily," he commented, more for Juinis' benefit than anything else. It had little effect on the Taellan.

"Well, let us go and find what so disturbed the lady," the Taellan said impatiently. Sparing a dark glance to Kallish, he flicked a speck of dust from one sleeve. "Neither the Prime nor I came here simply to leave."

"Naturally not, my lord," Arrow began, choosing her words with care, oath-spells waking. Protection of the Taellan was as much her duty as the White Guard's. For all that he was protected by a full, senior cadre, she could not allow him to wander down the street without warning. "There is something here, my lord. As you can see, there is a darkness in the street, and an accumulation of energy that is causing static in the air."

"And you have some idea what it is?" Zachary asked.

"Some things should not be spoken," Arrow answered. Juinis' eyes narrowed, irritated. The Prime cast a glance around the White Guard, seeing their intent, serious faces, fingers twitching for weapons, sparks of amber prominent in their eyes.

"What can you tell us?" There was an undertone promising violence if he did not start getting answers soon.

She shifted her weight, considering how best to answer, sword balanced between her shoulder blades, invisible to the 'kin in its dormant state even if its energy did draw their eyes from time to time.

"This street is watched," she began, her back to the street. "Along the left-hand side, there is a mostly intact house with a closed door. Outside that house there are runes drawn. By the same hand that set the spells on the mountain."

"Another trap?" There was no doubt in him, accepting her assessment. In contrast, Juinis was growing impatient with a conversation he did not understand, even in translation.

"No. They appeared more as containment. They are almost gone, though." And that was a worry.

"Containment?" Kallish was pale, mouth tight. The word in Erith had many nuances, and the warrior used the one which implied a prison.

"Yes, *svegraen*."

"I think a cadre of warriors should be able to deal with whatever is there," Juinis pressed. "We will get no answers standing here." He twitched his coat, settling the folds around him, and took a step forward.

"My lord," Arrow protested, side-stepping so that she was directly in his path. There was an audible intake of breath from the cadre, anger sparking in the lord's eyes. She ducked her head, made a respectful bow, ear tips burning. "My lord. There is great danger. If you wish for answers, then some of the White Guard and I should go ahead and clear the way." It was the best compromise she could come up with.

"You are presuming to tell me what to do?" His voice was low, all the arrogance of his long and pure lineage behind him. She bowed again, keeping her eyes down.

"By no means. I would clear a path that you may walk safely."

It was as much grace as she could manage. She had never had to become familiar with the niceties of the Erith Court where a quick tongue was essential. Set apart from the Erith in her human clothing, she was keenly aware of Zachary's interest and wariness. Juinis might be ignoring her warnings, not wanting to be seen as weak before the 'kin, but the 'kin were taking their cue from their Prime who was taking her seriously, and the unsettled White Guard.

The White Guard were on a hair-trigger, and dangerous for it, struggling with the conflict between their duty to protect the lord and horror at her presumption.

"My lord." Kallish broke the prickly silence, voice pitched low for Juinis. "It would be well to send her ahead." Neatly reminding the Taellan that she was disposable, Arrow thought sourly. At least the warrior had given her a gender. At the same time, Arrow had to admire Kallish's diplomacy offering the lord a way of saving face.

She realised that Juinis was not going to heed his guardian's sensible advice as the lord's colour rose, eyes flickering with amber.

"I will not hide behind any half-breed," he hissed to Kallish. Arrow suppressed a sigh. It seemed the lord's pride was more important to him. "What say you, Prime?"

Arrow clenched her jaw, holding in a useless exclamation. The Erith lord had as good as challenged the Prime's courage. A challenge that most powerful 'kin would not let pass. The most powerful 'kin alive lifted a brow, eyes assessing, and considered the matter with every appearance of calm.

"I'm inclined to listen to the lady," Zachary said at length. "We've encountered some trouble on the way, as I told you. Perhaps we should ask Arrow to go ahead a few paces?"

Arrow held her breath, waiting for Juinis' answer. It was a fair compromise, and perhaps Juinis would heed the Prime's advice where he would not listen to a White Guard cadre leader and a war mage.

"Very well." Juinis' colour was returning to normal. He gave Arrow an impatient flick of his hand, ordering her forward.

She inclined her head and turned, blowing out a breath as she hunted in her bag for chalk. Kneeling and drawing on her power, she drew a bold protective rune on the road surface. The lines held, glowing slightly as they set. Whatever was in the house had not crept this far.

Chapter Sixteen

It was an odd procession, and slow, Arrow going a few paces forward, drawing a rune, waiting for it to set before the group followed, waiting at the last rune before they moved. The White Guard had wards over the entire group, amber sparks crackling as Erith magic met the static charge of the growing pressure in the air the farther into the street they went. The 'kin were wary, hands on weapons, but walking within the Erith wards, more than one fang bared as the air became heavier.

When the static was bad enough that her hair was escaping its pins and trailing across her face, and she was still some way from the house, she paused, made an extra rune, and opened her second sight, overlaying on her first sight. The sensation of being watched was stronger, but there was nothing moving in the second world that she could see. At least not yet. She did her best to ignore the twist of her stomach, her bone-deep conviction there was something awful waiting ahead and kept moving forward. The Taellan had given his orders.

When she was only a few paces from the faded runes in front of the house, farther than she and Matthias had reached, the bold lines of her own rune fizzed and died, swallowed into the road surface. She tried another, to the same effect.

The group behind was still at the last rune she had drawn.

She stayed kneeling, put her hand on the road, hissing as the surface warmed, moving under her touch. It did not appear to move in either sight, rough surface cracked and broken. Her fingertips were telling her that it was smooth, vibrating under her touch, almost like animal hide. Across her back the sword pulsed, startling her, reacting to something she could not see.

Drawing a slow breath in, she opened her second sight fully, first world fading to shapes and depth overlaid with twisted darkness. Ahead of her, the house, barely contained by the fading runes, was a writhing twist, a blunt awareness watching through windows and the opening door. Something out of phase with this existence, brought through a magically-created fissure.

"Incursion!" A word she never thought she would have to say. The Erith's worst fears come to pass. A tendril, an awareness from the plane beyond, brought into this existence.

Behind her she heard Erith weapons drawn, felt the snap as wards were raised to full force, the low snarl of angry 'kin, and, distantly, an argument starting.

There was no time for that. The house's containment failed with a final shiver, runes fading to nothing, and the twisting mass surged out of the house. No longer just a sliver brought into phase, it was growing with each passing moment.

Freed of its bindings, it was enormous in the second world, presence looming and yet barely there to her sight, even with her senses fully opened. It slid down the house's front steps, along the pavement, growing as it moved, drawing in power from everything it touched.

Mindless and wordless, it was just hunger and want and age. So old. Weighted with centuries.

She rose to her feet, wards flaring silver. Tongue stuck to the roof of her mouth, ears ringing with the force of her pulse, limbs trembling, scream trapped in her throat. She wanted to run. Alone, her chances were slim. The sword at her back. The spell that was the final thing all Academy graduates learned.

In the midst of terror greater than any *baelthras*, a memory of the Preceptor's voice stern and cold at the final tests before the Trials, though she had not known about the Trials then. Fifteenth-cycle graduates do not run. Fifteenth-cycle graduates are the only ones who may, one day, be entitled to the cloak of a war mage. The last line of light between the Erith and the dark.

She wondered if the Preceptor had ever faced a demon, whether his iron words were borne of experience or book-learning. When it came to the Preceptor, she was no longer sure.

There was no running for her. Oath-bound to the Taellan.

And more. Incursion meant no-one and nowhere was safe. The surging black would destroy everything in its path. It might start with the Erith, but its hunger would not ease. The corruption would spread to humans and 'kin. Unchecked, the city would become a wasteland, the people who had struggled through plague and war cut down by something beyond their understanding. Hallveran had suffered enough. And once the city was gone, the black would roll out, gathering strength the more it destroyed. It was already so powerful it hurt to look at it.

And she had made a silent promise, what felt like months ago, to Marianne Stillwater, to find her killer. This thing was in her way.

Determination kept her back straight and facing towards her opponent.

Slowly, trying to make the movement look casual, she raised her hand to her shoulder. The darkness was a stride away, filling her vision, static crackle of its presence sending her hair in wild trails around her head and fizzing off her wards, sparks of silver cast across the darkness. Inside, the mass was something other, watching. Not the sharp awareness of sentience. Instead, it was primal. Hunger, want, and greed.

The sword hilt under her sweat-slicked palm was warm, eager to work. It might as well be a splinter. She was too small. Insignificant. The thing was growing even more.

Not watching her, though. Its attention was elsewhere.

Turning her head a fraction, she saw an Erith reaching forward, pale amber outline surrounded by wards, and a cluster of other Erith behind him, trying to reach him. Juinis. Drawn to the darkness as some Erith were, entranced, eagerly reaching for death.

"Get back!" she yelled, voice lost in the black, and drew her sword. The flare of silver caught the creature's attention for a moment, one long strand pausing in its reach for Juinis. The lord was still moving forward, brushing against the creature's smoky mass, bright amber dulled at once.

Panic flared. The death of a Taellan would be catastrophic. Arrow stabbed forward with her sword, light flaring as it met the dark.

She poured power into the blade. For a moment, it seemed to work. The darkness writhed, unheard sound echoing through her, shaking each bone, retreating from her sword.

Dimly, she was aware of the Erith moving away, physically dragging the lord, the sparks of 'kin magic moving away with them. Faint shouts reached her, another argument among them. They kept moving away. Leaving her.

Alone, the being's entire attention turned to her. Cold. Cunning. Spirits, it was big. As big as the mountain, rising over her until it was the only thing in the world. All focused on her, the only living thing in its reach.

It swarmed over her. Its presence drove her to her knees, sword wavering in front of her. Both hands on the grip. The sword tip pressed down. She called more power. Nothing came. Everything had been spent in trying to save Juinis.

The sword's tip was against the ground. Nothing, not even the oath-spells, shooting pain into her wrists, could make her rise.

Hunger and want enveloped her. No light. Wards gone. The barest sliver of her sword a physical weight in the second world, the only sign of life.

Deep inside, the seals ripped.

No.

She pushed back, settling the seals. They kept her hidden, kept her alive. Kept the Erith from seeing what she was. Kept the Erith, already wary at her very existence, from killing her.

The darkness pressed. She was flat on the ground now, that warm surface that rippled like a creature's hide. Her fingers ached from gripping the hilt.

The seals shifted.

No. She wanted to live.

The demon pressed harder. It was against her skin now, eating into her pores. Claws scored, tearing flesh. Bloodless wounds in the second world. Ripping her open so it could feed. It raged as it found nothing to eat, all her power gone, and dug harder. She was nothing but a heartbeat and pain.

The pressing dark closed in further, a tightening band around her lungs. No room to breathe. Vision wavered.

Deep within, something shifted. She wanted to live. She had always wanted to live. To feel the sun on her face, the rough texture of bark under her fingers, the current of power that ran through the world, the freedom and joy of spell-crafting.

She. Wanted. To. Live.

The seals inside tore with brilliant agony that had her gasping, back arching, eyes blind as silver consumed them. Between one heartbeat and the next, the well inside her roared to life.

The sword, an extension of her will, flared too bright to look at, slicing through the darkness that gripped her, cutting off talons and ties. The demon was screaming in a hollow non-sound that made her ears bleed, and she rose, struck again, cutting into it, seeking its heart. Finally remembering the spells she needed, blinding silver sparks showering over the creature, catching it, holding it.

"You will have no purchase in this place. Your anchor will be torn up. Your substance will be destroyed. Your soul will return to the place from whence it came. This I declare. This I bind. This I put my will to."

Her voice was the barest thread of sound, her power blazing, shaped by her will.

A war mage's spirit sword and a war mage's will. The most powerful defence the Erith had against the black.

The demon roared, shaking the earth, and she would not yield. The mass surged against her binding, a physical weight of spirit. And she did not yield. Every part of it pushed against her, sending her sliding backwards, feet digging into the ground. And she did not yield.

She repeated the spell, aching silver eyes unblinking, voice stronger, that well of power she had hidden for so long filling every part of her, sealing the demon-made scars.

The words poured out of her in a loop as she fought to get hold of the darkness, to find the heart so she could send it back to whatever realm it had clawed out from.

The darkness receded a fraction, coated in silver, tiny threads that would not yield no matter how much the thing twisted, groaning as the banishment spell began to take hold.

Three repetitions were supposedly key. She was well beyond that. Onto her ninth recital at least, voice croaking with effort. The thing writhed. The silver threads were thicker now, bars of a cage. With a last growling effort, the thing surged forward, trying to get past. Failed. Finally contained. She stepped forward, body moving smoothly as a warrior's, arm coming back then thrusting forward, pushing the gleaming length of her blade through the cage walls into the heart of the thing.

The solid dark mass convulsed, tearing the sword from her hand, losing substance, fragmenting into thousands of tiny pieces that faded as silver light shot through them. The noiseless roar dimmed.

Arrow felt the pressure lift from her chest, raised her silver eyes up and saw bright sky high ahead piercing the last of the darkness. Success.

Energy vanished, body tumbling boneless to the ground.

She lay on her back, panting. So that was a demon. The thing most feared by the Erith. And she had survived. Barely. Every part ached. The physical wounds may have sealed, but her mind was still catching up with that.

Her body felt strange. With the seals gone, utterly destroyed, the vast well of power inside that she had hidden so thoroughly and for so long was settling back into its proper place, mind turning, puzzle parts of her being properly fitted together at last. The dragging tiredness of carrying the seals was gone, replaced with the honest exhaustion of hard work.

The Erith would want her dead for certain, now. She had hidden for so long, since she had understood what they would do to her, how afraid they were of her difference from them and the silver power she carried. Seggerat and Eimille, their tempers blazing out of control, shouted an argument over her head, not caring she was there, hearing every word. Well, she had heard. And understood they would kill her if they thought she was dangerous. Her younger self had formed a plan and executed it, crafting the seals in the night and silence. So many years ago.

And the seals were gone. A memory.

She could not put them back even if she wanted to.

The silver heart of her power beat, silent and strong. She was exhausted but not drained. Still had enough power to defeat the Preceptor himself. If she could only bring her stupid body to move.

A tiny smile tugged her mouth. Her body would recover. A magician only needed her voice to work. The Erith might want her dead, but they would find that very difficult indeed.

Chapter Seventeen

"Arrow?"

The voice was muffled, hard to hear. Demanding attention. A shadow moved in front of the sun and she squinted up trying to make sense of the shape. Zachary Farraway.

"Prime," she said. Or thought she did. Her ears were not working properly. And her eyes ached. She sat up slowly, wincing at the effort. Ribs ached, too. Glancing down, she saw her clothing was ripped, stuffing of her jacket puffing out in white clouds, tears along her legs revealing brilliant silver stripes as her power worked to heal her. Another set of clothing that might not be rescued. Proof, if she had needed it, of how dangerous the *surjusi* was, that something of spirit could create physical damage.

"You're not injured."

Her ears were still full, yet she easily heard the disbelief in his voice.

"Healing," she told him. That was twice he had seen her heal by herself. An ability denied the Erith. He must know that, yet he just lifted a brow.

She saw the hilt of her sword not far from her foot. She leant forward and picked it up, the movement waking up the various wounds across her body, and she sheathed the sword. The strap of her messenger bag was still across her body, frayed in places, weight of the bag on the ground next to her.

Breathing carefully, she found the air dry, full of ash, fine flecks of deep charcoal coating everything she could see, remnants of the *surjusi's* passing. And through the ash a sweet scent she remembered well, and which made a heavy lump of her heart.

"There was a demon here." Zachary was pale, tight lines bracketing his mouth, crouching nearby so he could stare straight into her eyes. "And your eyes are completely silver. What in hell?"

"*Surjusi*."

"What?"

"*Surjusi*. Erith word." Her ears popped, a stab through her skull making her wince and reach up instinctively. Her hands came away bloody. She hunted through her bag for a clean cloth and wiped the worst of the blood away, hot itching inside telling her that her body was working to heal itself, make her functional and ready for the next threat. Sounds rushed in, too sharp and clear, skull ringing with a deep tone.

"Demon," he insisted.

"Human term. Limited. *Surjusi*." She drew up her knees, resting her arms on them, chin on her arms, not wanting to move and not sure she could. "Normally out of phase. Brought through."

"Deliberately brought here?"

"Yes. Not accident."

"What did that have to do with Marianne?"

"Do not know. Marianne here after *surjusi* contained," she told him, ringing in her head slowly dying.

"Marianne touched that creature? How did she survive?"

Arrow guessed that the *surjusi* had been contained, trapped behind the runes, when Marianne had been at the house. *Surjusi* were anathema to Erith, high magic the demon's preferred source of food in this realm. An Erith touched by *surjusi* could be drained of life, soul shredded in moments. Something about shifkins' natural magic gave them strong defence against *surjusi*, making them unattractive, although they might be influenced by the *surjusi*'s taint and could be killed by a magician wielding *surjusi*-tainted power. It was likely that the thing had not bothered to attack Marianne, although she would have been aware of it.

She told the Prime that. Or tried to. The ringing might have faded but her mind was still swimming, absorbing the separated parts of her back into one being. Setting the seals in place had been the hardest thing she had ever done in her life. If it had not been so necessary, the Erith almost comically terrified of a half-breed that had manifested silver power, she would have given up several times. Only the stubborn will to live had kept her going. She had left herself enough power to work magic, but not much more than that, crippling herself even before they had put the collar on her.

"And the silver?"

Arrow's face lightened into a smile, bitter-edged.

"I had to open myself to defeat that thing. Break the seals."

The Prime rocked back on his heels a moment, absorbing that information. He was wary. As he should be. Not concerned, though. And he should be, she thought darkly. Physically battered, she nonetheless had as much power now as she'd ever had tapping into the mountain.

"You hid from the Erith all these years. And your ability to heal yourself." He had noticed, of course. He knew the Erith far too well. "Nice trick." His answering smile was dark-edged. "You'll need to do something about your eyes, though. They're glowing silver," he told her, seeing her confusion. "Here." He drew a thick-bladed knife from a thigh sheath and turned it, using it as a mirror.

She blinked, startled. Her eyes were indeed pure silver, the contrast more startling because ash and blood coated her skin. Above that, her hair—unruly at the best of times—was in thick snarls, coated with ash.

A moment's focus and the glow died, returning slowly to the familiar silver sparks, a little brighter than before. It was unlikely that the Erith would notice. She concentrated a few more moments, mapping the sensations through her body, how it felt to have her whole power back and dampened down.

"Better." Zachary stowed his knife and rose to his feet. The silver coiled, wary. Secrets shared were dangerous. And yet Arrow thought he would keep hers. Why, she was not sure. Perhaps simply because he did not owe truth to the Erith. "The Erith are gone."

"Not all of them." She could not stay here forever. She managed to stand, turning to face the source of that sweet scent, fresh pain rising.

On the uneven road surface dusted with the sooty remnants of the *surjusi*, an Erith warrior lay partly on his back, legs tangled from running, one arm flung out; his sword was still in his grasp, unseeing eyes wide open to the sky, mouth open in a shout that had long since gone.

"You knew."

"There is a scent. You do not forget." Her voice choked. Moving carefully, she went over to the warrior. Etan nuin Sovernis. One of the youngest White Guard in service. A troublesome cadet as far as she had been concerned. He had taken delight, along with several of her classmates, in teasing her when she had been collared. Still. His past petty cruelty was no answer to the hurt in her chest. No one deserved this fate.

Gently turning him, she laid him out for rest, folding his arms over his chest, putting his sword under his fingers, careful not to touch his skin.

"How did he die?" Zachary asked. There was not a mark on the warrior's body in the first world. In the second world, he was torn into tiny shreds, the echo of his scream drawing tears to her eyes.

"Tainted and drained. The wounds are of the spirit." Taking another clean cloth from her bag, she carefully closed the warrior's eyes, closed his mouth, smoothed a stray strand of hair back from his forehead so that he looked more at rest, as though he might have been sleeping. Closing shaking fingers into a fist, she pressed it against her mouth, ache in her chest threatening to choke her.

"Was he a friend?" the Prime asked gently, experienced in loss.

"No." The ghost of what might have been a laugh rode her words, a few hot tears escaping to run down her face and trail through the ash. She glanced up at the Prime, seeing Matthias and Tamara a short distance away, faces sombre. "There are too few Erith that we should not mourn." She was too worn to be anything but honest. She swallowed, taking in his resting pose, the sleeves nearly bare of braids. "He was young. One of the youngest White Guard."

The 'kin waited in silence while she checked the warrior's pose and decided there was nothing more that could be done.

"If you would, stand back a little, please."

Zachary went to stand with his son and Tamara without complaint.

The silver power came to her call, warm and familiar, and she placed her hand over the warrior's heart. She did not speak the ritual words even in her mind, biting her lip hard enough to draw blood to hold the words in. The warrior's family would carry out the rites, and they would not want his rituals tainted by her efforts. For now, all she could do was prepare his remains for the journey.

The spell for a soul stone was simple and tore a little piece of her with it. The silver glow spread across the warrior's chest and flared, covering his entire body in a momentary blaze before fading slowly. When the light was gone, there was no body on the ground, just a dark, brilliant glimmer, and the first green shoots of *vicandula* forcing themselves up between the cracks in the road. The *vicandula*, a plant born of Erith magic, would remain as a permanent reminder of the warrior's passing, no matter what the humans might try.

Arrow gathered the glimmer in the plain cloth she had used to smooth the warrior's face, folding it with exquisite care before rising.

"What is that?" Tamara asked, unashamed in her curiosity.

"An Erith soul stone," Zachary answered, something in his voice making Tamara duck her head and step back, half hiding behind her mate. "It would be the honour of the shifkin nation to keep the vigil and provide transport and escort back to the Taellaneth," he offered with the tiniest of bows, in the Erith manner. Arrow gave him a small bow in return, cradling the cloth in both hands.

"That would be most welcome, Prime." He was as well-versed in Erith death rituals as in other Erith customs, and she could not help wondering, again, where he had come by such rare knowledge. "Do you have a container that I may use?"

"Of course." Zachary relayed instructions to Tamara which had her walking briskly to the end of the street where the muster vehicles—along with the other 'kin, armed and wary—waited. Arrow was impressed at the discipline as they held rank.

"You knew that thing was here," Zachary growled when Tamara was out of earshot, even for a 'kin.

"Not knew. Suspected. Hoped it was not true." The soul stone was a lead weight, a reminder of failure.

"A little warning would have been nice," Matthias snarled.

A few short hours before, the combined wrath of two powerful 'kin would have made her tremble. Now she held the Prime's gaze, refusing to back down.

"There was nothing you could have done. *Surjusi* are matters of magic. They cannot be defeated with your weapons. And to mention such a thing would spark panic. With no proof... Well, the city has suffered enough."

"There's proof now." Matthias was still angry. The Prime, holding Arrow's eyes, was calmer, thinking.

"Any more?" he asked.

"I cannot sense anything else but need to see inside the residence to be certain." Her eyes fell, imperfectly hiding the tremor that ran through her at the thought of facing another one of those creatures alone. The building seemed empty to her senses. She hoped that was true.

Tamara's return broke the uncomfortable silence. She was carrying a small wooden box made in 'kin style, apparently plain yet beautifully finished.

"This was a gift from the Hallveran muster," Zachary told Arrow. "Will this do?"

"It is beautiful. Shifkin craftsmanship is admired among the Erith. Thank you."

The plain cloth bundle fitted neatly into the box and Arrow was left holding it with both hands.

"Come, let's set the guard before we go into the house."

Zachary chose four older 'kin as the honour guard for the warrior's soul stone, their age betrayed only by the knowledge in their eyes and the weight of their presence in the second world. They bowed as one and accepted the charge with dignity, taking the box with another bow in the Erith style. It was not just the Prime who was familiar with Erith death rituals.

Another pair of 'kin produced flasks of coffee and, to Arrow's surprise, towels to wipe off the worst of the ash.

Stepping apart from the group, out of sight for a moment, she buried her face into the towel, inhaling the scent of 'kin. Pine forest and the tang of wild that reminded her of Farraway Mountain. It did not cancel out the sweet scent of Erith death, which would be tied to this place forever thanks to the *vicandula*. She allowed herself one, muffled sob.

Lifting her head, face cleaner, she found Zachary nearby, holding out a metal mug of coffee.

"Warriors know the dangers."

She nodded agreement, sipping coffee, throat burning.

"But?" he prompted.

"War mages are responsible for keeping the population safe from incursion and other magical attacks. I failed." The last words were forced out through stiff lips.

"So what? Give up? Crawl away and hide?"

"No!"

"Good," he said, satisfied, "you're no good to anyone wallowing."

He wandered away and she bit her lip, sorrow lifted by a clean wash of anger. He had provoked her, found a weak spot, and exploited it. There was no softness in him, rather a deep understanding of the way people worked. She wondered if that was what the Erith Queen had seen in the Prime that had led her to pursue peace against all odds and the loud protests of her closest advisors. Peace which had been secured. There were Erith and shifkin growing up with no direct knowledge or experience of war. The first generation to do so.

"Ready?" Matthias asked.

"Ready," she confirmed, handing the empty mug and soiled cloth to one of the 'kin with thanks.

The Prime led the way back along the street, pausing a moment at the *vicandula* which had already reached knee height.

"I haven't seen one of these before."

"*Vicandula*. An Erith gravestone," she told him. The first one that she was aware of outside Erith borders. She suspected that the Erith might establish a presence in Hallveran simply to tend this plant. A fallen warrior's grave was a precious matter to the Erith.

The Prime nodded, filing that information away, and moved on, Matthias and Tamara trailing after Arrow.

The human house was built in an old style, with shallow steps leading up to a raised ground floor, the bricked-in, blank space of former basement windows peering up at them from behind the stairs. Arrow lifted her eyes quickly from the basement. Too many bad memories. There had been a name carved next to the front door, now faded and worn. Rowan. Arrow stopped, entire focus on that one, innocuous name.

"Rowan," Matthias read, seeing Arrow's interest. "Human. Not a name I know. Arrow?"

"A name known to the Erith," she told them, brushing past him to the open doorway, needing to move. That name on a place which had housed *surjusi* was no coincidence. There was a human family Rowan with a long, bitter history with the Erith. One of the Ancestors.

"How?" the Prime wanted to know.

"I cannot tell you."

He took in her pale face, set jaw and the glitter in her eyes. "Well, who can tell me?"

"The Taellan if they choose. The Preceptor. Lord Whintnath." It was a relief to have a question she could answer. "Or the Queen herself."

He did not reply, following her inside.

It had once been a fine residence, the entry room having a polished marble floor and carved wooden stairs that rose two storeys above their heads. The staircase was cracked and broken, neither of the upper floors accessible. The marble floor was covered with debris. Bits of roof tiles, plaster that had fallen from above, parts of the staircase. Everything was covered with a thick layer of dust which showed clear sets of footprints leading from the front door to one of the doorways to the side.

Walking into the room, Arrow stopped again, held by what she saw in front of her.

The once-grand room had been re-purposed. The ceiling long since gone, a large uneven space had been cleared in the middle of the ruin, all the rubble from the collapsed ceiling pushed to the sides, the stone floor somehow intact, and onto that clear space the magician had written his spells. The chalk was patchy and faded, broken in one or two places, still potent. A spell she recognised, the shape of it clear in her mind from the last student days at the Academy.

"Stop!" She put out a hand as Matthias would have gone past her.

"It's chalk." Matthias frowned, puzzled rather than offended.

"It is the remains of a summoning spell. There may still be traps."

"A demon summoning?" The Prime was rigid beside her.

"Quite so."

"Dangerous?" A promise of violence under that voice.

"I am not sure. Give me a moment to see." She shrugged off her bag, leaving it in the doorway, and after a moment's thought drew her sword rather than chalk, the hilt fitting neatly into her hand, the blade shivering into being, blazing silver.

Opening her second sight fully, she stepped cautiously forward. The spell was dormant, thankfully. A walk around the room, checking each rune in turn and poking into corners where stray traces of power lay, did not reveal any traps. The search did reveal another sacrifice, a small pile of pale ash that had once been a breathing creature.

"There is no more power here." She sheathed her sword, the movement becoming easier with practice, eyes drawn not to the spell circle but to the remains of what had been a large, decorative fireplace. The grate was still there, full of debris that spilled onto the floor, but either side of the fireplace itself, the walls had been damaged, something removed.

Arrow put her hand onto the damaged wall. Nothing. No power, no residue from whatever had been there.

"Problem?"

"Not now." The past was another matter. There were businesses in Hallveran that made their way by robbing out old, abandoned residences. She had seen fireplaces like this before, the decorative surround removed for selling in barely legal warehouses.

"The dealers were here." Matthias shrugged slightly. "So?"

"I am not sure. Something." Some piece of information was stirring at the back of her mind, wanting attention. Something seen or heard. And this was a building that bore a name, all Erith knew. Possibly, the dealer had been entirely innocent, simply robbing an abandoned building. Possibly, they had known the connection, and there was something more sinister at work.

"Another sacrifice?" Zachary had seen the ash pile too and called her attention away.

"Yes." She abandoned the fireplace and returned to the spell, crouching by the nearest set of runes. They were flat in first sight, rounded and shadowed in second sight.

"This magician needs stopping." He joined her, staring at the runes, close enough that the clean scent of shifkin, crisp winter and pine forest, cut through the remnant of unclean magic. "That's Erith magic."

"Yes."

"Still think he's not Erith?"

"Any magic user can be trained to wield Erith magic. It is simply magic. A power." She paused, trying to tuck her hair back behind her ears. "As far as I know, this spell was only known to the Erith. So, somewhere, an Erith has been involved."

The rest she held behind closed teeth. Not just any Erith. A highly trained magician, which narrowed the numbers down considerably. Humans had their own ways of summoning demons, usually involving a lot more blood than had been spilled here. The summoning spell laid out on the floor was now only taught to fifteenth-cycle graduates. Nausea rose at the thought that a war mage had been involved in this. With the graduation came blood oaths, a solemn declaration of protection and vow to hunt out and destroy forbidden magic. If a war mage had been involved, they had betrayed their cloak, something she had not thought possible.

"Is the circle shape significant?" Tamara asked, crouched on the other side of the room. Her eyes were keen on the floor. With her ready smile, it was easy to forget that she had a sharp mind, more than a match for her mate.

"It is. A shape with no beginning and end allows for more power to be held. And there are two circles." Arrow straightened, pointing. "The white chalk was done first. Then the green second. See the strength behind the lines?"

"Same magician?"

"Yes."

"Two circles?" Zachary was quick. "Two demons? There were two here?"

"There was only one left. The first came through and helped the magician bring the second. Then one was left to watch."

"Where's the other?" Matthias had one hand on a weapon. She did not blame him, even if his human-made weaponry was useless against *surjusi*.

"Not here. Beyond that, I do not know."

"Can you track it?"

"No."

Soft growls of displeasure met that one word. She spread her hands, seeking the right words.

"A *surjusi* is a being out of phase with our reality. It was brought through enough to have a presence here, enough to do harm, but it is ... a negative. A space that makes no sense. Even outside." Her voice cracked a moment. "It was only when it was bound that I could see it. Not fully, but enough. Unbound, it is like trying to trap smoke."

"How do we find it?"

"The Erith will want it caught, Prime. The last incursion claimed hundreds of Erith lives before it was stopped."

"I remember," he said quietly, all anger gone. "The Erith were in a panic for months." Many Erith, a long-lived race, remembered first-hand living through incursions. If the Erith population discovered a new incursion, no matter how far from their borders, the panic would be worse. Arrow swallowed, all too easily imagining the damage that could be done when a population panicked. The devastated city all around them held many examples.

"So, how do we find it?" Tamara pressed.

"There are signs to look for. Disturbances. People acting out of character. Unexpected or unexplained violence. Reports of ghost sightings."

"Violence?" Matthias' voice was heavy. He looked across at his father. "The muster's reported more fights than usual." Arrow remembered that they had lost a young one the night before and bowed her head.

"The muster house is not far from here. Could the demon's effect reach that far?"

"Yes, Prime. The longer it was here, the farther it would reach."

"And it's been here perhaps as long as four months, if Marianne saw it." Zachary nodded, looking around the ruined room. "We'll need to update Justin." He named the Hallveran 'kin leader. Arrow kept her eyes on the runes. The Erith would want this kept secret from the other races, dealt with in secret, not wanting their greatest weakness exposed. And yet. This was, as far as she knew, the first incursion in human territory. More than the Erith were in danger and the 'kin had a right to know and be warned so they could be vigilant.

"The effects should fade now that the *surjusi* is gone," she added.

The 'kin were no longer paying attention, focus going towards the front door. A moment later, and Arrow heard the sound of raised voices and felt the hum of 'kin anger.

Chapter Eighteen

"It seems you're wanted," Zachary told her, moving to the house's main door. Matthias slipped out ahead to stand on the steps barring the path between the oncoming Erith warrior and the Prime. The warrior was striding impetuously towards the house, a pair of 'kin following him, trying to get him to stop. A young warrior she knew slightly, but who had not been part of Kallish's cadre. The 'kin had not laid hands on the warrior yet. Which was good as the warrior was flushed with urgency, hands twitching for weapons as he faced Matthias.

"Release her at once!" the warrior commanded. Matthias folded his arms across his chest and stared back, unmoved. Arrow was not sure how much Erith any of the 'kin understood, hoping they were not fluent as the warrior launched into an incoherent curse.

"*Svegraen*." She cut through his words as he turned his bitterness on the 'kin. "I am here. What is required?"

"Come now."

"What is required?"

"The lord is tainted. You must come now."

"Very well." Arrow's shoulders bowed, the weight of expectation back upon her. Little wonder the lord was tainted, infected by the black of the *surjusi*, as he had been in the process of throwing himself at the *surjusi* last time she had seen him. "Where is the lord now?"

"At the Taellaneth. Come."

"It will take me days to reach there," she protested.

"The Preceptor is holding the mirror relay for you. Come."

"Very well." Her stomach twisted. Her least favourite method of travel. She ducked back to pick up her bag, then stepped out into the cold.

Her small absence had given the warrior time to notice the *vicandula*. It should have been the first thing he noticed, Arrow thought. Any older warrior would have stopped to pay their respects at a fresh death site, no matter the urgency. The young warrior was staring fixedly at the plant.

"Who fell?" His voice was quiet, part of him broken.

"Etan nuin Sovernis," she answered, equally soft.

"The rites?"

"No ritual has been performed. I gathered his soul stone, and the shifkin nation have taken charge of it to transport back to the Taellaneth."

"I will go with them."

"As you wish, *svezraen*. I will advise the 'kin."

"Problem?" Zachary asked.

"Lord Juinis was tainted by the *surjusi*. My presence is required. This is Geran vo Sovernis. He wishes to accompany his kinsman's remains back to the Taellaneth."

"Of course. Matt, make the arrangements. Ask Justin for extra for the escort if needed." Matthias accepted the command with a brief nod. Zachary turned back to her. "Can we give you a lift somewhere?"

"I should make my own way, thank you." Eyes wide, she tried to imagine the dismay of the White Guard learning that the shifkin nation's Prime had been led directly to their mirror relay point in Hallveran.

"It's no trouble." An unexpected, wicked glint was in his eyes. "The old Wicksham department store, the metalworking shop at the river crossroad, or the residence on Oak Street?"

"The department store, if you please," she said, voice small. The White Guard were not going to be pleased to learn that the Erith safe houses in Hallveran were so well known among the 'kin that even the Prime knew them. He had not given her a complete list of Erith properties in the city, but from the gleam in his eyes, she thought he knew exactly where the others were, too.

She left the Erith warrior in close guard of the 'kin, the warrior seemingly bemused at the care the 'kin were taking of him and the precious cargo that he had insisted on carrying, eyes damp as he had taken the box from the 'kin.

She had no more attention to spare for his difficult journey as she entered the hollowed-out interior of the old department store. She had spent the previous night here, performing the spells necessary to create the sword, the building quiet, the air stale. Now the building's wards hummed from recent activity, the air thick with exhaust fumes as the White Guard had left their vehicles here, warded and locked, small in the vast space, the warriors themselves doubtless travelling direct through the mirror.

Arrow made her way to the enormous sheet of mirrorglass set against one of the few remaining internal walls, surprised to find such a precious object left unguarded. There were wards, but this was Hallveran and magic was not always straightforward. The sheet was at least as large as the one in the Preceptor's study, tall and wide enough to accommodate the largest Erith warrior, its surface rippling with amber and the Preceptor's personal sigil.

She did not touch the surface immediately, pausing to draw in a deep breath, trying not to choke on the exhaust, seeking to calm her stomach and squaring her shoulders before she reached out, mirror surface warm and sticky to touch.

The surface shimmered and cleared at once, revealing the Preceptor impatiently pacing back and forth in a chamber of pale stone. Arrow's stomach lurched again. She knew that room.

"There you are. Where have you been? Get through here now." He snapped his fingers to her and held his hand out through the mirror. Another deep breath and she took his hand, his fingers closing sharply around hers, pulling her forward with enough violence to take her off her feet so that she stumbled through the mirror in Hallveran and into the stone chamber in the Taellaneth.

Huddled on the floor, she concentrated on her breathing for several moments. Mirror travel was being torn into tiny pieces, shaken, then shoved back together again. Her mind and body were still trying to work out if she was back in the right order when she became aware of a third of White Guard carrying the Preceptor's precious mirror out of the room, and the Preceptor himself standing over her, an expression she could not read on his face as he stared down at her, taking in the *surjusi* ash, the torn clothing, and the sword.

"An incursion." His dismay was evident.

"Yes, my lord."

He had nothing to say for a long moment, staring into middle distance while she breathed, convincing her stomach that it was back inside her body and in the right place. There was no need to throw up. No need at all.

"Juinis wants healing," he said at length. "See to it. We will talk tomorrow. Prepare yourself for cleansing."

Arrow nodded and scrambled to her feet as he left, allowed out of the room's only doorway by the third of White Guard stationed there. The third were implacable, backs to her in a sliver of courtesy.

Sighing, fingers trembling, she undressed, shoving her clothes into the messenger bag, making sure all the stray bits of stuffing from her ripped coat were tucked inside. Her boots did not fit so she had to leave them next to the bag against the wall. Stripped of clothing, she moved to stand in the amber circle marked in the centre of the room, then back to the doorway and she began the second part of the process, the part she truly loathed. Setting aside all her wards and defences, pushing her magic down until she was helpless, utterly naked. She would rather go through the mirror again.

Once her wards were down, there was a rustle behind her. She did not need to look to know that a robed and masked magician had entered the room. Senses open, defenceless, she shuddered as the first score of magic striped across her back.

The cleansing magic was brutal, scouring every pore, rattling her teeth, stinging her eyes, sending her hair in all directions from her head, cleansing in the first world and the second. Biting her lip held in a moan.

The Erith probably had an actual ritual they used for their own kind, one which she suspected did not hurt. She could not see Lord Juinis or any of the other Taellan for that matter, accepting a command to "strip, take down your wards, and stand there" which had been her first experience of this room.

Satisfied that she was clean, any possibility of *surjusi* taint removed, the unseen magician left the room and one of the White Guard on duty threw something through the open doorway, and it landed on the stone with a soft hush of air. She turned and found the expected plain robe, confirmation to any who cared to know it that she was clean of taint.

The robe was thin, and, despite the fine Erith weaving, scraped against her too-sensitive skin. She gathered up her bag and boots and went to the door. The White Guard moved away without a word, leaving the building, their duty done.

In the corridor outside, the Chief Scribe was waiting, pacing up and down with restless flicks of his robe, movement stirring the flames of the five vigil candles that always burned here.

"At last. Come."

"Sir." Arrow nodded and followed him, stone chill against her feet. She gasped as the outside air bit through the cloth, curling her toes up in a futile effort at protection as the surface changed from smooth flagstones to sharp-edged gravel pieces.

The Chief Scribe had a carriage waiting, drawn by four Erith horses prancing impatiently in place, heads tossing at his brisk approach. Eshan pointed to the groom's perch at the back and stepped into the carriage himself. Arrow got herself onto the groom's perch, shoving her feet into her boots rather than carry them, then held on grimly as the carriage sprang forward, coursing through the Taellaneth grounds as quickly as the horses could run.

She was frozen through, teeth chattering, by the time they reached the Halsfeld manor, forced to leave her bag and boots outside and follow Eshan into the manor at a brisk pace. No time or inclination to admire a residence she had not been in before, gathering confusing impressions of a richly furnished residence full of laughter and tension, ending up in a room with a burning fire. The Halsfeld healer was in attendance, Lord Juinis wrapped in a magnificent velvet dressing robe settled before the fire, sipping Erith tea.

"Heal him," Eshan barked at her, making a bow to the Taellan, and leaving the manor.

Arrow drew a breath, toes thawing out in the plush rug underfoot, and assessed the Taellan. He was pale, cheeks hollow, expression more fixed than normal. She judged that he had had a fright and would likely be the better for it. He had also been cleansed already; there was no residual trace of taint that she could see in second sight.

"Well, get on with it," the Halsfeld healer snapped. His personal wards were flaring, nervousness clear. He was worried about being tainted himself.

"My lord." Arrow ignored the healer, made a shallow bow to the lord that would have earned her an instant reprimand from most of the Taellan.

The cleansing spell was unnecessary. Even the healer with his weak magic would have been able to tell. And there was an Academy not that far from here full of skilled magicians, most of whom knew far more healing spells than she did. All of that stayed behind her teeth and she spoke the quickest, simplest healing spell, careful to allow only a trickle of power to fuel it, setting the magic over Juinis as a silver net.

Once it had absorbed into the lord, he moved restlessly, more life returning to his eyes.

"It is done, my lord."

"Then why do I still feel so weak?" he asked peevishly.

"Your personal reserves would have been fighting the taint, my lord. A meal and some rest and you will be returned to yourself." Arrow bowed slightly. The healer could have told his master, remaining silent instead, twitching, fingers playing with the strap of the bag that lay across his body. More concerned about his own health, she judged, and wondered how he had survived so long in a Taellan's household.

"Go," the healer ordered her. "I will see to the lord."

Arrow bowed again to the Taellan, ignored the healer, and walked out of the residence before she was tempted to say something imprudent. Shoving her feet into her human-made boots, she shrugged on her ruined coat, slid the messenger bag across her body and began the long trek back across the Taellaneth grounds to her own residence, hoping she did not encounter any Taellan, White Guard, the Chief Scribe, or the Steward, who would all reprimand her for her attire. She was tired and anticipated a long day tomorrow with the Preceptor.

As she walked, she remembered that she had left her pack in Hallveran, and the only Erith clothing she had in the Taellaneth was the outfit with the coat that had been ruined by snake venom, presently crumpled along with her other laundry waiting for her to have the time and courage to face the laundry mistress to request cleaning and mending. It was possible that the laundry mistress would have some other cast-offs that she could have. The last time Arrow had been forced to ask the laundry mistress for fresh clothing, she had spent so long listening to the woman shriek that her ears had rung for the rest of the day.

Dragging herself across the Taellaneth, she realised she faced either the probable wrath of the Taellan and disappointment of the Taellaneth Steward at her damaged clothing or dealing with the laundry mistress. This late in the day, she took the coward's option of returning to her residence to think on it a bit more. To her surprise, she found not only her pack leaning against the wall outside her residence, but also a small hemp sack next to it which contained a waterskin and more food than she usually saw in several days. There was nothing to identify where the unexpected gifts had come from. She murmured a thanks to the uncaring air and took her hoard inside, steps lighter.

Chapter Nineteen

Insistent hammering at her warped and ill-formed door woke her far too soon. Opening it, wrapped in an old blanket, she found it was barely daylight and there was not one but two Taellaneth messengers outside, although it was hard to say which was the more displeased by her appearance.

"Good morning." She managed a polite tone.

"Preceptor Evellan requires your attendance," one said.

"The Taellan require your immediate attendance," the other countered, glaring at the first messenger.

"Very well. Please convey to the Preceptor that I will join him after I have attended the Taellan. And please convey to the Taellan, or the Chief Scribe, that I will be there as soon as I can." She stepped back, intending to close the door, blocked by the second messenger's foot.

"Immediately."

"I cannot present myself to the Taellan dressed in a blanket," she told him, exasperated.

The messenger looked as though he would dispute that, then cast another glance up and down her person.

"An eighth candle."

A bare ten minutes in the human world. A ridiculously short period of time for her to get into her Erith clothing with its numerous buttons. Arrow set her jaw.

"I will be dressed as soon as I can."

"An eighth candle," he insisted as she shut the door in his face.

Precisely an eighth candle later, he began hammering on the door again, so powerfully that the wood, already weak, cracked, a hairline fissure running up the centre of it.

Mostly dressed, just her coat to fasten, Arrow opened the door with a hiss, narrowly missing being hit in the face by the messenger's raised fist.

"Now," he told her. The other messenger had gone.

"Fine," she snapped, the bottomless pool of silver warming inside her.

She stepped out of the room, closing the door behind her, noting the fist-sized dent as well as the crack. The door had fitted badly before, and now most definitely needed repair. Which she would have to negotiate with the Steward. Far easier than dealing with the laundry mistress, but yet another unpleasant conversation ahead.

"You cannot be outside like that," he said, horrified. Her coat was open, her hair unpinned, a handful of pins shoved into one pocket.

"Then, please go and report my inadequacies to the Steward and make sure you tell him I was permitted only an eighth candle to dress for the Taellan." There was an edge to her voice that she had not heard before, temper that had been dormant for years stirring at the petty bullying, no longer afraid of what they might do. The messenger paled, swallowed, and ran off.

Arrow bit back curses. She needed to compose herself if she were to survive the Taellan and Preceptor. Walking at a brisk pace, she made her way to the main building, fastening her coat properly and haphazardly pinning her hair as she went. The coat was horribly creased, still, every wrinkle highlighted in the bright morning light. Perhaps she should have braved the laundry mistress after all.

Arriving at the room which the Taellan generally used for their business, the Taellan were nowhere to be seen. There was an open door farther along the corridor with the scent of Erith tea and hum of conversation creeping from the doorway.

Prepared for a long wait, Arrow went into the meeting room, startled for a moment to see it was not entirely empty. Kallish nuin Falsen, dressed in her day uniform and her hair sleek down her back, not a single crease visible, waited by one of the high windows. Arrow made a half-bow in the warrior's direction and received a nod in return, further surprising her before she took her own place, standing in one of the shadowed alcoves where servants waited.

She used the time to review the events of the past days, considering what the Taellan needed to know, and whether the Preceptor would see through the paper-thin shielding she had hastily constructed where her seals had been. They were not pleasant thoughts.

More than a half candle later and the Taellan entered, all ten of them, talking among themselves and taking their places around the table with no sense of urgency, one of Eshan's scribes following them in and settling himself into an alcove in a similar pose to Arrow. Lord Juinis, restored to full health, was accompanied by Gret vo Regresan and Eimille vel Falsen, both the older Taellan's personal wards shimmering at the edge of Arrow's sight, protecting themselves against any possible residue the lord was carrying. It was a calculated show of support by the two older Taellan. Many of the others were keeping a prudent distance from the Halsfeld lord.

Once the lords and ladies had settled in a rustle of fine fabric, the elder called the meeting to order with a wave of his hand, beckoning the scribe forward first. The scribe updated the Taellan on what should have been a minor dispute between landholders in the Erith heartland. It did not sound urgent to Arrow's ears, not even considering that the lands bordered one of the Consort's personal properties, and yet the Taellan treated the matter with solemn attention, asking a series of questions that never seemed to end.

By the time the scribe was finished, Arrow was calm and resolved in what she would and would not disclose. The Taellan ignored the Erith warrior and Arrow was summoned forward at Seggerat's gesture. As soon as she stepped forward, a barrage of questions arose, voices running over each other. The melody of the Erith language and voices did nothing to hide the demand. The Taellan wanted to know everything about the malevolent spirit. Where had it come from? What was its purpose? Had she truly banished it? Would it return?

"My ladies and lords," Arrow bowed, "I have not yet had time to consult with the Preceptor and the Archives in this matter." Even as she spoke there was a dull thud at the door, the familiar sound of a knock muffled by the room's wards.

Without waiting for a reply, the doors opened, wards crackling and hissing at the breach.

Evellan came into the room, robes brushing off the ward static as he walked. The doors closed behind him at the flick of his wrist and spoken command, the room's wards settling at a further command, an open display of power that he rarely indulged in. Quietly amused by the open shock on some of the Taellan's faces at the abrupt entrance, Arrow made her bow and stepped back at his approach to let him speak.

"Preceptor Evellan." Seggerat rose to his feet, voice cool. "Is there something amiss?"

"Something amiss?" The Preceptor's voice was silky quiet in the room, its tone one that his students would know and dread. Arrow wished she could take a few more steps back.

"Yes, my lord." Seggerat managed to convey his irritation without raising his voice or changing his apparently polite tone.

"There has been an incursion. A *surjusi althem* in this realm for the first time in over a hundred years. And you..." The word dripped scorn, encompassing the entire table. "...you think to deal with this without informing the Academy?"

"Ah. I fear there has been a misunderstanding," the elder said smoothly, and Arrow's apprehension transferred to him. When he was smooth, he was dangerous.

"A misunderstanding? Was there not an incursion? Are you not here this morning to discuss the incursion? No misunderstanding so far." The Preceptor had banked his anger, yet it still burned enough to draw displeased frowns from many of the Taellan.

"We do not think to deal with this without informing the Academy. That would be foolish. Rather, we are to hear our agent's report and determine a response."

"Your agent in non-magical matters only, my lord." Evellan could be smooth, too. "And by the mere fact she now wears a spirit sword, I can assure you that magical matters are involved."

"A sword?" The elder lost some of his composure, annoyance flushing his cheeks as he turned to glare at Arrow. "A sword in this chamber?" More than one of the Taellan glanced at her shoulder. Few of them were powerful enough in magic to fully see the sword, just aware that there was something there.

"A spirit sword, my lord, which I am permitted to carry," Arrow reminded him.

"No weapons in the meeting chamber!" Gret surged to his feet, outrage surpassing Seggerat's. Arrow required a great deal of self-control to keep from glancing across at the living weapon that was Kallish nuin Falsen.

"Weapons are permitted when carried by the White Guard and war mages, my lord." Arrow kept her voice as neutral as possible, torn between amusement at their discomfort and irritation, her temper still prickling that they had yet again so clearly and completely forgotten her training.

"Magical matters," the Preceptor reminded the room. After a long, tense moment, Gret settled and Seggerat twitched his formal robe into place and took his seat once more.

"Magical matters," he acknowledged.

"Arrow, where have you reached in your report?" the Preceptor asked, glancing around for somewhere to sit. There were no other chairs in the room, so he simply stayed where he was, with a good view of the room.

"I had not begun, my lord, other than to inform the Taellan that I had not had an opportunity to consult with you or the Archives."

"You are quite certain that you encountered a *surjusi althem*?" Eimille vel Falsen asked, clinging to a last glimmer of hope.

"As certain as I can be, my lady." Arrow drew a breath, saw the Preceptor's raised brow, and went on, "and I should also report at once that there were two *surjusi* summoned."

The room erupted in a rapid-fire round of questions, exclamations, and alarm, the Taellan talking over each other across the table, pelting questions at Arrow too fast for her to follow. For the first time that she could remember, Seggerat failed to restore order with a glance and resorted to rising to his feet again, palms raised. Even that failed to bring quiet.

Unable to act, Arrow watched with close attention and interest. Since she had last observed the Taellan, Juinis had been tainted, there had been an attack on the House Falsen, and the House Sovernis had lost one of its youngest. She had now brought confirmation that there had been an incursion. It was more danger than the Taellan had faced in her memory, and long-dormant tensions between some of the most influential Erith alive were coming to the surface, showing just how fragile their cooperation was. As she watched, the Lady Sovernis reminded Gret vo Regresan of an old obligation due to her House. From the colour of Gret's face, the reminder had not been appreciated.

"Stop!" The Preceptor's voice cut through the babble, laced with a touch of power. The Taellan turned their collective attention on the Preceptor, varying degrees of shock and disbelief across their faces. Evellan's robes flared around him, the ever-present shadows swirling in restless curls.

"There is no point in being truly upset until we know what we are dealing with," the highest authority in Erith magic stated with admirable patience.

"Lord Evellan." The elder inclined his head in a rare show of respect. "Continue," he told Arrow in a completely different voice and seated himself with a rustle of fine cloth.

"Elder. Lords and ladies." Arrow stepped forward again. "It would perhaps be easier if I tell you what I have learned, rather than describing events." She did not wait for permission, foreseeing a debate that could last an age.

Instead, she catalogued in as even a voice as possible, the triple-layered trap of spells left on Farraway Mountain, the attack by *baelthras*, the attack by the magician with his invisible weapon, and the discovery of the ruin in Hallveran with summoning spells for not one but two *surjusi*. She said nothing about Juinis' taint, or being pulled into the crossbow's world, or the breaking of the seals she had kept hidden from the Erith more than half her life.

The telling took a while, but under the weight of both the Preceptor and elder's stares, the Taellan remained silent, attention fixed on her.

There was a short pause when she reached the end then the Preceptor stirred.

"The same spellworker throughout?"

"The trap on the mountain and the summoning at Hallveran, yes, my lord. I do not know about the attacker on the mountain as there was no clear trace."

"Erith?" Seggerat wanted to know.

"I cannot be certain. The summoning spell was Erith, and the runes used on the mountain were Erith."

"There had to be some involvement of Erith, then." Kester vo Halsfeld spoke up, apparently quite calm.

"I believe so, yes, my lord."

"Where are the *surjusi* now?" the Preceptor cut back in.

"The one left at the house is gone. The other, I do not know. I speculate that it accompanies its summoner." That the *surjusi* was still tied to its summoner was the only explanation she could think of that made sense for why there was no widespread panic or taint. The *surjusi* would follow its temporary master for as long as the magician kept the spells refreshed, waiting until the magician made a mistake before slipping its bonds and escaping. An untied *surjusi* would cut a direct line through the second world for the Erith borders, drawn by the promise of a feast of high magic.

"Who we cannot identify." The elder had a pinched expression, not hiding his dissatisfaction.

"That is so," Arrow agreed. There was a restless movement around the table, the full impact of her report beginning to sink in. Arrow did not blame them for their pale faces and trembling. At least one highly skilled magic user, with an invisible weapon, the ability to translocate and the aid of a *surjusi*. She would quite like to hide but suspected she would receive different orders. And the White Guard would be doubling their patrols as soon as the elder had the opportunity to speak with Lord Whintnath.

"You discovered the *surjusi* in Hallveran by following Marianne Stillwater's trail?" Kester again, seeking clarification.

"Yes."

"Do we know why the lady was there?" The elder picked up on Kester's line of thought.

"No. I do not think she was looking for *surjusi*. She was on some other quest."

"Who cares what she was there for?" Gret burst in, dismissive. "She had no ability to summon the thing or control it."

That gave rise to another round of questions from the Taellan, discussing the matter amongst themselves across the table, Arrow and the Preceptor forgotten. The Preceptor was following the conversation, but from his abstracted expression, his mind was clearly on other matters. Arrow gave up trying to follow the twisted paths of logic that the Taellan were following. They were worried, and not thinking clearly.

"Can we find out why the lady was there?" the Preceptor asked into a momentary quiet, tone mild. Arrow was not fooled. His eyes were keen.

"I believe it would be helpful to try." Arrow hesitated a moment, then decided there was no choice. "The residence in Hallveran had the name Rowan outside it."

The Taellan fell silent again at the name, drawing the same conclusions she had, and also taking in a collective breath, mouths opening. The Preceptor moved. Not subtly. He took a firm step forward, shadows swirling, and the Taellan remained as quiet as obedient students.

"Rowan." The Preceptor turned the name over.

"It is not possible," Eimille said flatly, eyes sparking amber betraying her unease. The oldest of the Taellan, she had lived through more than one incursion, had lived through the damage caused by the original Rowan and the other few humans the Erith referred to as the Ancestors. The Ancestors had somehow learned summoning spells, then succeeded in breaching Erith borders, intent on slaughter. Too many had died. Generations ago, in human terms, but the Descendants were still monitored by the Erith because it was the same lifetime for many Erith, and the Erith did not forget.

"It may be coincidence," Kester conceded, "however, it would be prudent to follow up the matter."

"I agree. I will inform the Queen. Kester, inform Lord Whintnath that we require the Descendants be traced."

Kester nodded, accepting the elder's order, and Arrow's eyes strayed to the silent, watchful warrior still waiting by the windows. Surely a better choice to relay messages to the White Guard's commander. She had a sinking feeling of why Kallish was there.

"The summoning spell is advanced magic. I will have all those with the necessary skills accounted for." Evellan's voice was rough. Many of them would be magicians he knew well, like Gilean vo Presien or his fellow students, or students he had personally taught. He did not want to believe that one among them had broken their oaths any more than she did.

"As swiftly as possible," the elder prompted, earning a sharp stare from the Preceptor.

"I will go over the spellwork with Arrow, see what we can learn," the Preceptor added, effectively reserving her services for himself.

"I expect to be kept informed," the elder said, lifting his chin, eyes sparking amber. Evellan lifted one dark brow, locking eyes with the head of the Taellan. Arrow's feet twitched, wanting to move out of the way.

Whatever Evellan would have said was interrupted by a knock at the door, swiftly followed by the entry of Eshan. The scribe's face was more than usually pinched as he made his way across the room and whispered in the elder's ear. Both then looked at Arrow with almost identical expressions of distaste.

"The Prime has requested your presence..." The elder's voice was sharp. "...as he feels there is unfinished business."

"We have not yet determined who killed Marianne Stillwater," Arrow reminded him.

"He has sent a group of shifkin to deliver the message and wait for a response. You are ... requested to report to him tomorrow." The elder's mouth was white, words forced out.

"Here?" Lady Sovernis cried, "Those savages are here?"

"At the main gate." The elder did not look at the lady, attention still on Arrow. "The Prime expects our compliance."

Arrow said nothing. Either the elder would agree or he would not. A coil of apprehension settled in her. The elder was capable of letting his pride keep her here against the Prime's wishes. With the use of Erith magic and possible Erith involvement in Marianne's death, that would not be wise. More than that, the Prime's open demand for her presence suggested something else had happened outside the Erith borders.

"The shifkin are determined and experienced trackers and warriors." The Preceptor's voice was thoughtful. He was not speaking to anyone in particular, making the remark to the air.

"Very well. You may go and see what the Prime wants." The elder was ungracious, lips still thin. "Relay the message," he ordered Eshan, ignoring the curl of Eshan's lip as he was demoted to mere messenger to the shifkin.

"Arrow." The Preceptor caught her attention. "Let us be clear. The *surjusi* cannot be allowed to roam. You will use whatever resources and means you need to stop it. Kill the summoner and send that thing back where it belongs."

"Yes, my lord." The weight of his command settled on her and she swallowed nausea. It was not the first time the Preceptor, or the Taellan, had sent her to kill something. It did not get easier.

"Before we finish, one final item of business." The elder's eyes flicked to Kallish, who came to attention smoothly. "*Svegraen*," the elder said, contempt on his face.

"My lord." Kallish bowed. Arrow glanced around the table and saw contempt reflected in other faces too. Kester's face was closed, a mask hiding his true feelings.

"You were charged with the protection of one of our number," Seggerat continued, and Arrow's uneasy feeling crystallised. Surely, the Taellan were not going to hold the captain responsible. "You failed in that protection, allowing the Taellan to become injured. Worse. Tainted."

"And allowed a member of your cadre to fall," the Sovernis lady put in, doubtless concerned the elder would forget that insult.

Kallish nuin Falsen said nothing, holding quite still, spots of colour blooming along sharp cheekbones. Arrow could not tell if that was shame or anger, but she had no doubt of her own feeling.

"You have taken the warrior's report?" she asked the elder, her cool tone one she had never dared before in this company. The elder's intense, displeased glare pinned her, drying her mouth, but she held her ground.

"We have Lord Juinis' own account."

"I was injured," the head of House Halsfeld protested, fury shaking his voice.

"You were ..." Arrow snapped, patience gone, forcibly biting off the next word and clamping her jaw shut for a moment before saying in a more moderate voice, "reckless."

The silence was absolute. To Arrow, the moment distorted as, lightheaded, she realised she had just lost her temper with the entire Taellan. There was no way to take the words back, to unsay them, and no apology that would earn her forgiveness. And she found that she could not form the words, let alone the will, for an apology—even in her mind. The Taellan might be stung by the injury to one of their number, and the Lady Sovernis by the loss to her House. They had not stood on that street. They had not faced what the warriors had faced, and not for the first time. So, she did not bow. Instead, she straightened her spine, waiting for the wash of fury.

It broke over her head at once. The elder rose to his feet again, along with half the Taellan, all voices raised at once. Picking out individual voices was almost impossible but they all had in essence the same question. How dare she?

When the storm had died for a moment, at the elder's insistence, silence returned. Every pair of eyes in the room was fixed on Arrow.

"The Taellan was warned once and warned twice and still persisted in walking into danger, lords and ladies. Erith are taught to bear the consequences of their own actions." Arrow heard her voice shake and, with a little skip of her heart, recognised that it was not fear. Rather, she was furious. Juinis, used to every protection and comfort of an ancient House, might truly believe that his White Guard protectors had failed, but no proper enquiry had been made and Kallish's sense of honour and her training would not let her question the charge.

"Warned?" the elder said, low and dangerous but to Arrow's sharp ear, not wholly outraged. To charge the lord with being reckless was to remind the Taellan that all Erith, whatever their station, were expected to be guardians of their own conduct and measure their words and actions, not rush heedlessly into danger. Juinis had settled back into his chair, the flush in his cheeks no longer entirely from anger. His silence spoke for him, a fact she was sure the elder did not miss.

"By a senior White Guard and by a war mage," she confirmed.

"War mage. Abomination!" The comment came from one of the Taellan, disgusted. Arrow thought it might have been the Sovernis lady, prickling under the loss of one of her House. The who did not matter. It was a widely held view in this room.

Without surprise, Arrow realised that Seggerat was going to deal with her outburst by ignoring it. Accustomed to near-absolute power, she was regarded as a necessary evil and nothing more. She was sure that, if asked, the elder would say he did not wish to give her credence.

The elder settled at the table once more, composure restored, and turned his attention to the warrior.

"You are demoted. Kester vo Halsfeld will carry the order to the commander and you will be reassigned. Dismissed."

"My lord." Not a hair out of place, Kallish executed a flawless bow and left the room, eyes straight ahead.

"You have much to do." The elder's voice was silky.

"Elder." Arrow did not bow, just inclined her head, fury still riding her.

"Report to my study. I will be along shortly," Evellan ordered, voice casual, eyes sparkling with amusement. Arrow suspected the amusement was at her expense, some part of the long-term game of power he was engaged in with Seggerat.

"My lord." She gave him a small bow and left the room, stalking along the corridor. Coming across one of the messengers, she sent him to the gate with a more cordial message for the shifkin if they were still there and requesting details of when and where she should meet them, details that she was confident Eshan would forget. For the first time she could remember, after a close look at her face, the messenger did not argue but simply swallowed hard and ran.

Clean air on her face was just what she needed, the scent of the Erith garden soothing her as she descended the shallow steps at the front of the main building. The pale stone sculpture stared back at her and she walked around until she stood facing the mage, stopping a moment to look at the familiar face, his eyes fixed on his enemy. The sculpture was larger than life, casting a shadow over her as she paused, feeling the resonance of the courage shown by the warriors and war mage more acutely than ever, having seen what they faced. She bowed her head in silent respect and turned, intending to make her way to the Academy.

Just out of view of the main building, she acquired a shadow.

"They are sending you after the *surjusi*?" Kallish's voice was cool.

"They are, *svegraen*. Tomorrow, I think. Today, I must share information with the Preceptor."

"Such things should not be faced alone." There was something in the warrior's face that held Arrow silent for a moment. Some memory too dark to be spoken. The warrior held out something. "When you find it, call."

Arrow took the item held out with automatic thanks, looking down to find a small grey communicator disk in her hand. She looked up to find the faintest trace of a smile on the warrior's face, amusement at her shock.

"Not alone," the warrior repeated, inclined her head, and strode off leaving Arrow open-mouthed, fingers clenched around the precious chip of stone. A White Guard emergency beacon keyed to Kallish if she was not mistaken. Arrow had never seen one before. The White Guard protected them almost as fiercely as their medallions.

She tucked the beacon into an inner pocket sealed with a spark of magic and had to force her hand away. Not alone. The warrior could not possibly know the full extent of what those words meant. Arrow glanced back at the statue barely visible through the trees, the warriors close around the mage, each holding their post. Her throat tightened. Not alone.

Voices, a pair of White Guard on patrol, broke her mood and she made her way briskly towards the Academy.

Chapter Twenty

She arrived at the Academy before the Preceptor and, mind busy on other matters, almost ran into Gesser vo Regresan. He was less than pristine, robes marred with chalk dust, faint trace of a bruise across one cheek.

"Runt!" He seized her arm, fingers digging in hard enough to bruise. "Come with me."

"I cannot. I am needed—"

"I do not care. With me. Now."

Arrow dug her heels in, forcing him to stop or drag her bodily along the corridor. He stopped, glaring at her, disbelief across his face.

"I command you. Now."

"I cannot. I have an appointment with the Preceptor."

"Evellan?" he sneered. "What could he possibly want with you?"

"I cannot tell you that."

His grip tightened and she pulled away, moving him a step before he dug in his heels in his turn, twisting her arm to an uncomfortable angle where her shoulder would dislocate if he pulled harder. From the glint in his eyes, he knew precisely what he was doing.

Her wards flared, cascading silver over him, and he hissed, loosening his hold and giving her a hard, angry shove so that she stumbled back several paces. She stopped, facing him, wards visible. His bullying was normally a private thing.

"What is the meaning of this?" The Preceptor's silky quiet voice startled them both.

"This runt refused a command." Gesser twitched his robes into place, straightening, hair somehow smoothing itself.

"Arrow is under my order." The Preceptor's voice was still smooth.

"What could you possibly want with it?" Gesser's lip curled. "I require a demonstrator."

Ah. The tenth-cycle class. The chalk dust and bruise made sense. Arrow bit her lip. Apparently, Gesser's concentration under distraction had not improved if students were able to hit him so easily.

"You are a senior student. Arrow is a graduate. Do your own demonstrations. Arrow, this way."

Arrow said nothing, following Evellan down the corridor. That was twice Gesser's will had been crossed, and this time publicly. There had been no retaliation last time. This time, there would be.

"I want you to draw the runes you saw in as complete a form as you can. Not whole, you understand."

"I understand," Arrow said. Even without a mage's will behind them, whole runes had their own power and the Preceptor did not want any of the unclean spells alive in his study. "Which runes, my lord? The ones from the mountain or the ones from Hallveran?" They were walking along an open corridor, a number of curious students wandering between lessons.

"Both, of course. Get to it, the door is open."

"Yes, my lord."

Arrow went into his study alone, a rare occurrence, and found that he had added a workbench, a waist-high, long, wooden table. There were writing supplies on the bench. A large stack of the parchment-thin rice paper the students used to practice and a pyramid of chalk were ready for her.

His desk was also in the worst state she had ever seen it. Piled high with homework, scrolls and parchments, as well as some empty potion bottles. She frowned at the mess. The Preceptor famously would not permit anyone to clean for him, yet always seemed to have matters under control. Thinking back, she tried to remember if she had seen or felt Teaching Mistress Seivella's presence anywhere. Despite having her own reasons to dislike the lady, Arrow knew that Seivella and Evellan were close, too close according to some students, although Arrow did not believe that gossip and the lady was generally conscientious in her duties at the Academy. Whatever had taken the lady away from her duties must be serious, and her lengthy absence unplanned.

If she had the time, Arrow would go and sit quietly in the refectory and listen to the student chatter. What they said and what they did not say. Another time. For now, she had work to do.

Sometime later, she was kneeling on the floor, making sure that the last of the summoning circle runes was correctly placed, when the door opened behind her. Weapons oil and cardamom. Heat ran up her face. Her loss of temper before the Taellan resurfaced. With the heat of the moment gone, she was faintly embarrassed by her loss of composure, but mostly irritated with the Taellan for their cavalier disposal of a good warrior's service.

"Arrow." Kester's voice was bright. "Evellan not here yet?" He glanced across at the untidy desk and frowned in his turn.

"I have not seen him for a while, my lord." She rose, glanced down and grimaced. Her already wrinkled outfit was now covered in chalk dust and even more creased.

"These are the spells you saw?" He did not appear to notice her discomfort or dishevelled state, stepping past her to look at the large circle of papers she had created on the floor.

"The spells from Hallveran, yes. The others..." She tilted her head to the papers laid out on the bench. "...are from the mountain."

"They do not look complete," he observed. He had his hands folded carefully behind his back, appropriately wary of touching spell runes.

"That is because only a fool draws complete blood magic." Evellan entered the room, the door closing softly behind him. "Good," he said, seeing the papers laid out. "Talk me through this, Arrow."

She began with the runes from Hallveran, as they were closest. She had made each rune incomplete when drawing, a skill which was hard-won. So used to drawing the complete rune, or the complete spell, holding back that final line or two was difficult.

The Preceptor knelt on the floor beside her, shadows spilling around him, brushing against her wards, amber in his eyes prominent.

She waited for him to test her. To demand how she, apparently a mid-powered mage, had been able to banish a *surjusi*. To discover that she had never been a mid-level mage, the warm coil of silver purring contentedly inside.

The question did not arise.

The Preceptor paled as the day wore on, shadows becoming more restless, face drawn. He had lived through the last incursion, too, she recalled.

"This is far worse than I feared," he said at last, voice raw. He rose, moved away from the papers, withdrawing to stand beside his desk, grimace crossing his face as he looked at the piles waiting for his attention.

"The magician is skilled," Arrow agreed.

"Skilled? Skilled! If any one of my students had half the talent he has…" Evellan bit his lip and stared out at the gathering dark.

"But one person," Kester put in unexpectedly, drawing a sharp glance from Evellan. "Only one. However powerful, that is something."

"Young thing." Evellan shook his head and came back to the room. "The mountain spells, Arrow."

So, she talked him through the black-and-white shapes and bloody red runes.

"*Urjusi* again." His lip curled. "The remnants are cleansed?"

"On the mountain, yes, my lord. I did not have time to do so at Hallveran."

"There is a cadre and mage on their way to tend the *vicandula*. I will make sure they cleanse the Rowan residence." Evellan made an apparently careless gesture towards his desk. The orb flared a moment, spark of amber lit in its depths. A reminder for later. It was a rare day that the Academy's head needed such a device.

"The warrior's family wanted to have the *vicandula* moved to the heartland," Kester said. He sighed. "Lord Whintnath has had to explain matters to them."

"I could not leave Etan nuin Sovernis' body as it was." Arrow felt heat in her face, stung into defending her error. The *vicandula* rose when the soul stone was made, and not before. Transporting the body to the heartland would have given the family a tangible marker for their grief.

"That is what Whintnath explained. It has been such a long time that some things have been forgotten." Kester's voice was heavy. Like her, he was too young to remember the last incursion. Perhaps training with the White Guard, alongside veterans of more than one incursion, had given him better insight.

"I have seen enough. Arrow, burn the papers. Get whatever you need from the Academy supplies."

Arrow gathered the sheets and piled them into the grate, setting them alight with a spark of power, waiting until they had all burned to fine ash before she left.

She had survived the day. The Preceptor had not noticed her increase in power. No one had challenged her or called her an abomination for hours, and she had not broken any bones. In the Taellaneth, a day worthy of note and worth celebrating.

Leaving the Academy building to return to her residence, she drew that small spark deep inside, wanting to hold on to it, knowing it would not last. There were mundane tasks to be done, basic housekeeping in her residence and, worst of all, she needed to get her laundry done.

Glancing around, she saw the dormitory building of the Academy, a number of smaller windows lit up, no doubt students studying or just gossiping into the night. A warm and welcoming place, Vailla had described it. Arrow had already been installed in the outbuilding. While the Academy might have allowed her to study, not one single Erith family, high-born or low, would have put up with the abomination being housed in the same building as their young. In the past, Arrow had envied the students their warmth and the friendships they seemed to form so easily. Now she envied them their innocence. Magic was new, exciting, full of wonder. Not full of the bitter aftertaste of *surjusi*, summoning spells and unknown, lethal magic she had no idea how to combat.

Her mood sank lower as she approached the laundry house, full basket a barely noticed burden. Despite the hour, the laundry mistress was still in her domain, nasal voice carrying out of the open doorway.

"...do not expect to have to tell you again!" Wendara, one of the oldest Erith Arrow had ever met, far older than Eimille vel Falsen, was taking her anger out on one of the younger laundresses, a tiny Erith woman who was new since Arrow had last been here.

She stood still with her bundle, waiting to be noticed. Even here, the laundry workers exhausted, it would not take long. A few moments later, every eye in the room found her.

"I have no time for you." Wendara's tone matched Seggerat's for indifference.

"Mistress, I am needed. Taellan business, and Preceptor's orders," Arrow began. She did not have the time or energy to spare to do her own laundry again.

"I do not care!" The shriek sent all other inhabitants of the vast room huddling down, shoulders bowed, making themselves as small as possible while they continued to work as hard as they could. No one wanted to catch Wendara's eye.

"Mistress," she began again. Wendara had seen the clothes in the basket, and the state of them. Snake venom, dirt, road salt from the human world, and a few spatters of blood.

"Lazy, stupid, incompetent creature. How is it you manage to ..."

The silence was shocking enough that everyone momentarily stopped working. Arrow turned her head. Something that silenced Wendara was something worth seeing.

Kester vo Halsfeld was in the doorway, faint frown creasing his brow. He must have come here from the Preceptor's study, faint chalk marks along one sleeve.

"Arrow." He nodded to her. "Mistress."

"My lord." Arrow made an awkward bow around her laundry.

"I heard a raised voice. Is there a difficulty?" the Taellan addressed Arrow.

"There is too much to be done without this creature adding to the work," Wendara spat with as much venom as the snake.

"You do all seem to be working late," he commented in a quiet voice that had Arrow's defensive wards prickling. Young for a Taellan, yes, but not stupid.

"We are." The laundry mistress was tone deaf.

"And yet not one item of power is being used?"

"Teaches bad habits," Wendara answered readily, confident in her reasoning. "This lot are slovenly."

Arrow cast her eye over the room, noting the tired faces, stooped shoulders, and swollen hands. The room was always the same. Full of soapy steam, the harsh breathing of exhausted workers and Wendara's nasal tones. The large, magically driven washing vats remained unused in favour of the much smaller washing boards and tubs that required manual labour.

"It seems you are quite dissatisfied with your position, Mistress Wendara," the Taellan went on in that mild tone.

"I? Not I."

"The Taellan does not require its servants work half to death, Mistress. Use those devices..." He nodded to the vats. "...wherever you can. And deal with Arrow's laundry at once. The Taellan requires her service."

"The Steward ..." Wendara began, face paling. Arrow's ears pricked. What might the Steward have to say?

"I will speak with the Steward." Kester inclined his head to her, and then to the silent, staring workers, some of whom were close to tears. "Good evening to you all. Arrow, walk with me."

"My lord." Arrow hastily put her basket of laundry down in front of the astonished and speechless laundry mistress and went after the Taellan, struggling to catch him as he was striding into the night at a fast pace.

"How long has that been going on?" he demanded, still walking.

"As long as I have been at the Taellaneth."

"It will stop."

Not sure what was required of her, Arrow said nothing, holding in her questions from long-ingrained habit, and now that her temper had cooled, from concern she might be rude. She was still oddly disappointed with him for not speaking up in Kallish's defence earlier.

He halted amid the trees at the edge of the Taellaneth's prize garden, staring out across the glimmerlights. The brighter lights of the manor houses were faintly visible.

"I cannot stand bullies."

"No, my lord?" The confidence was unexpected, her hasty words in response out before she could check them, whatever demon had taken hold of her in the Taellan's meeting room that morning rising up again.

"No." He had taken no offence, instead seemed almost amused. "The White Guard understands that we serve at the Queen's will, and the Taellan in her absence. There are many ways of living with honour."

Arrow turned that over in her mind for a moment. The spark of anger at Kallish's demotion was still bright. She discovered that she had enough self-control to say nothing and used it.

"You do not agree?"

It took her a moment to form a reply.

"I have not given the matter much thought. My lord."

"Mages do not wish to live with honour?" He sounded curious. She had no idea what he could see on her face. She could see nothing apart from his silhouette in the trees.

"They may do."

"But you do not?"

"I have not had the opportunity to find out." The spark flared, bright flame burning now. She took a quick breath, waiting for the oath spells to wake and stab her wrists. Talking back to a member of the Taellan was not proper service.

"I am sorry."

The sincerity struck her silent again, ears burning in embarrassment. The silence stretched, brittle and full of some meaning that escaped her completely.

"Have I made matters worse at the laundry?"

"Your instructions were direct and should be followed. But the Steward will require to intervene."

"He cannot be unaware."

"Mistress Wendara wears more than one face."

"I see." A half-laugh in the dark. "Well, that explains the difficulty you have with your appearance." She clamped her jaw shut, ears prickling with heat under her hair. Another difficult silence. "I should seek out the Steward."

"In the main building. He is likely still in his office. Do you ..."

"I will find him. Thank you. You should rest. There is much to do." He moved, and she could not follow it fully in the dark. "Good night, Arrow."

"Good night, my lord." Ears still burning, Arrow waited for him to move away before heading back to her residence. There was indeed much to do, a never-ending list of tasks when she would much rather dissect the odd conversation she had just had, wonder when she could expect another reprimand from the Steward over her appearance, or consider the interesting concept of how a demotion could be honourable.

Chapter Twenty-One

Back in human clothing, Arrow met Matthias and a half-dozen heavily-armed shifkin at the Taellaneth gates the next morning. With the grace of an evening to herself, she had had time to consider what she had learned, and what was missing. She had also woken to find a small miracle in the shape of her laundry, clean, pressed and mended, outside her door.

There was a grim task ahead, to stop the *surjusi* and the summoner, her stomach twisting at the thought of taking another life. But it had to be done.

"Hey, Arrow," Matthias said genially. The shifkin had parked their vehicles a prudent distance from the gates, still within Erith bow shot, and were being deliberately provocative to the gate guard, if Arrow was any judge. One 'kin perched on the roof of a vehicle with a human-style newspaper open in his hands. A trio played cards on the front end of one vehicle, the remaining 'kin apart from Matthias leaning against the other vehicle, sharpening knives on a whetstone.

"Good day to you." She stepped out of the Taellaneth's gates and heard them slam shut behind her. There was a faint creak from one of the watchtowers and she looked up to see a pair of Erith archers poised, bows drawn. Matthias was aware of them, eyes gleaming with unexpected and rare mischief as he waited for her to join him.

"You got the message?"

"I was advised that the Prime wished for my presence," she confirmed.

"They didn't show you the note? Shame. Pa spent a while composing it."

"I believe it had the intended impact." Her mouth twitched. She wished she had seen the note.

"We brought your car back. From the township. Your mechanic seemed distressed." His eyes still gleamed.

"Yes. Thank you." Arrow could only imagine the mechanic's reaction to armed 'kin appearing with one of his precious vehicles. "I wondered what had happened to it." One of many loose ends she had tried to gather overnight.

Matthias' face lightened into an unexpected grin before he turned to business.

"Pa's at the muster house in Lix. We can meet him there."

"Has something happened?" she asked.

"More of nothing. No new leads. Still can't figure out where Marianne was in that missing time. ATV rental records are a mess. No help. Four months. We should be able to find some trace of her." Matthias was frustrated. Arrow hesitated before speaking again.

"Would it be possible to go and see Lucy Steers?" She kept her eyes on him as she spoke, not sure how widely known Marianne's defection was. "She did not tell us everything," she added when Matthias stayed silent.

"Sure." Matthias' humour vanished with his agreement. She wondered what he felt about Lucy and her presence in Marianne's life. "I'll get Pa to meet us there."

"Thank you." She got into the passenger seat of one of the vehicles at his direction. He took the driver's seat, the other 'kin fitting into the second vehicle at some unseen signal. They drove back along the road towards Lix.

"Do you mind off-roading? I hate Lix traffic."

"Off-roading?" She repeated the unfamiliar term. "I do not know."

"Hold on, then."

Arrow had thought that the drive down Farraway Mountain was the most terrifying experience possible in a vehicle, and now discovered that it was in fact Matthias Farraway's idea of off-roading. The vehicle veered sharply off the smooth road surface and bumped over the rough ground that surrounded Lix, jolting wildly. She gave an undignified squeak of fright more than once, clinging on to her seat with both hands.

Avoiding Lix traffic, driving over rough ground, they arrived at the other side of Lix in record time, Arrow breathless and Matthias grinning again. He was whistling cheerfully as he drove them through the estate to Lucy's house.

The Prime was waiting outside next to a sleek black vehicle of his own. It was only then that Arrow realised the other vehicle that had been outside the Taellaneth had not followed them.

"They'll go back to the muster house. We can call them if we need them. But it's Lucy. Doubt that we'll need back-up." He sounded confident. Arrow was not so sure.

"Arrow." Zachary opened her door for her, something which no one had ever done before. She thanked him, stepping out on trembling legs. "You look a bit shaken up. Matt's driving that bad?"

"It was unusual," she conceded, drawing near-identical grins from both.

"You wanted to see Lucy." He turned serious.

"I want to know more about Marianne's last task. The one that took her to Hallveran."

"Good. So do I. Lucy's in." The gates opened as he approached, glancing over his shoulder at Matthias.

"Don't worry. Easier if I wait here." Matthias nodded, and stayed with the vehicles.

"Easier?" The question was out before Arrow could check it.

"Lucy and Matt can be prickly," Zachary said calmly, not checking in his stride up the driveway. Arrow supposed she should have guessed that. Matthias was intensely loyal to his father.

The front door opened as they approached, and Lucy stepped out to meet them, arms folded across her stomach. She was as immaculately presented as before, jaw set in a stubborn line.

"What do you want?" The hostility was not targeted at either Zachary or Arrow.

"I have questions for you about Marianne's last task."

"I have nothing to say to you."

"Lucy," the Prime began.

"No! She's dead!" Lucy's lip trembled, eyes spilling over with tears. Arrow traced the red in her eyes and wondered if she had been crying all morning.

"Yes, she is," Zachary said gently. "And we are trying to find out who killed her."

"Well, it wasn't a client," Lucy snapped.

"May we come in?" Arrow asked.

"Can I stop you?" Lucy asked bitterly.

"Of course. If you do not wish us inside, we can talk here," Arrow answered. Lucy glared, temper overriding grief.

"Fine. Come in. Let's get this over with."

Arrow followed Lucy's straight back and sharp strides through the hallway she remembered from her previous visit and into a large, light room with soft furniture that looked like it was never used, the only personal touch a set of framed photographs on a side table. Marianne and Lucy in happier times, Marianne's face alive with laughter and mischief, Lucy smiling freely without any constraint of grief or anger. Lucy perched at the edge of one chair, Zachary took another, and Arrow settled on the one nearest to her.

"So?" The challenge was still there.

"Marianne had a commission, you said, which took her to Hallveran and as far as the north island. What more can you tell us?"

"I told you. It was ordinary, apart from the travel. Client wanted something. Marianne found it."

"Details, please." Arrow's eyes narrowed. Lucy's outrage had shifted. An actress playing a role, now, rather than the furious and hurt woman who had met them at the door. Some instinct told her to keep pressing.

"Fine. A series of jobs. Paintings. Carvings. Not very valuable. No idea why he wanted them. All over the place. Hallveran. Cyrus. North island."

"Do you have photographs of the items? Information on where they were found? Details of the client?" Arrow pressed.

"Damnit. It's my business. I can't just hand over …"

Lucy stopped at the sound of 'kin anger. Zachary was perfectly still, attention fixed entirely on her, the growing sound of his anger filling the room.

"Stop it." A low, snarled command. "Give Arrow all the information she wants."

"You are not my leader."

"You were sleeping with my mate. You have no right to her secrets," Zachary snapped, temper flaring, old anger and bitter hurt coating his words. Arrow did not think that Lucy saw the hurt, though, pale with her own rage.

"You wouldn't let her go! She asked you."

"She asked. She knew the answer before she asked. The only reason she asked was because you insisted."

"You said no!"

"Stop." The weight of the Prime's power washed over the room. Arrow found herself immune again, but Lucy was not. She gasped, glaring at Zachary.

"This is my house ..."

"And you're hiding. What are you hiding, Lucy?" His voice was soft, the gentle quiet of a hunter.

Lucy did not answer with words. She stood up, stalked out of the room, threw open a door somewhere else on the ground floor of the house, then was absent a few more moments before she stomped back into the room, a thin sheaf of papers in her hands which she threw at the Prime. He made no move to catch them. The papers spread out as they fell, landing in a messy pile around his feet along with a small plastic object Arrow did not recognise.

"Happy?"

Arrow paid them no heed as they locked eyes over her head, her own attention on the papers.

"Danes." Forgetting dignity, Arrow knelt on the floor, gathering the papers. "Danes. Hugh Danes."

"The name means something?"

"He is known to the Erith." Arrow answered, most of her attention on the information sheet that had come to rest at her feet. Hugh Danes. Doctor. Surgeon, in fact. Wholly human. His address was listed, in one of the wealthier parts of Lix.

"Like Rowan?" The Prime's voice was hard. Arrow glanced up to answer him and caught a strange expression on Lucy's face. She rose to her feet, the sheet with Hugh Danes' information crushed between her fingers.

"You know," she told Lucy.

"I know lots of things."

"Arrow's right. Hell. Whatever this is, you know. This got Marianne killed. Don't you care about that?"

The sharp crack was Lucy's palm meeting Zachary's cheek. He did not move, staring at her, eyes bright with power.

"Well?" he asked.

"Hugh Danes is my cousin," Lucy admitted, voice tight. Arrow felt a shock go through her.

"But you know the name Rowan as well."

"Old friends of the family," Lucy sniffed. "Never liked them."

"And Hessman?" Arrow discovered that she could growl almost as well as any shifkin. Lucy's paling face told its own story. "This is awful," she muttered to herself.

"What's wrong?"

In her distraction, she had spoken in Erith, but the Prime's sharp look suggested he had understood her.

"Hessman. Danes. Rowan. The Descendants." She shivered. Awful did not begin to describe it. Descendants of humans who had threatened the Erith before.

"Arrow, I have no damn idea what you're talking about." And was fast running out of patience.

"Where are they?" Arrow demanded of Lucy.

"I don't know."

"Lucy Steers." Arrow laced power into her voice, drawing a wary glance from Zachary and a terrified stare from the human woman.

"I don't know," she repeated, but this time Arrow believed her. "That's Hugh's address. The Rowans haven't lived in Lix for years. Just Hallveran. Not even sure there's any of them left after ... everything that happened there."

"Hessman?"

"There's a Hessman that lived near Danes. Long time ago."

"Somewhere to start at least," Arrow muttered, releasing her power, and kneeling again to gather all the papers and the strange plastic thing. Some human technology. All together Marianne's file, she guessed. A few pages of handwritten notes and some printed text. "This is the last commission that Marianne Stillwater undertook. There are no others?"

"No."

"Anything else you need to tell us?" Zachary could do silky soft as well as the elder.

"Get out of my house."

"If anything springs to mind, call," Zachary ordered.

"Go to hell."

"I mean it, Lucy. There are things going on here that are more important than your jealousy and temper. Call."

"Out."

Zachary raised his lip, showing white teeth, before turning on his heel and stalking out.

"You too," Lucy snapped at Arrow.

"He speaks the truth. There is a serious danger that we believe Marianne came across. More information would be useful."

Keeping her voice calm and Zachary's absence seemed finally to break through Lucy's rage. The human woman hugged herself again.

"Is it my fault?" Lucy's temper vanished like smoke, leaving her raw and vulnerable.

"I do not know. I intend to find out why she died." Arrow heard her voice hard and cold. This human had no idea what she was dealing with, she was sure. And may have caused the death of her lover. "I will share what I can," Arrow added, momentary sympathy prompting the offer.

"Thank you."

Arrow decided there was nothing more she could say or do. Holding Lucy's attention with her power was one thing. Using magic to force Lucy's mind open and reveal her secrets was quite another, one of the forms of forbidden magic. She would not betray her oaths as a magician, even on the trail of *surjusi*.

She left the house, bundle of papers in her arms. She followed the Prime back down the driveway and out of the gates to the vehicles. Matthias straightened at his father's expression.

"Anything I can do?"

"Yes. Track down Hugh Danes." Zachary held a hand out to Arrow and she passed over the sheet of paper, creased from her grip. "Find out where he is and what he's doing right now."

"I'll need to get to the muster house to run this." Matthias took the information. "Keep it quiet?"

"Yes. Go. Arrow and I will follow."

Matthias drove off without further question, leaving Arrow holding the papers next to a tense and furious Prime.

Zachary paced restlessly along the street. Reasonably sure he was not going to harm her and too curious to wait, Arrow flicked through the papers so reluctantly provided. There was less here than she had hoped. Handwritten notes, difficult to read, with a few prominent names. Notes, she thought, detailing the places that Marianne had visited searching for whatever her client had wanted. Printed copies of a few e-mails updating the client, and a copy invoice from a shipping firm in Hallveran, sending some package back to Lix. It was a shock to see one of the Descendants so casually referred to, the mere name carrying resonance for the Erith and not lightly used within the Taellaneth. The White Guard would want to see this. She thought it unlikely that the Prime would allow this material to be given to them.

She puzzled over the plastic device, turning it in her hand.

"Lucy didn't tell us everything." Zachary's voice by her ear startled her. At some point, he had started reading over her shoulder.

"The last communication, this invoice, is four months ago. When Marianne disappeared. And Lucy did not give this to us when we spoke to her first." Had actively concealed it, in fact, lying so well that Arrow had not picked up on it. Nor had Zachary.

"Doesn't look like much. What's that?" Zachary held out his hand for the plastic thing. "Ah. Flash drive."

"Flash drive?"

"Computer memory. You plug it in ... It's a way of storing information," he explained, mouth twitching at her puzzled expression. "I'll get one of the techs to print it off and get you a copy."

"Thank you." She stared at the small thing, wondering how much information could be kept on something about the size of her thumb. "I had hoped there would be something here to help understand what happened."

The low thrum of shifkin anger held Arrow motionless for a moment. Only a moment. Zachary was not angry at her.

"Lucy's hiding things. But. They loved each other," he said. That old anger was back in his voice. He caught her startled expression and laughed, little humour in it. "You're young. Things don't always last. No matter how well they start."

She ducked her eyes in instinctive respect. He usually carried his age lightly or hid it well along with his power. In this leafy street, he bore every one of his many years as a leaden coat. As she scrambled for something to say, he sighed softly, all the age tucked away again. He leant back against the vehicle, forcing himself to be still, folding his arms and glaring at the pavement.

"I can't believe that Lucy would hurt Marianne."

"Not deliberately, perhaps," Arrow agreed. "She may not have realised how dangerous her cousin was."

Zachary absorbed that in silence for a while, still tense. Likely fighting a similar impulse to Arrow. She wanted to march back into the residence and demand answers. Why would Lucy be helping Marianne's killer?

"Marianne was stubborn. Impatient. Too damn curious for her own good. She was also absolutely loyal. Trustworthy." It struck Arrow as a curious assessment of the woman who had left their mate bond. Zachary made a small sound that might have been a laugh. "Yes, loyal." Bitterness coated his words. "She was a better friend than partner."

There was a world under those simple words. A brief glimpse into the tangled personal life and complicated politics of the shifkin Prime. Leader of a nation that did not accept weakness in those in charge. A leader who described his straying mate as trustworthy and had not publicly revealed her betrayal for ten years. Matthias knew, unhappy at a stranger being let into his father's secrets. But Matthias did not know all his Prime's secrets. Perhaps Marianne had been the only one who did. Trustworthy. Loyal. A true friend, to Arrow's ears.

"She didn't deserve this," he added, uncannily following Arrow's line of thought. He was showing her a side that she suspected very few people got to see. The trust warmed her.

For a long moment, Arrow could not think of a single thing to say, too much crowding her mind.

"We will find who did this, Prime."

"Yes. And end them. Let's get to work. Where next?"

She paused, catching his attention. "There is somewhere here I would like to visit."

"Something relevant?"

"I do not know. When I was last here, there was something. I did not have time to follow it. It was like Erith magic, but not. A little bit like what I felt on the mountain."

His attention sharpened. "Let's take a look. Might as well do something." There was a snarl under those words, and a sharp look back in the direction of the house hidden by trees. "Drive or walk? Which way?"

"Drive would be quicker. Along here and left to start with."

Chapter Twenty-Two

They left the vehicle tucked under a large, spreading, evergreen tree that mostly hid it from view, going ahead on foot. There was no snow here, a light breeze freezing her skin, skeletons of trees poking up at the sky waiting patiently for spring. Winding through the bare branches, tightly woven hedges and high stone walls that concealed other residences was the faint trace she remembered from before.

The Prime seemed happy to follow her lead, although he had armed himself before they left the vehicle and checked that his mobile phone was on and receiving a signal. He padded silently beside her, heavy boots making no sound. She was clumsy and loud by comparison, constantly stepping on frozen leaves or branches, footfalls loud.

At length, they came to the border of a residence that had clearly not been used for some time. The hedge was overgrown, spreading out across the pavement, plants too dense for them to push through, an effective barrier in the first world. In the second world, the grounds were circled with old ward spells.

"Here." She tried to make her voice as soft as possible, not wanting to alert any possible listeners. She kept walking, one hand sliding into her bag searching for chalk, the other checking her pocket where she had put Kallish's communicator disk.

The residence had one of the largest grounds that they had seen, and it took a little while longer to reach the gates, tangled with vines. Worn from time and weather, the metal name plate was damaged, some letters missing. H. E. S.   A. N.

Ice filled her. Hessman. There were other human names that would fit. Arrow dismissed the possibility. Hessman. The name of an Ancestor on a property with Erith magic woven into its wards.

"Looks empty," Zachary said. He had glanced at the nameplate and was now focused on the residence that could just be glimpsed through the trees. Blank windows looked back at them.

"It is guarded," she told him, stepping back out of view of the house, fingers tightening on the disk. The White Guard would want to know.

"There's no one here." The Prime crouched in the shadows beside her, making his own assessment. "No scent at all, which is wrong."

"The wards are old. Laid perhaps decades ago. Perhaps as recently as twenty. Still active. Not listening," she clarified, "or watching. There to defend."

"Bet you can get through them." The Prime's eyes glinted.

"Most likely." She nodded, continuing her assessment. He growled irritation. Busy trying to understand the spellwork, Arrow ignored him. "Ward spell variant," she said to herself, her own wards shimmering to life. "Clever." And skilled. Decades old, and the skill level used to draw the wards here was almost at the level used on the mountain.

"Shall we go?" The hunter wanted to move.

"A moment, please." Torn between hope that she was not overreacting and hope that she was not using the gift for nothing, Arrow took the communicator from her pocket and activated it.

"Arrow?" Kallish's face appeared a bare heartbeat later, the warrior's tone urgent and quiet.

"*Svegraen*. It appears that Marianne Stillwater had taken commission from Hugh Danes. Her business partner is cousin to Danes. And I have discovered a Hessman residence with Erith magic in its wards not far from Marianne's house in Lix. I fear the Descendants may be active in Lix and your aid would be welcome."

"Will you be at that location a little longer?"

"Yes. The Hessman residence, which I wish to investigate."

"We will be there soon."

The connection severed. Arrow put the spent disk back in her pocket.

"You called the guard." Zachary did not look displeased, watching her with a thoughtful expression she was coming to know.

"The Descendants," Arrow began, waiting for the oath-spells to wake and cripple her. They remained silent. A welcome side benefit of having breached her own seals, perhaps. "The Descendants," she said again, testing, and continuing when no pain rose, "have history with the Erith. Their Ancestors breached the Erith borders and attempted an incursion in Erith lands."

"Humans?" Zachary was astonished.

"Quite so. The White Guard have kept watch on them, but perhaps not closely enough."

"You think the Descendants are involved in Marianne's death?"

"And the *surjusi*. Possibly. I would like to investigate this residence."

"Let's go." His face was alive with interest and anticipation.

They went back to the gates, Arrow drawing power to her fingertips as they walked, watching the reaction of the wards in the second world. Every spell line that she could see remained dormant, uninterested in a magician brushing past the perimeter. Reaching the gates, she used her hand to draw a rune for opening in the air, trace of silver power following her movement, then pressed the rune on the lock. It was gentle magic, no harmful intent present, and the gate opened without protest, rusty hinges creaking in the first world and no disturbance in the second.

Arrow walked up the curving driveway to the residence with Zachary as her silent shadow, nearly invisible in the second world, too, as he had his own power contained. The residence was a tall, square construction several storeys high. They circled it carefully. Almost one entire wall, facing away from the road towards the extensive garden, was glass.

"A tower?" Zachary muttered, disbelieving. "Like a genuine old castle tower?"

"Not for defence," she noted, nodding at the window.

"Still. A tower?"

"This means something in the human world?" Arrow asked, genuinely confused. Among the Erith, watchtowers were common. They were functional buildings, not residences. She could not understand why a wealthy human, able to afford the large stretch of land here, would want a tower.

"Load of romantic nonsense," he said dismissively. "Humans used to build castles a bit like this. With smaller windows."

They arrived back at the front door, an impressively large wooden construct banded with thick iron that seemed to be designed to keep out an army.

Whatever its original purpose, the door opened easily at Arrow's push. The wards around and through the building were restless, less compliant than the ones at the gate.

"We are about to make noise," Arrow said, watching the spell lines vibrating.

"Magic?"

"The building has different wards to the gate. Taking them down will be loud."

"Good." The satisfaction in his voice carried clearly into the second world.

She pushed aside a trail of spell that wanted to know who and what she was, her own wards rising.

"There is no darkness here," she told him, "no *urjusi* or trace of *surjusi*."

If the Prime answered, she did not hear him, her attention focused on the residence's ward spells that were flaring to life all around them. Even without forbidden magic they were powerful, testament to the abilities of the magician who had set them. A small exercise of will, a word of command, and the defences fell. Not before there was a flicker at the edge of her sight, a flare in the second world that any magician nearby would sense.

"The wards are down. The effect was large." She came back mostly into the first world, second sight overlaid.

"Then we should move." Zachary was through one of the doors as he spoke, moving with the spare efficiency of a predator. Arrow followed.

The residence was both dull and odd. The air was stale, yet every surface was free of dust. The building was in good repair and yet several doors stuck, reluctant to open. There were no personal effects anywhere, even in the bedchambers, and yet the air resonated with the echoes of the building's inhabitants. And apart from the wards which Arrow had cut through, there were no other signs of magic inside.

"Nothing." Zachary was irritated. She did not blame him.

They were standing halfway up the stairs where there was a wide, carpeted, landing set with a pair of comfortable chairs, bathed in sunlight through the spelled glass that rose the entire height of the building. Even on this dull winter day, the stairwell was bright with light, pale bricks along the internal walls angled so that the sun focused down to the stone floor far below. The stairs were an open construction, a mix of wooden treads and barely there metal supports.

Arrow tilted her head, wondering why the builders had chosen this particular wall for the window. The building was not quite high enough to see over the tops of the surrounding trees, the nearest a short distance from the building, letting the light in. So, the window was not here for the view. And the internal walls blocked the light from going into the rest of the building.

She was trying to work out what way the building faced when there was a dark flicker at the edge of her second sight. Tilting her head again, she focused. Underneath the trees in the grounds, something watched them. Something vaguely human-shaped, distorted by a mass of focused power that was growing larger as she watched.

"Down!" she yelled, following her own advice and ducking behind one of the chairs, not waiting to see if the Prime followed her advice.

The tangled mass of power, unclean mage fire, hit the glass with an impact that reverberated through the whole building, the spelled glass shuddering before it gave in quiet surrender, glass shattering into glittering shards that fell in bright, ringing rain, darkness of the tainted power fizzing out, power spent, winter-cold air rushing in.

Arrow's wards flared, forming a protective dome, spelled glass sparking as it fell.

A low, dark sound nearby and she saw the Prime lying prone, a shard of glass as long as an Erith warrior's forearm pinning his arm to the floor, head tucked in, back sparkling with bits of glass.

"Prime." She extended a hand. He took it without question and she extended her wards to cover him as the rest of the glass fell.

Another blot of power thumped against the wall over their heads. Sticky, dark mage fire. Shadowed in the second world. *Surjusi* taint. Arrow pulled power, speaking the command for her own mage fire, risking a peek over the arm of the chair she was hiding behind.

Under the trees, the dark shape had resolved into the too-familiar shadowed shape of Marianne's killer. It stood still, watching.

Arrow rose to a crouch, careful to keep hold of the Prime, shields extended, and sent her own bolt of mage fire out into the garden. To her surprise, it struck, coating the magic user's shields in silver before fizzing to nothing. The magic user staggered back into shadow as she readied another bolt, and a moment later, she felt the displacement of a translocation spell.

"Ethtar." She spat the curse.

"He's gone?" The Prime was not surprised.

"Yes. Translocation."

"I hate that spell."

"Yes." Arrow paused, checking with all her senses. "Definitely gone." She let the mage fire die and turned as the Prime let go of her hand. He simply pulled the glass out of his arm with a grimace, dripping blood on the carpet.

"Building's on fire," he remarked. The mage fire had taken hold. In his haste, the magic user had forgotten the usual constraints on the fire and it was seeking new fuel. The upper storey was smouldering as the magic burrowed into the building. Arrow sighed. Whatever clues the tower held were about to be lost.

They made their way downstairs in silence, Zachary dripping blood as they went. Overhead, the smell of burning grew. One bolt of untamed mage fire. The entire building would burn.

As they reached the front door, it burst open, a human magic-user rushing in, weapon drawn.

"Halt!"

Zachary snarled and, before the human knew what was happening, had the man pinned against the wall beside the door, one arm twisted up behind his back.

"Y-you are trespassing," the human spluttered, "and I am placing you under arrest for criminal damage." Arrow gave him credit for bravery as well as foolishness.

"We did not set the fire," she said mildly, glancing up at an ominous creak. "I suggest we continue the conversation outside. The ceiling may fall."

Zachary dragged the human out of the house and across the overgrown grass. The man, who wore a uniform that was faintly familiar, seemed to Arrow's amusement to have forgotten he was armed, weapon held limply at his side.

"How did you know we were here?" she asked.

"You are under arrest ..." he began again, stopping when Zachary shook him.

"I am not in a good mood," the Prime murmured close to the human's ear. The man turned chalk-white, visibly trembling. "How did you know we were here?"

"M-Mr F-Farraway, sir? I didn't recognise you."

"Answer."

"There was an alert at the watch station." He managed to get the words out.

"There must have been an alarm," Arrow said, irritated with herself, finally recognising the human's uniform as that of the estate watchmen. "Electronic?"

"Y-yes. All the h-houses are fitted with them." The human's gaze went past Arrow and Zachary and his eyes widened. Arrow turned and paused, understanding his dismay.

The entire residence was on fire now, mage fire burning far hotter and far more quickly than any normal blaze. Dark, unnatural flames were licking the surface of the building, finding their way along the walls, seeking fuel.

"You should step back a little farther," Arrow suggested, planting her feet, opening her second sight and silently cursing the magic user for his carelessness. The magic user had not cared what his fire burned, only that it burned. The nearest trees were too close, and the fire would quickly spread without someone to stop it.

She did not wait to see if the Prime and human had moved, drawing a quick containment spell in the air before her, lines clear in second sight, and sending it out with her will; she watched the silver lines catch at the edges of the mage fire. The mage fire twisted. She pushed more power into the spell, the heat of the fire raising sweat on her skin, her own containment failing and eyes sliding to silver as she worked. The well of power inside rose at her will, seemingly endless, and strands of power lapped around the mage fire, holding the sticky substance.

There was no easy cure. Unyielding patience was required. It took a long time, even in the second world where the passage of time was difficult to measure, before the mage fire finally died, running out of fuel. Arrow released her containment with a sigh of relief, shoulders sagging. At her back, several prudent paces away, she could sense the disciplined minds and amber wards of White Guard, although she was not sure how long they had been there.

There was still power left in her, but even that endless pool of silver required rest. She closed her eyes, feeling the ache of silver as an overused muscle, and drew on the memory she had made in Hallveran of how it felt to have the silver hidden. Only when she was sure she was balanced again did she open her eyes, turning to her companions.

Kallish nuin Falsen and a cadre of warriors waited in a loose semi-circle, apparently relaxed at parade rest, eyes watchful. Not all the same warriors as had been in Hallveran, she noted. Behind them, Zachary was waiting, arm either healed or bandaged under his clothing, and beyond him was a pair of black vehicles and the shifkin that had met her at the Taellaneth that morning.

"It is done," she told the cadre, voice rasping with smoke. She coughed, eyes watering. In the second world, she had not been aware how close to the fire she had been. Her clothing was covered in ash, natural ash this time, smoke-scented.

"Good." Kallish moved, offering her a waterskin. Arrow took it with thanks and cleared her mouth, almost choking as she found she had been given cooled Erith tea rather than the plain water she had been expecting. The Erith guarded their tea jealously. She took a long drink, not sure when she would next get the chance, and returned the skin, with more thanks.

"Have you been here long?"

"A while." Kallish's voice shaded to cool. "Gathering took longer than expected. Some changes were required to find the right warriors." And Kallish was apparently in charge of a cadre, still, despite the Taellan's demotion. Arrow wondered what had happened, and how. The warriors with her were quietly resolute, awaiting orders. And not one was glaring at Arrow. The right warriors, indeed.

"There was a human here," Kallish remarked, breaking Arrow's thoughts, "who the Prime questioned. The human wanted to send for human firefighters…" An undertone in the warrior's voice told Arrow she had greatly enjoyed that idea. "…which the Prime dismissed and then sent the human away. The shifkin arrived shortly after on his command." Human firefighters could have spent weeks tackling the fire and not put it out. Arrow guessed that the human had been a low-level ward keeper, not skilled enough to recognise mage fire. She shook her head. Humans were unprepared for a *surjusi*-powered magic user.

"The human was a gatekeeper for this estate and arrived when the magician had attacked the house. It seems there was a human alarm set." Arrow felt heat in her face. A stupid oversight.

"Annoying." The warrior nodded her understanding. "This was the Hessman residence?"

"As you say." Arrow turned to stand with the warrior, eyes widening at the extent of the damage. There was almost nothing left in the second world. In the first world, the once-fine tower had been reduced to smouldering sticks, not even the enormous front door surviving in recognisable form. It was also difficult to see and Arrow blinked, wondering if her eyes were coated with ash, too. Glancing up at the sky, she realised that it was late, darkness almost fully set.

"It burned for the day." The warrior followed her glance then tilted her head. "The Prime is keen to speak with you."

"I imagine so." Arrow made her way back to Zachary who was frowning.

"The magician left." It was not a question. "We tried tracking him." He tilted his head, indicating the 'kin. "But nothing. Not a single scent or trace."

"Another translocation spell," Arrow confirmed. Kallish was beside her, listening keenly as she tried to follow the conversation. Before Arrow could translate, Kallish beckoned one of her cadre across, a warrior Arrow did not recall from Hallveran. She blinked as she recognised him as the warrior who had led the third trapping the snake in the scribe's archive, startled when he made a small bow, a mark of respect, in her direction.

"Xeveran, translate, please."

Xeveran's grasp of the common tongue was nearly as good as Arrow's, and she could not help wondering how a warrior had acquired that knowledge, even as she was grateful for his presence.

"Is there a way to stop him translocating?" Zachary asked.

"There are some methods. All require close proximity," Arrow began, then looked at Kallish, "unless we could add a binding spell to arrows?"

The warrior looked thoughtful. The White Guard's archers were adept at tying spellwork for fire to their arrows. A small binding spell should not be too difficult.

"Something to try. We will prepare some."

"Good. If we can trap him, that's a start. How do we find him?"

Arrow had no answer to that. The magician was heavily disguised, not one trace of his personality—if it even was a he—slipping out of his disguise. She had nothing to track in the second world, and the 'kin had nothing in the first world.

"There were no clues in the residence?" Kallish asked.

"Nothing. It was very ordinary."

"Hadn't been used for some time," Zachary added. "Gate guard said it was built by the Hessmans. Been in the family over two hundred years. Current owner Matthew Hessman. Hasn't been here for at least five years. Guard had no idea where he is, and no contact information."

Arrow and Kallish absorbed that information in silence, Arrow's eyes drifting back to the building.

"Something wrong?" Kallish asked, eyes keen, glint of amber in the fading light.

"That window."

"Window?"

"The side of the building was all glass."

"In a tower?" Kallish was sceptical.

"Yeah. Stupid design," the Prime agreed.

"And very costly," Arrow put in. "A lot of skilled magic and craftsmanship to create a window with no view. And no purpose."

"Perhaps the architectural archive will have details?"

"I am not sure humans keep such good records, *svegraen*. But it would be useful to know." It might reveal some more detail of the humans who had built the place, or finally put to rest the nagging instinct that there was something important about that window.

"Agreed. I'll get Matt on it." Zachary's brief smile was a flash of teeth in the gloom. Arrow could only imagine how much Matthias would enjoy more paperwork after a day spent indoors.

"Did Matthias uncover anything useful?"

"Not so far. Damned man has vanished."

Arrow's stomach chose that moment to gurgle, reminding her that she had not eaten that day, audible to everyone and drawing a soft laugh from the Prime. Her face was burning, and she knew that all her companions could see that.

Before she could stammer an apology, matters were taken out of her hands. Zachary and Kallish decided to leave patrols at the ruined house and return at first light to continue the search. Arrow was not sure what they hoped to find after searching during the day while she had been suppressing the fire but trusted their judgement. Neither 'kin nor Erith gave up easily.

Whilst they planned, she thought about Zachary's wish to trap the magician, and some ideas formed.

"Arrow? You've been quiet."

"I have some ideas to help trap the magic user and *surjusi*," she said, "but I will need supplies and a place to work."

"We will use the Erith safe house," Kallish said. "There is a workspace there."

"If you need anything else, let me know." Zachary held out a white card and Arrow took it with an odd sense of familiarity. Rather than the outdoors shop details, in the bare light left to her, she could see only a series of numbers on the card. The Prime's personal number. A rare honour. None of the Taellan had this.

She ducked her head, hiding what was no doubt a foolish, pleased expression, and tucked the card away in a pocket.

Plans made, details settled, they separated, Arrow finding that the White Guard had brought their own sleek black vehicles. Kallish left a third of her cadre along with some of the shifkin to watch the house, and expertly steered Arrow into the back of one of the vehicles, transporting her across Lix to the Erith safe house.

Having two thirds of a cadre at her disposal was a heady experience. Xeveran took her list of requested supplies and headed out with his third while Kallish and her third settled her in the property's kitchen with food, then made sure the property was secure and the workspace prepared.

Finishing the last of her meal, full of food, Arrow listened to the quiet noises about the building as the third made their checks. They had activated the building's wards, too, making sure nothing would get in without their knowledge.

This must be how it is to be a recognised war mage, Arrow thought, savouring the last of the Erith tea. A cadre around her, her requests granted. The other side of that protection was her obligation to stand against the darkness. That thought prompted her to rise and seek the workspace.

Chapter Twenty-Three

With her inferior senses and inability to track the *surjusi* in the first or second worlds, there was nothing she could add to the hunt. What she could do, better than any of the 'kin or the Erith warriors, was magic. She had a secure workspace and access to as many supplies as she could wish for. So, after a few hours' sleep, she began creating containment spells, weaving her magic into potions and powders, filling the containers the White Guard had found for her.

Focused spellwork soothed her, requiring her absolute attention, easing the frustrations of the past days.

She finished another jar of powder and stretched, small of her back stiff. A quiet cough distracted her before she could move on to the next containers waiting in line. Looking up, she found Kallish in the doorway, shape indistinct in shadow. Arrow blinked, realising it had grown dark while she worked, and she could in fact barely see what she was doing. She had spent the entire day here.

"Lights, *svegraen*," Kallish requested and the most junior of the cadre slipped past her with a taper, lighting the old-fashioned lanterns hanging around the walls of the room. A room designed for spellcraft, it had no windows in the walls.

"*Svegraen*," Arrow greeted Kallish, and stretched again, all the muscles across her back and shoulders tight and sore. "Is there something you need?"

"We have food, and the shifkin have just delivered this for you. It came from something called a flash drive."

Arrow took the large, heavy envelope and cleared a space at the end of the workbench.

"A flash drive?" Kallish prompted.

"Yes. A curious object. Apparently, a storage device for computers." Arrow opened the envelope and tipped out the contents. A thick sheaf of papers, with a covering note from Zachary, letting her know this was everything that they had found on the flash drive.

"How large was this device?" Kallish asked, eyes on the pile of papers.

"No larger than my smallest finger."

The warrior's eyes gleamed with interest before she ducked out of the room, returning a few moments later with a plate piled high with food and a tall wooden beaker. Arrow murmured an absent thanks, attention on the papers. She barely noticed Kallish handing her a fork and leaving the room.

Far into the night, Arrow had finished skimming through the papers, Marianne's full file on the commissions she had received from Hugh Danes. Danes had detailed several items that he wanted Marianne to find. Including wooden panels that, Danes said, came from Hallveran.

In the middle of the papers, she had found a series of photographs. Wooden panels, the size impossible to tell from the photographs, firstly grouped together, a series of four. Covered in dust, clearly having been stored and neglected for a long time, then individually captured going through various stages of cleaning until they were sharp and fresh. She cleared more space and spread the pictures out along the workbench. The panels depicted slightly different scenes, detail sharp and fresh, and finally at the last set of restored pictures, there was a sense of scale; a human-made measuring ruler laid alongside the panel.

Frowning, Arrow made a rough calculation, bits of information coming together. Wooden panels from Hallveran. The missing panels from the ruined fireplace in the Rowan house in Hallveran. Long since taken away.

Marianne's reports to her client showed that the panels had been found in a warehouse in Hallveran, one of the semi-legal human businesses that sold items robbed from deserted homes. Marianne had arranged for the panels to be shipped to her client, and there was an acknowledgement from the client, pleased with the success. Then nothing. The trail of correspondence ended.

Arrow could all too easily picture the next part. Something about these panels had piqued Marianne's interest. She had gone to the Rowan house, wanting to see where the panels came from. After all, she had been in Hallveran already. And had found something beyond her experience.

That fit, Arrow thought. It fit what she knew of Marianne, a bold and enquiring mind.

The shifkin female might not have fully understood what was going on in the panels, perhaps guessing some of it. A group of humans performing magic. The Ancestors, Arrow guessed, a depiction of the plan they had formed to perform forbidden magic in the Erith heartland, steeped in power, and to destroy the Erith.

The assault had nearly succeeded. Even defeated, the Ancestors' actions had the potential to ruin the Erith's relations with humans.

Very few Erith understood what the Queen had been about, letting the Descendants live. There may only have been six humans in the heartland when the spell was performed, but it was clear that entire families had been involved in the preparation. Families denied more land because humans had spread out over those they had been granted, and there was no more space in the human world, not in Lix anyway—and the Ancestors did not want to move. Families such as the Ancestors who wanted their own land to farm, or live, had nowhere to go, forbidden from using the open space that bounded the Erith lands. The human authorities would not permit it, enforcing their tentative agreements with the Erith, who had pushed back all breaches of their borders with brutal force.

The gaining of more land was a shallow motive, Arrow had always thought, aware that such things seemed to matter to some humans. Perhaps the Queen had thought so, too, leaving some of the families alive, those who had not been involved. And rather than declaring war and annihilating the human population, as many Erith called for, she had secured a formal treaty with the humans which had governed their relations ever since, ensuring peace and lucrative trade. And no more human encroachment into Erith lands.

A shadow against the light caught her attention. Kallish came into the room, the warrior as immaculate as ever.

She showed the photographs to Kallish and explained her theory.

"It was a bloodbath," Kallish said after a long period of quiet, attention still on the photographs. "Foolish humans who did not understand that they would destroy their own kind as well as the Erith."

"You were there, *svegraen*."

"And many of the warriors here now."

"I am sorry."

"All long before your birth." Kallish was not dismissive, just pointing out the fact. "We hoped that the humans would forget over time. Several generations past, in human terms."

"It seems not." Arrow sighed. The Erith had several blind spots when it came to dealing with other races. "Perhaps they do not know exactly what happened. All the humans involved were dead. They just had their own suspicion." She remembered the bitter hostility in Lucy's face and understood it better now. "And where there are no facts ..."

"Geese will make their own tales," Kallish finished the Erith saying, equally grim. "I will suggest to Lord Whintnath that some education is in order."

"They have not found the Descendants yet?"

"A few. None involved." Kallish gathered up the papers. "I will have copies made for the commander."

"And I should update the Prime and Preceptor." Arrow rubbed her hands across her tired eyes.

"It will not help with the hunt," Kallish said practically. "Rest first, report later."

Her wish to report to Zachary the next day was thwarted by the news, relayed by a brief, personal visit from Matthias, that Lucy had disappeared. The 'kin were now dividing their attention between the hunt for the *surjusi* and trying to trace the human female. He took the news of the wooden panels having come from the Rowan residence with a nod, mouth tightening, and went on his way, tense and unsettled. Perhaps wondering, as Arrow was, among other things, just how long it was going to be possible for Zachary to hide the relationship that had existed between Marianne and Lucy.

She made a short report to the Preceptor after Matthias had left, half expecting to be summoned back, surprised when he did nothing more than tell her to continue. He looked tired through the communicator's amber shimmer, face shadowed.

His own news for her was equally disheartening. The Academy had traced and accounted for all of the Erith magicians capable of a summoning spell and were satisfied that none had been involved.

The Queen had chosen not to inform her people, and had ordered a discreet, wider, enquiry into any Erith capable of handling the power necessary to summon *surjusi*. As the days passed, the Taellan were becoming convinced that the problem was in the human world, not their own, despite the attack on House Falsen. As a precaution, though, the Erith borders were raised, using the excuse of the attack, powerful ward spells that normally lay dormant now maintained by teams of magicians.

The Erith liked to believe that the borders could be maintained indefinitely, but the hard truth, Arrow knew, was that the border was too large and trained magicians not numerous enough. The White Guard were also stretched to their limits, having doubled their patrols and also tasked with investigating every report of unusual activity as a possible sighting. It was only a matter of time before the Erith population at large realised what was happening and panic started. Previous incursions had seen neighbours and family members turn on each other, terrified of the taint that could kill with a single touch.

With too much to think about, Arrow took refuge in the workspace again, continuing to make her potions and powders until the light faded once more. The cadre moved quietly about the building, leaving her alone with her thoughts.

She sat in the workspace, wooden stool uncomfortable enough to keep her awake, cradling a mug of coffee in her hands. The White Guard had been puzzled by her request initially, and now she had seen most of the cadre try the drink with varying results.

The workbench in front of her, waist height for ease of working, was covered with pre-prepared physical spells. Enough to trap a magic user and *surjusi*. She hoped. The supplies were finished. The cadre would get more if she asked, she thought. Trapping a *surjusi* was too important to take any chances.

Tilting her head back, she saw the setting sun through the skylight, casting its last rays onto the workbench and throughout the room. There were no windows in the walls, just that large, reinforced skylight for natural light. The walls were scattered with remnants of some previous magician's less successful spellworking, so she supposed the precaution was wise. There were lamps set along the walls so she could work into the night.

She froze, mug halfway to her mouth, and looked up at the skylight again, then down to the workbench. The window.

"*Svegraen!*"

The urgency in her voice had an entire third through the door in moments, hands on weapons, casting alert glances around the room. They found her frantically dragging empty boxes from under the bench, packing her spells.

"The residence. The residence, *svegraen*," she said urgently, fingers trembling as she tried to fit one more pouch into the box in front of her.

"What is it?" Kallish's presence was a wash of cool.

"The magician is at the residence, *svegraen*."

"The Hessman residence?"

"Yes. Yes. Quickly."

"Pack all this up," Kallish ordered her third, waving to the dozens of pouches and jars. "Xeveran! Bring the vehicles around. Arrow, you need to advise the Prime." And, wonder of wonders, the cadre leader produced a sleek mobile phone from one of her pockets. Arrow stared at the device in something like horror. The only telephones the Erith admitted to possessing were at the administrative complex outside the Taellaneth, and then only traditional telephones. Kallish's calm cracked into a tiny smile. "Emergency use."

"Naturally." Arrow took the phone, wondering how many other human technologies the warriors had tucked away for emergency use, and dug out the Prime's card.

The White Guard were geared up for war when she finished her brief call with Zachary. Long hair was pinned back, armoured coats securely fastened and shimmering with the tell-tale presence of defensive wards. Arrow stepped outside into darkness and bit back a curse at her inferior eyesight. There was a spell she could use to enhance her sight, if the Taellan had not forbidden that she apply her magic for personal use, a restriction almost as annoying as the oath spells themselves.

Settled into the back of one of the vehicles with Kallish, she bit her lip, wondering if being able to see to fight a magician and *surjusi* was really personal use. It did not take long to decide that it was not. The spell took moments to execute and she spent the rest of the short journey adjusting to her newly enhanced sight. Not perfect, not nearly as good as 'kin or Erith sight, but better. At least she should not walk into things.

They arrived at the gates of the Hessman residence shortly before the 'kin.

The Prime was dressed in combat clothing and had brought a dozen 'kin with him, mostly armed. Two were in loose clothing, their change close in their eyes. The 'kin greeted the Erith warriors with respectful nods as the groups gathered around the Erith vehicles outside the residence gates, air filled with the taste of smoke from the ruined residence.

"What's up?"

"The magician is here."

"Where?" The snarl in Zachary's voice sent her back a step before she checked the movement.

"Somewhere on the grounds."

"You don't know exactly?" He did not question her certainty that the magician was here, and she steadied under his confidence.

"Not yet. Here, we need to distribute these. Everyone should take some." Arrow pulled a box out of the vehicle.

"You've been busy," Matthias noted. His eyes widened as warriors opened every Erith vehicle, revealing box after box of pouches and fragile pottery jars.

"What's this?" Zachary's eyes were keen. "A new weapon?"

"Pre-prepared containment spells," she corrected. "They do not require any activation. Just throw. They should stick."

"Should?"

"It is the strongest containment I can conjure," she said, back straightening, then shrugged, "but untried."

"*Svegraen.*" Kallish had been following the conversation through translation, and now brought the second of her cadre forward and instructed him to see to the distribution.

"Where do we start?" Zachary asked, on his toes as the last of the pouches were distributed. Erith archers were readying their bows, checking the strings were taut, 'kin going over their own weapons with similar proficiency. Glancing around the group, Arrow thought that between them they would be able to take on an army. She hoped it would be enough for a *surjusi*.

"Over here." She led them through the grounds of the house. There was no active magic she could sense, any spells in the residence sundered by mage fire, and no sense of being watched. She was not sure that could be trusted.

"The lawn?" Zachary asked, sceptical.

"That window." She pointed to where the window had been.

"You're stuck on that window. Why?"

"It makes no sense. Unless it was not a window at all." She drew a breath, hoping that she was right and was not about to look very foolish before all these competent warriors. She knelt on the ground and put her hand on the earth, seeking. "I think it was designed to send light to something underneath."

Both Zachary and Kallish's faces lit with understanding and they barked similar-sounding orders to their warriors. In short order, the group was spread out, warriors casting their attention in all directions.

In the middle of them, Arrow sent her senses out into the ground. Searching through earth was difficult given the density and weight of soil.

At first there was nothing, just soil. The occasional earthworm. Even a mole, startled by the pressure of her magic. And then. There. At the edge of her search. Something unnatural. She rose and quickly moved closer to the house, kneeling, and repeating her search. There. That was not grass.

"*Svegraen*, there is an unnatural section of ground here."

"Understood." Warriors gathered, weapons ready, Kallish moving to stand at Arrow's shoulder as Arrow peeled back the not-grass. It was feather-light, woven to let light through, cloying to touch, and as it gave way, a dense sheet of glass was revealed, gleaming dully in the limited light.

"This is a skylight." Zachary crouched next to her. "There must be an entrance somewhere."

"Possibly in the residence." Arrow glanced across at the ruin and grimaced. "Though it will be difficult to find. This is not warded," she added, surprised. There was not one trace of magic on the glass. Which was why days of searching had not found it, the unnatural covering indistinguishable from the rest of the grass unless it was moved.

"A cellar," Zachary speculated, eyes glinting. "Wonder how big it is?" He glanced up to his people. "We'll go in here. Matt, explosive charge. And get ropes ready."

The 'kin moved in, some setting small packets of explosives on the glass, some readying ropes for the descent into the dark, tying off the ropes on the thick trunks of nearby trees, the rest readying their weapons to stand alongside the Erith archers, waiting.

"Can you muffle the sound, Arrow? Don't want the whole neighbourhood on us," Matthias said.

"A moment." Arrow gathered power, crushed chalk in her hands and spoke the spell as she let the crushed chalk fall on the glass. "Ready."

Chapter Twenty-Four

The explosion was a noiseless concussion of force against her skin, glass disintegrating in silent, sparkling rain as it fell a long way into the dark.

Warm air rushed up out of the hole, carrying with it a familiar stench. Arrow covered her nose in a futile attempt to block it, stomach churning.

"This is the place."

"Looks like it," Zachary agreed, eyes glinting.

"The crossbow came from here."

"Crossbow?" Kallish asked.

Zachary did not waste time asking if she was sure, just nodded grimly.

"Lights," he ordered. The 'kin with ropes pulled short sticks from their belts, snapped them, and sent them down. The sticks glowed, light growing stronger as they fell until they landed on a floor of packed earth.

Arrow moved, kneeling at the side of the hole, sticking her head over to see underneath, opening her sight and trying not to breathe in too much. To her surprise, Kallish gripped her shoulder, hard, ready to pull her back.

"I cannot sense anything. Apart from the smell." Which must surely be worse for the 'kin, although they showed no reaction.

"Let's go." Zachary nodded to the 'kin attached to ropes.

Shifkin slid down the ropes without hesitation, forming a loose circle facing outward, throwing more light sticks into the dark, widening the visible area; the pair that had not been armed shifted to their animal forms, the others standing with weapons ready. There was nothing but blank, earthen floor so far. Two thirds of White Guard went next, Arrow being carried—without being sure how it had happened—by the second in Kallish's third, a stocky male who set her down as if she were fragile glass before moving aside to let more 'kin follow, including the Prime and Matthias.

At some unspoken agreement, the remaining third, and a few 'kin, remained above, watchful, shapes silhouetted against the night sky, when Arrow glanced up.

The darkness stretched seemingly endless and untouched in all directions, around the glowing sticks. Even as she tried to see if there was an end to it, one of the 'kin threw a light stick as hard as he could. It tumbled, spinning, flickering as it turned, long into the distance before falling naturally to the ground, a dim spot to Arrow's eyes.

"It's huge." Matthias sounded impressed. "Not just a cellar. Big as a whole bloody building."

"How in hell has it stayed hidden for so long?" Zachary countered, then glanced about. "We need to search it. Find its size. And that damned magician."

"I cannot sense him. Or any *surjusi* taint," Arrow added, "but that does not mean much." Her nose wrinkled. Now that she had her feet on the ground, the stench was worse and there was residue of old magic against her skin. Nothing active.

The magic was the odd blend that she had sensed in the wards above. Partly Erith, partly human. Along with the stench in the first world, the traces of magic in the second world carried the unmistakable twist of forbidden magic.

"Yeah, he can appear out of nowhere," Matthias agreed, bringing her attention back, raising his weapon to his shoulder, eyes sharp. A few quick hand signals and the 'kin flowed forward, Erith with them.

Just beyond the light from the glowing sticks, they found the first wall, dense earth perfectly smooth, embedded with mirror pieces that glittered light back to them. Arrow glanced up and back, spotting the skylight not far away. During the day, the mirror pieces would reflect light better than any lamp, and not require fuel. The cadre set a makeshift torch in front of the mirrored wall, demonstrating how effective the mirrors were as light spread out in a warm pool.

There was a shuffling sound in the darkness and Arrow's stomach twisted, remembering the crossbow's home. That awful something moving in the dark. All the warriors, 'kin and Erith, sharpened their attention.

"Light," Kallish ordered. It took Arrow a moment to realise the order was for her. She crushed a piece of chalk and threw it up, speaking the spell then blowing, sending the chalk dust out. Light particles bloomed, the chalk rising with the spell, searching for the far corners of the vast underground room.

"Nice trick," Matthias said approvingly, not taking his eyes from his surroundings.

The light was not bright even with her enhanced sight, just enough to see better. Irregular shapes appeared in the gloom, bulky boxes covered in tarpaulin, wooden shipping crates scattered on the earth floor, some open, packing straw spilling out.

Soft shuffling met Arrow's ears again. Around her, the warriors twitched, following the noise, eyes glinting 'kin greens and browns and Erith amber.

And then out of the darkness, a voice.

"Hugh? Hugh? Are you here?"

Arrow knew that voice. Lucy Steers.

"What in hell?" Zachary muttered. "Wait here." He flowed into the dark, melting into shadow, presence betrayed moments later by an undignified squeal, then uneven footsteps as he came back to the light dragging an unwilling Lucy. She had lost her groomed perfection in the time she had been missing, hair tangled, skin chalky white in the poor light, dressed for winter in a heavy, dark-coloured, practical coat.

"Wh-what are y-you doing here?"

"You first." Zachary gave her a shake, enough to send her stumbling back when he released her. "Thought you didn't know anything else?"

"I don't."

"Lies," he snarled, baring his teeth.

Lucy's chin lifted a moment, jaw set, and she opened her mouth to respond.

A dark mass, the size of a warrior's head, flung out of the shadows. Mage fire.

There was no time to issue a warning. Arrow pushed her wards out, silver flaring as the mage fire hit, falling to her knees at the force of the unclean magic, darkness spreading in thick strands over the silver, burning into her wards and hissing at the grating sense of another magician's power against hers.

Lucy screamed and huddled down on the earthen floor.

"Stay still. Hear me? Do not move." Zachary put all of his power into the command and Lucy shook under it, head bobbing.

Another bolt of mage fire hit.

"Fire," Kallish ordered, sounding tense and controlled.

Erith arrows hissed into the dark, struck something. Or somethings. A pair of archers fired amber-bright arrows after, streaks of brilliance that lit the scene as they flew.

The vast cavern stretched out into the distance, full of more piles of boxes and crates that went on and on, blocking clear sight. A distance away, in the shadow of a towering crate, a darker patch huddled, the indistinct shape familiar. A disguised magician.

The archers needed no orders. More bright arrows flew, anchoring into crates around the darkness, providing a clear target, ordinary, lethal arrows whipping through the air with them, striking the darkness. The thing moved, rising with a howl that made Arrow glad she was on her knees. Rage and pain. Something else to add to her nightmares. A faint, inky shimmer traced the defensive wards around it, the taint of unclean magic or *surjusi*, she was not sure which yet. Another dark blot of mage fire gathered within the shadows.

Still kneeling, panting with the effort of maintaining the ward, Arrow gathered her own power and threw mage fire back. Brilliant silver sprayed across the inky shields. The magic user howled again, more pain than rage this time, and his wards fell.

The White Guard needed no instruction, another volley of arrows pinning the magician to the ground before a pair of swordsmen rushed forward, one slicing into the dark with an amber-bright blade, the steel's wards flaring as they met the dark. The single, clean stroke severed the thing's head. A lucky stroke, or experience, Arrow could not tell.

As soon as the head was cut, the camouflage faded, revealing a pale human form with wispy strands of dark hair thin across a distorted skull, too long and appearing almost twisted, tatters of dark clothing scattered across limbs that also seemed too long for a human.

"Not Hessman," the nearest warrior reported, then promptly ducked as something non-magical shot out of the darkness near him, personal wards flaring amber. A strike thudded against the crate where his head had been. A crossbow bolt. Plain, ordinary, and deadly.

The warriors quickly returned to Arrow's wards as more crossbow bolts followed. Arrow winced. The bolts were easier to deal with yet still took energy and concentration.

More shuffling sounds, this time above. The warriors were focused on seeking the crossbow wielder, archers standing with their bows ready, 'kin with their weapons raised. Arrow glanced up, blinking to make sense of what she was seeing.

There was a metal pulley system of some sort on the roof high above, faintly traced by the light from her chalk, with chains and wrapped bundles dangling haphazardly from a roof-mounted beam, something moving among the chains. As she watched, it grew larger, made more sense to her eyes. Two arms, two legs, shimmering yellow eyes, long brown fur, and teeth bigger than her hand.

"*Surrimok.*" Her voice came out weak. She had never seen one before. Mountain dwellers in the Erith heartlands. Cunning. Deadly. Vicious. And here in an underground cavern. In Lix. She would rather face *baelthras*.

"Xeveran, above," Kallish snapped.

Her cadre moved, focused on the threat descending rapidly along the chains. The creature, with its adapted hands and feet, was not hampered at all by unfamiliar metal rather than tree bark.

As Xeveran's three archers loosed more arrows, Zachary swore.

"What in hell?"

"*Surrimok*. Mountain predator."

"How do we kill it?"

"Keep shooting," she answered, grim, pouring more effort into her wards as the crossbow bolts continued. Non-magical, still draining.

The flat crack of gunfire, sounds muted by the earth all around, joined the slice of arrows through the air. The creature let out a bass roar that shook the earth, making Arrow huddle down and every 'kin apart from Zachary and Matthias pause for a moment, arrows and bullets mostly bouncing off its thickened, fur-covered hide. A few struck home, one arrow poking out of a joint as the creature hung a few feet above the Erith, warriors now armed with spears.

It dropped off the chains in an impossible leap, avoiding the waiting Erith, landing instead on a pair of 'kin, clawed hands tearing, roaring again when the 'kin's body armour denied it purchase. Out of the darkness, the two wolf-form 'kin leapt, dragging the creature off their wounded, snarling as the *surrimok* shook itself free.

A ring of Erith warriors and 'kin closed in.

Arrow watched closely, mage fire sparking in her hand, waiting for a clear shot, not sure the warriors needed her help as the *surrimok* roared again. Lowering her hand, she began to breathe again when a dark shadow at the corner of her sight snapped her head around.

Before she could make sense of what she had seen, another blast of unclean mage fire spun out of the dark. Her wards sparked, flexing dangerously under the pressure. Her own mage fire died as she focused on her wards. Hands pressed onto the earth to keep her kneeing, she poured strength into the wards, quivering with effort as the assault continued. Blow after blow of sticky, corrosive mage fire. Scratching against her wards, drawing weals across her body in the second world as she fought to keep her wards up. Sweat coated her.

Not one but two other magicians, one considerably stronger than the other.

"Can you do something about the mage fire?" Zachary asked.

"Not while I hold the ward." Her words came out faint, with pauses between. The great well of power inside was fully open, nowhere near drained. There was only so much she could focus on at once.

She could not follow what happened next, concentrating on holding the wards, gritting her teeth as the mage fire bit. It was not eating into her skin, she told herself. It just felt like it.

Moments later, the pressure on her wards eased, the familiar amber weave of White Guard wards rising over the group. Lifting her head, she saw Kallish's third kneeling in a group, faces tight with concentration and effort and the remaining third descending the ropes left by the 'kin, amber shimmering about them already. They slid into position alongside Kallish's third the moment they touched the earth, sheen of wards visible in first sight as the two thirds focused. Xeveran's third were still battling the *surrimok*, which was fighting to the last.

With ten Erith warriors taking over the burden of warding the group, she rose, lips forming the spell for mage fire, pulling more power, mage fire blinding silver in her hand, and cast the fire in the direction of the stronger magician, immediately followed by another cast at the other magician. Unseen in the dark, her second strike hit, sending a shower of sparks over a standing figure who screamed, twisted, and fell, huddling on the ground, silver consuming his unclean wards.

Ignoring the crossbow bolts still shimmering against the warriors' wards, she moved forward, another bolt of mage fire coating the weaker, huddled magician. The stronger magician's focus turned to her. He threw a larger mass of mage fire, the lethal magic blending with the shadows as it hurtled towards her. With only her own person to protect, her wards shimmered and held, the effort not enough to make her pause, even if her skin felt raw under her clothing. Another bolt of mage fire at the weaker magician and he gave a final, awful, gurgling sound before going still, camouflage sliding away. Dead. Another emaciated human male, hair almost gone, body just as distorted as the first, clothes in tatters around him. Also dark-haired. Not Hessman either.

"Hugh." A low moan from Lucy, still huddled on the ground where Zachary had left her. One question answered.

In the time it had taken to defeat the weaker magician, the third of White Guard had finished the *surrimok* and were now focused on hunting down the stronger magician, 'kin interspersed with Erith as they moved soundlessly across the floor through the dank air. The amber shimmer of the wards was shot through with dark from the tainted mage fire.

The magician's shape moved, a sinuous twist, in the first and second worlds. Watching. Waiting. Patient with the experience of age. Arrow hissed at the chalk-on-blackboard sensation of the thing pressing against her wards. Senses open, mouth full of the taste of rot, she registered the infinite black of *surjusi* awareness. And a smaller spark of human intelligence in the middle of it.

Not tied together by an anchor as she had assumed, with the *surjusi* following the human under the human's command, as long as the spells held.

The fool human had not tethered the *surjusi*, she realised. He had swallowed it down. Nausea rose, and she swallowed, mouth and throat dry. No time now.

She moved forward after the warriors, flung sideways as something quick and enormous thumped into her, barrelling her aside, slamming her into one of the crates. Blinking, she caught herself on one of the rims of the boxes, exposed metal nails cutting into her skin, gaping up at the unfamiliar two-legged, furred shape standing over her, clawed hand raking towards her head.

Surrimok. Her mind caught up with her eyes. Adults lived in mated pairs. Stupid oversight.

Ribs broken. Again. Lungs aching. Punctured again. Wards flared, bright, biting.

The *surrimok*, far larger than the other, the female, then, and deadlier, hissed, eyes blinding. So much hate. Claws swept down and raked at her wards, invisible weals rising on her skin as the creature's magic cut into her own.

Move, move, move.

Too much pain. Blood choked her throat, frothing. She gathered power, pushed, and screamed, pink foam bubbling at her mouth, ribs snapping back into place again. Mage fire was a mere thought away, the spell already cast, and coated the fur above her, sliding into the creature's mouth. The *surrimok* burned above her, raining sticky, molten ash on her exposed skin and hair. Burning flesh. Stomach churned. So much death.

Surrimok dead, she kept herself upright by one hand clutching the box she had been thrown against, bleeding fingers staining the wood, and looked for the others.

The warriors had finally remembered the containment spells she had made. The stench of the air was cut with the clean scent of her magic as powders and potions slammed into the magician's wards. The warriors' accuracy was excellent. So were the magician's defences, the *surjusi* rearing up in the second world.

In the first world, the magician writhed under the containment. The silver flickers of Arrow's power were building a net around it. Slowly. Inside the gradually tightening net, the magician twisted, sending out more mage fire, assault carrying *surjusi* taint, and the fire finally fractured the warriors' defences, more than one falling back with a cry as the unclean stuff touched their skin. The rest of the warriors, 'kin and Erith together, did not pause, pressing forward, showering the magician with spells. And still he did not go down.

His camouflage was failing, bits and pieces of shadow falling away to reveal what might be glimpses of an arm or a leg underneath, more showing as the disguise fell away. Pale human skin, limbs lengthened and distorted, a face that looked melted, features twisted in malice, and pale hair. Hessman. Finally.

A mass of something dark and unholy spiralled out from him, coating the nearby warriors, Erith and 'kin alike, visible in both the first and second worlds. The *surjusi* unleashed.

Arrow felt herself sliding down the crate, that well of energy she had thought bottomless beginning to fail as she forced her body to heal enough to move. Getting her legs to support her, she took a few shaky steps forward, unseen, so that when the magician made another break for freedom—the thick coat of containment spells not enough to hold him—she was there.

The capture was inelegant. She simply fell forward, hand reaching out, fingers closing around and holding on to what she thought was an arm. It was bony and too hot under her hand, what should have been human skin feeling rough against her palm. The momentum of her fall pulled the magician down and they tumbled to the earth together.

"Containment," she said. Her voice was raspy, throat still clogged. She made it back to her knees, gripping as tightly as she could, the magician pulling against her grip.

Another shower of spells rained down on the magician, far shorter than the last.

"That's the last of it," Zachary told her, coming to crouch beside her.

Chapter Twenty-Five

It was, finally, enough. The magician was held firm, snarling, silver net encasing him, the final bits of his camouflage falling away to reveal an emaciated human male, bits of blond hair sticking out in tufts around a misshapen head. His body was too long, limbs knotted and moving oddly as he crouched, knees to his chin, hands twisted into claws digging into the ground beside him, trapped by the spells coating the scraps of clothing he wore and his mottled skin, bruised and discoloured. Satisfied he was confined, Arrow released his arm, wiping her hand on the earth in reflex.

"What in hell?" Matthias was at his father's shoulder.

"*Surjusi*." Arrow's voice was weak. "He took it into him."

"Demon-ridden." Zachary supplied the human term.

"The others were bad. But this." Matthias shook his head, revulsion clear.

"Too much power for a body not meant to contain it."

"I have questions." Zachary's voice was dangerous.

"Ask. We do not have long."

Even as she spoke, another volley of crossbow bolts fired out of the dark, held by the warriors' wards, so thin the amber was barely there in places.

"Find him," Zachary snarled to his people. The 'kin melted into darkness without a word, not one remaining as he stayed among the Erith by the broken human body.

One of the thirds raised a stronger battle ward, amber shimmer streaked with the darkness that marked *surjusi* taint. Cleansing was needed, and soon. Yet every warrior held, outwardly calm, firm against the dark. Arrow wished, one day, she could display that courage, too. She wanted to run away, screaming.

Instead, she stayed with the broken body, watching the demon-tainted human struggling to breathe with a ribcage that looked as though it had snapped and reformed more than once. The man had gained the power of a *surjusi*, flicker of a too-old intelligence behind his unseeing human eyes. Arrow wondered if he thought the price had been worth it.

"You killed my mate." Zachary's voice was soft. Almost disinterested. It made Arrow want to run even more.

"Killed many." The voice was broken, too, rasping.

"Marianne Stillwater." Arrow shifted a little, closer to the Prime, lacing power into her own voice. "Shifkin female. She found your house in Hallveran. You chased her."

"Good hunt." A gleam of pitch in the human's blue eyes, the demon twisting. "Little wolf. Tasted sweet." The low whimper a short distance away was Lucy, all but forgotten.

"He is lying," Arrow said, disgusted.

"Yes. Can you bind him to truth?"

"I can try."

She fetched chalk from her bag, spoke the necessary words and cast chalk dust over the figure. He writhed, screaming, the sound too deep to be coming from his hollow chest.

"Why did you kill my mate?" Zachary asked again.

"Got in the way. Silly little wolf. Sneaking into places. Seeing things. Questions. Questions. Questions."

"What did she see?"

"Saw us." The darkness swirled again. "Knew us."

It was a sorry explanation for a sad death, Arrow thought, resting her arms on her knees, taking as deep a breath as her sore ribs would allow. Marianne had been too curious for her own good. It seemed Zachary agreed as he stepped back, lip curling.

"Are there more?" she asked.

"Always more. Tasty."

"Are there more *surjusi* on this plane?" she clarified, power in her words.

"Plenty waiting. Brother. Sister. Little children. All hungry. So hungry." The voice deepened, shaded to something otherworldly, and Arrow's hand moved instinctively to her sword hilt. The thing was stronger than it looked. Far stronger than the fragile human body it had ridden and ruined.

"Who is us?" Her attention snagged.

"No us. No us. Us. No. Us."

"Who is us?" she demanded, fingers tightening on the hilt.

"No. Us. No." The demon was to the fore now, human blue gone from his eyes and he surged up, pushing against the containment, the strands of the spells creaking in the second world, some fracturing. The physical body it was using was weak, but the spells were weaker. Freedom was a mere moment away.

Erith amber blazed, the warriors recognising how close the thing was to freedom, weapons drawn, the cadre moving to form a circle around the creature, each warrior's face set and determined. Zachary rose to his feet, eyes blazing brilliant green, unable to see the breaking of the containment, sensing something wrong.

In the centre of the ring, watching the containment failing, the Preceptor's commands ringing through her, Arrow drew her sword and thrust it forward, words of the banishment spell pouring out of her as her sword held the thing to the ground. It writhed under the spirit blade, shrieking in an awful mix of human and demon pitches.

Three repetitions this time, and the body finally went limp. All darkness faded, leaving a heap of skin and bone, face turned to the earthen ceiling above, fading blue eyes clouded.

"Definitely dead?"

"Yes, Prime." Arrow's voice was faint, shoulders slumped, taking two attempts to get the sword back in its scabbard. "Most definitely dead."

With the monster defeated and the danger passed, the enormity of more death pressed on her, edges of her vision blurring. Too many dead around her. And too many by her hand. There had been no choice, but the stain of it corroded her inside. Will alone kept her up. The draw of the dead filled the second world, a too-familiar grey, the weight of their wants and unfulfilled lives pressing on her. There was a price to pay for death. She wondered if the White Guard felt it too and she had no words to ask that.

The 'kin were coming back into the light, dragging a human corpse with them, one of the 'kin carrying a modified crossbow and quiver of bolts. Matthias gave his father a brief nod signalling all clear. The body this time was recognisably human, no indication of any taint, an unfamiliar face. Lucy glanced at the body, bit her lip, glanced away. She was pale and visibly trembling.

"Michael Hessman," Kallish observed, eyes on the heap in front of Arrow and Zachary. "Hard to tell but the colouring is the same."

"Demon-ridden." Zachary's voice was heavy with what sounded like sorrow. He shook his head. "Idiot."

"Foolish," Kallish agreed, Xeveran providing a rapid translation. "Not the first fool to want power and not count the cost."

"And the others?" Arrow asked.

"Danes. Rowan. The one with the crossbow was another Rowan," Matthias told her. "We recognise the faces from research." Kallish nodded her agreement. Every White Guard cadre leader would know the Descendants by sight.

"Space is clear?" Zachary was just checking.

"No more living things," Matthias confirmed. "It's huge. A little way in that direction..." He pointed. "...ground slopes up in a roadway. There's a vehicle door. Probably leads to the street. Couple of vehicles we need to check plates for and some stuff I'm not touching without Arrow."

"They could have been here for years." Zachary stared at the body.

Had been here for years, Arrow amended quietly in her mind. The ruined tower above had been two hundred years old, built to provide light below in a time when artificial light had not been available. She wondered what other surprises the Descendants' residences would hold when the White Guard searched them. Treaty or not, the Queen would not allow this to pass without reprisal. The humans, so long used to the Erith as exotic neighbours, were about to get a harsh lesson in Erith justice.

"Yeah." Matthias sounded worn.

"And we might never have found them." Zachary's voice held a threat, words cast in the direction of the human. "Come here." There was no power in his voice, but Lucy rose to her feet and walked over to him, pulling her heavy coat more tightly around her, lifting her chin again in silent defiance. "This is what happens when people play with things they don't understand," he told her, pointing to the mangled remains.

"You killed him." She was glaring at Arrow, voice shaking. Not fear.

"He carried a *surjusi* within. Willingly," Arrow answered. "You would call it a demon."

"No. I don't believe it."

"Look at him. Look at how deformed his body had become. That is no human disease," Arrow said, then sighed as Lucy's chin stuck out.

"Demon-ridden," Zachary said softly, close to Lucy's ear. "And now look at your cousin."

"I saw him. Dead as well."

"Deformed, too. Tried to play with demons." Zachary's voice was still too quiet.

Lucy's attention finally turned to him, and some of her defiance faded.

"Which we would have known about if you had told us the truth."

"I don't owe you anything."

"This one," Arrow said, pointing to Hessman's remains, "killed Marianne on the mountain. He hunted her across the mountain until she had run her feet raw. Then he shot her with a crossbow." Arrow paused to steady her voice. "It was a weapon made from body parts and powered with blood magic."

Lucy's face was white, eyes burning as she stared at Arrow.

"I didn't know." She swallowed hard, lines of her throat standing out.

Arrow believed her. Zachary did, too, face twisting in disgust.

"How did you know about this place?" Arrow asked.

"We played here as children. A few times. It ..." Lucy looked around, swallowed, nose wrinkling. "It's changed a bit since then."

"And didn't think to mention it." Zachary's voice was silky soft again.

"Would it have made a difference?" The bitterness in Lucy's voice made no impression on the Prime. She seemed furious.

Arrow remembered the quiet question, is it my fault? and thought that Lucy was mostly angry at herself, hating everyone else because that was easier than accepting that she had contributed to her lover's death.

"It would have saved us some time," Zachary said, "and you'd still be a friend of the muster. As it is, you're disavowed."

"Y-you ..." Lucy's mouth opened again but no sound came out as all the 'kin apart from Zachary turned their back on her.

"Get out," he told her.

"I dropped my torch when you grabbed me," she protested. He dug into one pocket, producing a small flashlight, and handed it over. After another glance up at his set face, and a long look around the silent Erith and backs of the 'kin, she turned on the torch and walked out of the circle.

"One assumes that the human female was not widely known about," Kallish said quietly.

"One assumes correctly. It has not formed part of my reports."

"I see no reason to mention it."

Perfectly in accord, Arrow and Kallish waited as Lucy's torch disappeared into the dark and the 'kin settled, anger on several faces. Not directed to their Prime, she noticed. The glares were following Lucy's progress into the dark. She had wondered how he had managed to keep it a secret from his people and it appeared that it had not been much of one. It said something about the regard they had for him that they had kept quiet, though.

"Injuries, *svegraen*?"

"Some minor wounds. And cleansing needed," Kallish answered. For the first time, Arrow heard weariness in the warrior's voice. "We had hoped not to have to face *surjusi* again."

Arrow could find nothing to say to that.

She stared at Hessman's body and wondered again if the human had thought the price for his power had been worth it. Every limb was distorted, fingers twisted so that he probably had not even been able to feed himself. If he had eaten at all. He was so thin, merely skin over bone and sinew. Her eyes snapped back to the misshapen fingers. There was no possibility that this thing had handled the chalk with the skill necessary for the runes on Farraway Mountain. He might have managed the containment spell in Hallveran, straight after the *surjusi* had arrived. The *surjusi* distortion would have been mild then. But the mountain recording had shown him shuffling and awkward in his gait.

A cold certainty settled. Someone else had drawn the runes. All of them. Someone who had knowledge of high Erith magic. Us. There were more.

And with that conclusion, there was a new, vital question as to how he had survived so long with that *surjusi* inside him. Nothing in the history that Arrow knew suggested he, or the Ancestors, had been powerful magicians. His body had not been made to carry that much power and had survived far longer than she would have guessed possible

She took a step forward, crouching by the corpse, inspecting what she could, and found an answer to that—and another troubling question.

"It's done, then," Zachary said over her head, sounding as weary as she felt. Perhaps he felt the weight of the dead, too.

"No more *surjusi*." Arrow nodded.

"We never found where Marianne was for four months."

"I believe she was already dead, not long after she hired that vehicle in Hallveran."

"Explain, please?" Zachary crouched beside her.

"I wondered how this thing survived so long. The *surjusi* should have killed the human long ago. Too much for a human body." She glanced across and found that, once again, he perfectly understood. "But there are Erith spells to preserve matter. In particular, there is an Erith spell which is meant to preserve remains so that the family might say their goodbyes." She pointed to the dead thing and the rune carved into his chest. "Like that. Only it would have been invisible normally. I speculate that it was carved there to combat the *surjusi* taint. A marking like that on Marianne Stillwater would have preserved her remains for months."

"We didn't see the magician carving anything onto her." Zachary rubbed a hand over his face and through his hair, rising to his feet.

"Spells can be spoken, too," she reminded him, rising as well, pressing a hand to her ribs as they twinged, and regretting it at once as a fierce stab shot through her.

Zachary's face was drawn as he followed her reasoning, probably remembering, like she was, that there had been no sound with the reconstruction spell and it was impossible to know if or what the shadowed form had spoken on the mountain. She also kept to herself that a few minutes with Marianne's body would have confirmed the spell. They might have known, much sooner, the correct time of Marianne's death. Four months since Marianne had found the Rowan residence in Hallveran and run herself half to death across the mountain. Heading for Zachary. It was the only explanation that made sense. Chased. Hunted. And killed so close to her goal.

"Dead before we knew she was missing. We might still not have found her." Zachary was grim, glaring at the body in front of him as though he wanted to kill it again. "I've had searchers out." A few of the 'kin twitched, ducking their eyes, embarrassed by their failure, a feeling Arrow was deeply familiar with. "I've not been pleased at the lack of finding. An impossible task. Impossible to track a dead woman." The 'kin settled, faces set.

"I am sorry that there are no better answers," she said.

"At least we have some." He turned slightly to face her, and she mirrored him, face to face. "You will convey to the Taellan in whatever terms that they will understand, that we will have an accounting from the Erith as to how Erith magic came to be used to kill our mate and violate our territory." It was not Zachary speaking but the Prime, his power coiling out.

"Prime, it will be done." Arrow made a small bow before she could check the motion, Erith Court manners ingrained.

"And you will tell the Taellan that we have come to value your service." He was still speaking as the Prime. Her jaw dropped. "We would be extremely displeased to find that anything had happened to you."

She closed her jaw, words failing her, and simply bowed again, eyes pricking with unexpected tears. Valued. And an unsubtle offer of protection. An invisible yet tangible net that the Erith dare not ignore. Her throat tightened. The Prime understood far too much about the way the Erith thought and operated if he knew so clearly how vulnerable her position was.

"The mage is under our charge," Kallish said unexpectedly. Xeveran had clearly given her a translation. Arrow turned to stare at the warrior, astonished, and caught the edges of a straight look between Kallish and Zachary. Across races and language barriers, they somehow understood each other perfectly, Kallish making a graceful, shallow bow and Zachary dipping his chin in respect. Arrow frowned, not quite sure what had gone on.

Around them, the White Guard held their ground, alert and on watch despite the taint creeping through them. None were wholly taken over. The few struck by mage fire had countered it, not without cost. There were injuries of flesh and blood, too. All would survive. How well was a question for another day.

The 'kin were equally battered, including the two in animal form, the same set, determined expression on their faces. Holding ground, waiting for orders.

An old White Guard saying crossed her mind. The battle is done. Take the win. Trouble will find you soon enough.

For now, she set aside the future, the likely fury of the Taellan, the possibility of discovery of her own secrets so long held, the probability that there was another dangerous magician still alive. All would come in time. All for another day. Today, they had held.

She drew a long breath, ache of healing bones catching her again, eyes gritty from lack of sleep and using so much power, throat tight with the echo of the loss she had felt on the mountain. A strong-willed, vibrant woman, too curious for her own good, had died to lead them here. Arrow had found her killer. The promise was kept. In the privacy of her own mind, she offered an Erith blessing for the dead and saw, shifting in the shadow, the ghost of a chocolate-brown wolf with bright eyes that winked at her and padded away, disappearing into nothing.

There would be questions. An investigation. The Preceptor would want to inspect this place himself, to understand how a *surjusi* could come so close to the Erith border. The White Guard would want to know how Descendants could form a conspiracy under their watch. The Queen herself would need to be involved, to be fully informed. The Taellan would doubtless want to shout at her for some imagined misdeed. Eshan was probably already plotting her next unpleasant task. Cleaning spiders out of what remained of his archives, perhaps, once Evellan was done with her here.

But the Prime had offered her his protection, the protection of the Erith's old enemies. She would live.

And for now, she was whole in mind and nearly whole in body. She would heal. The day had been won. She was alive. It was enough.

THANK YOU

Thank you very much for reading *Concealed*, The Taellaneth - Book 1. I hope that you enjoyed meeting Arrow.

It would be great, if you have five minutes, if you could leave an honest review at the store you got it from. Reviews are really helpful for other readers to decide whether the book is for them, and also help me get visibility for my books - thank you.

Arrow's story continues in *Revealed*, The Taellaneth - Book 2, also available at Amazon.

If you want to know what I'm working on and when the next book will be available, you can contact me and sign up for my newsletter at the website: www.taellaneth.com.

CHARACTER LIST

Note: to avoid spoilers, some names may have been omitted, and some details left out.

The Erith
Diannea vel Sovernis - member of the Taellan; head of her House
Eimille vel Falsen - member of the Taellan; head of her House
Eshan nuin Regersfel - Chief Scribe to Taellan; adopted member of House Regersfel
Etan nuin Sovernis - White Guard; adopted member of House Sovernis
Evellan - Preceptor, head of Academy
Geran vo Sovernis - White Guard; member of House Sovernis
Gesser vo Regresan - assistant Teaching Master; son of Gret
Gilean vo Presien - war mage
Gret vo Regresan - member of the Taellan; head of his House
Juinis vo Halsfeld - member of the Taellan; head of his House
Kallish nuin Falsen - White Guard; cadre leader; adopted member of House Falsen
Kester vo Halsfeld - member of the Taellan; Juinis' brother-by-marriage
Seivella - Teaching Mistress at Academy; deputy to Preceptor
Seggerat vo Regersfel - elder of the Taellan; head of his House
Serran vo Liathius - powerful mage; founder of the Academy
Vailla vel Falsen - member of House Falsen

Whintnath - Commander of the White Guard

Xeveran - White Guard

The Shifkin

Andrew Farraway - member of Farraway muster, Matthias' twin and Zachary's son

Con - member of Farraway muster

Jace - member of Farraway muster

Marianne Stillwater - mate of Zachary Farraway

Matthias Farraway - shifkin enforcer; mate of Tamara, Andrew's twin and Zachary's son

Tamara - member of Farraway muster, mate of Matthias

Zachary Farraway - Prime of shifkin nation; mate of Marianne Stillwater, father to Andrew and Mathias

Others

Arrow - mixed-blood, Erith-trained magician

Hugh Danes - human

Lucy Steers - human

Matthew Hessman - human

GLOSSARY

Erith words and phrases

Arwmverishan - abomination

Baelthras - six-legged predators

Brother by *vestrait* - Brother by marriage (not the same as brother-in-law) – applies to Kester who became Juinis' brother when Juinis wed Kester's sister

Cadre - a White Guard unit, made up of three thirds

Ethtar - curse word

Graduate - an Academy student who has completed all fifteen cycles; highest standing of Erith-trained magicians

High magic - any form of magic, generally human or Erith, which requires a spell to work it, whether written, spoken or drawn

Natural magic - innate magic which can be used without a formal spell, for example the shifkin ability to change form

Nuin - signifies someone adopted into a House, not part of the blood family, for example Eshan nuin Regersfel

Surjusi - unclean spirits, lethal to Erith

Surrimok - mountain-dwelling predator in mostly human (or simian) shape; yellow eyes, hands and feet adapted for climbing, and long fur.

Svegraen - term of address and respect for a member or members of the White Guard; literal translation is "warrior"

Taellan - refers both to the group of ten high-ranking Erith who make up the council of government for the Erith, answerable only to the Queen and her Consort, and also to an individual member of the council

Third - a group of five warriors making up part of a cadre

Urjusi - unclean magic

vel / vo - female / male versions of signifier of high-ranking member of a House, usually the blood family or their *vetrai* or *vetral*, for example Eimille vel Falsen and Seggerat vo Regersfel

Vestrai / Vestrait - married / marriage

Vestran - betrothed

Vetrai - wife

Vetral - husband

Vicandula - plant, also known as Erith gravestone

War mage - mage who has completed all fifteen cycles of the Academy and graduated in the discipline of war mage; entitled to wear the cloak of a war mage; swear oaths to protect the Erith

White Guard - elite warriors, undergo rigorous training, rank depicted by braids on their uniforms

ALSO BY THE AUTHOR

(As at January 2024)

The Taellaneth series (complete)
Concealed, Book 1
Revealed, Book 2
Betrayed, Book 3
Tainted, Book 4
Cloaked, Book 5

Taellaneth Box Set (all five books in one e-book)
Taellaneth Complete Series (Books 1–5)

The Hundred series (complete)
The Gathering, Book 1
The Sundering, Book 2
The Reckoning, Book 3
The Rending, Book 4
The Searching, Book 5
The Rising, Book 6

Ageless Mysteries
Deadly Night, Book 1

False Dawn, Book 2
Morning Trap, Book 3
Assassin's Noon, Book 4
Flightless Afternoon, Book 5
Ascension Day, Book 6

The Grey Gates
Outcast, Book 1
Called, Book 2
Hunted, Book 3
Forged, Book 4
Chosen, Book 5 (expected to be available early February 2024)

ABOUT THE AUTHOR

Vanessa Nelson is a fantasy author who lives in Scotland, United Kingdom and spends her days juggling the demands of two spoiled cats, two giant dogs and her fictional characters.

As far as the cats are concerned, they should always come first. The older dog lets her know when he isn't getting enough attention by chewing up the house. The younger dog's favourite method of getting her attention is a gentle nudge with his head. At least, he would say it's gentle.

You can find out more information online at the following places:

Website: www.taellaneth.com

Facebook: www.facebook.com/taellaneth

Made in United States
Troutdale, OR
08/11/2025

33555355R00142